CW01083017

THE WIDOWS' GUIDE TO BACKSTABBING

AMANDA ASHBY

Storm
PUBLISHING

This is a work of fiction. Names, characters, businesses, places, events and incidents are either the products of the author's imagination or used in a fictitious manner. Any resemblance to actual persons, living or dead, or actual events is purely coincidental.

Copyright © Amanda Ashby, 2025

The moral right of the author has been asserted.

All rights reserved. No part of this book may be reproduced or used in any manner without the prior written permission of the copyright owner. This prohibition includes, but is not limited to, any reproduction or use for the purpose of training artificial intelligence technologies or systems.

To request permissions, contact the publisher at rights@stormpublishing.co

Ebook ISBN: 978-1-80508-797-7
Paperback ISBN: 978-1-80508-799-1

Cover design: Emily Courdelle
Cover images: Shutterstock

Published by Storm Publishing.
For further information, visit:
www.stormpublishing.co

ALSO BY AMANDA ASHBY

The Widows' Guide to Murder

Domestic thrillers

The Stepmother
The Ex-Wife
I Will Find You
Remember Me?

Romance – adult

Once in a Blue Moon
What Were You Thinking, Paige Taylor?
Falling for the Best Man
Dating the Wrong Mr. Right
You Had Me at Halo

Romance – young adult

How to Kiss Your Enemy
How to Kiss Your Crush
How to Kiss a Bad Boy
The Heartbreak Cure
The Wedding Planner's Baby

Middle Grade – paranormal adventures

Midnight Reynolds and the Phantom Circus
Midnight Reynolds and the Agency of Spectral Protection

Midnight Reynolds and the Spectral Transformer

Wishful Thinking

Under a Spell

Out of Sight

Young Adult – paranormal adventures

Demonosity

Fairy Bad Day

Zombie Queen of Newbury High

ONE

Saturday, 15th March

'Connor, did you move my basket of plastic fruit?' Cleo's loud voice rang out through Little Shaw library, and several people looked up in annoyance.

Ginny, who had been on her way to the returns room, grimaced and brought the book trolley to a halt. She wasn't sure why Cleo needed a basket of plastic fruit for a library display about dinosaurs. Or why Connor would know where it was.

He obviously agreed, since he didn't bother looking up from the non-fiction section where he was shelving.

'I know you can hear me.' Cleo's voice went up in pitch, and her eyes flashed with irritation. *Oh dear.* Ginny's gaze locked on the wicker-handled basket that was poking out from under the table, just inches from Cleo's sensibly clad feet. Sighing, Ginny abandoned the trolley and hurried over to keep the peace.

In the five months since she'd become library manager in the small Lancashire village she'd moved to after her husband's death, she'd freshened the interior, updated the online catalogue, and hosted multiple community events. But she still hadn't figured out a way to stop one opinionated volunteer and a reticent young staff member from bickering.

'Is this what you're looking for?' She retrieved the basket, which was indeed filled with glossy plastic apples and lurid purple grapes that glistened in the March light filtering through the narrow windows.

'Oh, yes. Now I remember. I put it there to stop William from eating them. That man has no self-control.' Cleo scattered plastic grapes across the table, which was covered with craft magazines and a very large poster announcing the time and date for the thirty-year anniversary of the Little Shaw spring fete and gala.

'Pots and kettles,' Connor murmured.

Cleo's nostrils flared but she refused to look in his direction, for which Ginny was heartily relieved.

'It's to encourage people to donate to the Friends of the Village stall,' Cleo continued. 'Speaking of which, I told Sandra that you could provide three dozen jars of jam. She was very pleased, though passed on a reminder to sterilise the jars before you use them. Sandra and her husband are the force behind the fete, and they've never had a bout of food poisoning come out of it yet. They take their obligations very seriously.'

A small muscle in Ginny's cheek flickered. Not because she resented being told how to safely make jam or that she'd agreed to donate some for a good cause. But because she and Connor had spent yesterday afternoon creating a very similar display table to promote the very same fete.

She stepped forward, but before she could speak, Tuppence appeared in the doorway. Relieved of the distraction, Ginny waved her friend over.

Tuppence was one of the three widows who had befriended Ginny after her move to Little Shaw seven months ago, and in that short time they'd all become very close. They'd helped show her that even though nothing would replace the gaping hole Eric's death had left, Ginny could have a future to look forward to.

Which might explain why Ginny had decided to embark on a new career as a village librarian at the tender age of sixty. And solve a murder case. Though there was only one of those things that she intended to pursue from now on, and it wasn't murder.

'Goodness. Why do you have two displays for the spring fete and gala?' Tuppence demanded in her no-nonsense manner, her eyes bright. She was wearing pink trousers, a white linen shirt with tiny purple love hearts, and a floppy hat over her silver curls. 'It seems excessive.'

'Doesn't it just.' Connor finally glanced up from his shelving. Ginny gave him a warning look.

'This one is to encourage people to donate things for a good cause.' Cleo's mouth puckered together as she nodded towards the other display. 'And is quite different from *that* one.'

'If you say so.' Tuppence shrugged and then peered around the place. 'By the by, it's empty in here. Where is everyone?'

'Probably outside enjoying the sun. It's been quiet all day,' Ginny explained. She was still getting used to the ebb and flow of library life, and how it revolved around the weather and local events. Not that she could blame anyone. After a cold, grey winter, it had been a relief this morning to wake up to a pale blue sky and the first hints of spring, and Ginny's fingers had itched to tend to her garden.

'Excellent. Does that mean you can come to Harlow's after all?'

'Harlow's Haberdashery?' Cleo's gaze swept over Tuppence's cheerful outfit. 'Don't tell me you're going to enter something in the sewing category?'

'What if I am?' Tuppence demanded, and Connor drifted closer, no doubt hoping for a fight. 'After all, I've won several red rosettes for my watercolours. Maybe it's time to stretch my wings. Why? Worried about the competition?'

'Not from you,' Cleo retorted, and Ginny stepped between them.

'Tuppence is reupholstering her sofa and asked me to look at fabric with her.'

Cleo's mouth flattened. 'Doing it herself? I hate to think what it will turn out like.'

'That's lucky, since I shan't be inviting you around to sit on it,' Tuppence returned. 'Besides, I found a great tutorial on YouTube. I wanted to do a course IRL, but it was too expensive. "IRL" means "in random life". That's what the kids say. Isn't that right, Connor?'

'Not even close.' He gave Ginny a pained look and disappeared back towards the counter.

'I wonder if I said it wrong?' Tuppence frowned and Ginny took the opportunity to move her away from Cleo.

'I'm sure it was fine. Poor Connor's tired. He moved into a flat in the village and his roommates are very noisy.'

'Earmuffs is what he needs. We should get Hen to knit him some.'

Ginny wasn't quite sure that would appeal to an eighteen-year-old boy who mainly dressed in black, so instead told her friend she needed to get her bag and coat and give Connor a few last-minute instructions about closing the library, and to remind him not to wind Cleo up.

She found him in the returns room. 'Relax, Mrs C. It's about time you stopped doing so many extra hours. There's only fifty minutes to go and I'll do my best not to commit murder,' he assured her with a rare smile.

'I know you will... or should I say *won't*?' Ginny grinned and went back out to the library floor. Despite his young age and fondness for monosyllables, Connor had proved incredibly reliable. The last thing he needed was her undermining his confidence.

She made her goodbyes and joined her friend outside. The

planter boxes were filled with early daffodils, and an old-fashioned ice-cream van was at the park next door, where a line of excited children was waiting.

'Right… I'm ready to go,' she said then looked around, half expecting to see Hen and JM. 'Where are the others? Are they coming?'

'No, it's just us.' Tuppence started to walk, eyes dipped.

Ginny bit back her surprise as they went past the long line of children, towards the quaint bridge that led to the village high street. The four women usually spent every Saturday afternoon together, weeding the cemetery, but had been forced to cancel for the second time, thanks to several funerals taking place. Turned out March was a busy month. So, when Tuppence had called earlier that day to invite Ginny to help with some fabric, she'd assumed the four of them would be going together.

'I thought Hen would've jumped at the chance. She loves that shop. The last time we walked past it, she told me about the new quilt she was planning, and all the fabric she would need.'

'That's why she didn't want to come. She said she couldn't trust herself. Ever since Alyson moved out of the cottage, money's been tight.'

Oh. Ginny couldn't help but feel partially responsible for that. When she'd first arrived in Little Shaw, she'd managed to get muddled up in a murder investigation to convince the police Hen's beloved daughter, Alyson, was innocent. And while they'd succeeded, Alyson had decided to take an extended trip through Asia with a friend to recuperate from her ordeal.

Which had left Hen, who relied on the extra rent, counting pennies.

'I understand. And I suppose JM doesn't have much interest in craft.'

'*It's a perfectly nice hobby for someone else,*' Tuppence

recited, capturing JM's rather regal tone. Ginny bit back a laugh as they reached the other side of the bridge.

An ancient stone church sat at the top of a cobbled lane, and running along the narrow stream was a seventeenth-century pub called The Lost Goat. There were several wooden tables and chairs set out in the charming beer garden that over-looked the water, but despite the weather, they were all empty. Ginny hadn't been in recently but had heard the new managers were struggling to draw a crowd.

A chalkboard had been placed by the door announcing all kinds of specials, including two-for-the-price-of-one early-bird dinners.

'That reminds me, JM has invited us there on Monday night. Are you free?'

Ginny, who still tended to spend most evenings either read-ing, doing a crossword or trying not to talk to her dead husband, said that she was. 'But I don't even know what kind of food the new chef does.'

'That makes two of us, but at half price, I'm sure it will be lovely. I'll tell JM to book us in,' Tuppence said as they reached the high street.

Most of the businesses closed at lunchtime on a Saturday, but Harlow's Haberdashery was open until five and had several wicker tubs of end-of-roll fabrics outside. It was in a red-brick building with a large awning hanging over the white wooden door. Decorative bunting had been draped across it, and one of the windows held a poster for the spring fete and gala.

A second window was adorned with another poster, of a man in his mid-sixties with a shock of thick, grey curls and a lavish moustache that stretched across his cheeks. He was dressed in a black Victorian-style suit with a striped waistcoat, a large fob chain, and had a beaver hat tucked under one arm. Underneath the photograph was the announcement that 'Little Shaw Spring Fete and Gala Society is pleased to announce that for the thirtieth year in a row, Timothy Harlow will be our celebrity judge.'

Ginny supposed it made sense to have the haberdashery shop owner judge the entries, though she had no idea what made him a celebrity. Was it the outfit? Or was he famous for something else?

She pushed open the front door and stepped inside. Her arrival was announced by a tinkling bell. The interior was crammed with large glass jars of buttons, cubed wooden shelves of homespun wool, and an old oak cutting bench next to the counter.

No wonder Hen had declared a self-imposed ban. It would be easy to spend a fortune in the stylish shop. Despite having lived in Little Shaw for seven months, Ginny had never been inside before, mainly because she'd stubbornly brought as much as she could of her old furniture – and old life – with her when she'd moved here.

But since the first anniversary of Eric's death had passed, she had been considering some changes. Until this morning, she'd been thinking of a fresh coat of paint, but now the idea of curtains, cushions and new upholstery swam in her vision.

There was no sign of anyone behind the counter, so Ginny continued to walk around, running her fingers along a soft red version of William Morris's 'Strawberry Thief', before inspecting a duck-egg blue Laura Ashley with delicate flowers. There were more large wicker barrels of fabric, as well as a French Louis XV armchair with stripped-back walnut legs and reupholstered squabs in a straw-coloured linen. It was stunning and she studied the small, gilded frame perched on the seat. *Vanja Petrovic Upholstery Services*. She didn't recognise the name, but the address was local, and his work was exquisite.

Was this what had inspired Tuppence to attempt her own reupholstering?

Ginny turned to ask, only to discover her friend wasn't

there. That was odd. She scanned the shop, but on finding it empty, she went outside to where Tuppence was pressed against the wall of the post office next door, her hat pulled low over her face.

Ginny lifted up the hat and frowned. 'Is something wrong?'

'Wrong?' Tuppence fumbled around in her bag and withdrew a heavy-looking parcel, not returning her gaze. 'Of course not. Why would you say that?'

'No reason.' Ginny eyed the parcel that Tuppence was now hugging tightly to her chest.

'Okay, so there might be a *small* problem.' Tuppence looked guilty. 'When I said I wanted to look at fabric... what I meant was I want to *exchange* some fabric.'

'I see. But isn't it best if you go inside to do that?'

'Definitely, though the other... *even smaller*... problem is that last time I was in there, I got banned.'

'Banned from a haberdashery shop? Whatever for?'

Colour rose in Tuppence's cheeks. 'I should probably have mentioned that I was stuck on how to replace the batting and couldn't find a good YouTube tutorial, so I popped along to Vanja's upholstery course. He does it in conjunction with Timothy Harlow every six months. I've always wanted to attend, but it's outrageously expensive. Though after being there for an hour, I could understand why people pay the money. He's really very good. But that's when I noticed that everyone at the workshop had the same print I did.'

'Are you sure it wasn't just a practice fabric? Like calico?'

'No, definitely not.' Tuppence tugged open a corner of the parcel to reveal a folded length of fabric. It was a delightful pastoral toile of blue and white with each scene showing a deer grazing in a forest. 'It's called "Deer in a Woodland Delight". And it was jolly expensive.'

'It's beautiful,' Ginny said, truthfully. 'Though how did so many people end up with it?'

'No idea, but that's the reason I wanted to exchange it. Unfortunately, while I was leaving the workshop Harlow noticed me climbing out of the window.'

'The window?' Ginny repeated faintly, starting to get a better understanding of the problem. She could all too readily imagine Tuppence sneaking in and out of an upholstery course by climbing through a window. And while Ginny had numerous questions, mainly involving health and safety, now wasn't the time. 'When was this?'

'Oh, one night this week. Monday, I think. Problem is that when I went into the shop the next day Harlow refused to exchange the fabric. Quoted that Latin phrase at me.'

'*Caveat emptor...?* Let the buyer beware?' Ginny said.

'That's the one. Said that I should be grateful to own something so exquisite and that he was insulted I was questioning his taste. Worse, he wanted to charge me for going to the course.' She looked squarely at Ginny. 'I thought you could explain the misunderstanding.'

'M-me?' Ginny's stomach dropped, not quite sure how climbing through a window could be seen as a 'misunderstanding'.

'Of course. He'll listen to you. You're so calm and clever and have a knack of not getting people's backs up.' Tuppence thrust the parcel at her and gave her a pleading smile.

Ginny reluctantly took it. She'd never considered her ability to keep the peace as a special skill. In fact, she'd always felt like it made her weak and too willing to fade into the background, so it was strange to have people admire it about her.

Then she let out a groan. 'That's why you didn't want JM to come with us?'

'I thought she could be my last resort. She can be quite formidable,' Tuppence admitted with a rueful grimace, that Ginny could well understand. Their friend had done half a law degree back in the seventies and had a habit of misquoting legal precedents to anyone who would listen. And while at times it was useful, at other times it was like adding fuel to a an already burning flame. 'And you know how Hen can be.'

Ginny nodded. While JM was a loose cannon, their other friend was a bleeding heart and would be more likely to agree with everything the shop owner said and pay for the full course into the bargain, despite how stretched she was financially.

Which only left Ginny. She hated confrontation, but she owed her friends so much, and it was clear Tuppence couldn't afford to buy more fabric, if her tight jaw was anything to go by.

'Okay, I'll try. But I can't promise anything.'

'Thank you.' Tuppence handed Ginny a slip of paper. 'Here's the name of the fabric I'd like instead. I did tell him I would be back today for it, so he might have calmed down since we last spoke.'

'You think so?'

Tuppence swallowed. 'Maybe... but if he *is* still angry, I'm sure you can explain it. And don't let him scare you. Timothy Harlow's a grumpy old sod, but his bark is worse than his bite.'

'What if he's not working today?' Ginny peered over to the poster in the window, and to Timothy Harlow's condescending smile. Was that the reason he'd been selected as the head judge? Because he was bad-tempered and wouldn't be swayed by people? If so, it didn't bode well for her.

'He is,' Tuppence assured her. 'It's only him and his daughter, Megan, but she never does Saturdays. He might be grateful to have a customer. It seems as slow here as it was in the library.'

Ginny wasn't convinced that he would be pleased to get a return when it was a quiet day. All the same, she took the slip of paper and stepped back into the shop.

'Hello?' She walked to the counter. On the wall were numerous large black and white photographs of the old textile mills and weavers' cottages that were so much a part of the area's history. Further along were other photos of various men standing outside Harlow's Haberdashery throughout the years.

There were numerous newspaper clippings of Harlow at London fashion events, and at the far end was a more recent photograph showing a slim woman with tired eyes and a shared jawline.

Was this the daughter? It was possible, though despite the resemblance, Megan didn't seem to have her father's vivacious-ness, or his flare for costume, if her plain skirt and shirt were anything to go by. Then again, until recently, Ginny's own wardrobe hadn't been much different.

She felt an unexpected stab of solidarity with the woman.

There was also a wall calendar hanging up, displaying the month of March, with each of the fourteen previous days neatly crossed out, as if they were part of a countdown. Though there was nothing marked under today's date. Did that mean he merely crossed off each day once it was over?

Nearby was a dressmaker's mannequin draped in the same toile that Tuppence had bought, as well as a slim stand of tapestry threads, several of which had fallen to the wooden floor. Ginny bent and collected them up. They'd probably blown off when she'd opened the door. She put them on the counter, along with the parcel, and walked to the simple velvet curtain that blocked off the back area.

There was still no sound of movement coming from there.

'Hello?' she called again, unsure what to do next. If Timothy Harlow was as bad-tempered as Tuppence suggested, he wouldn't appreciate her walking into his backroom. She turned to the window in time to see Tuppence staring in at her, eyes full of hope.

Ginny swallowed. She was stuck between an eager friend and a missing haberdashery shop owner. Sighing, she pushed aside the heavy fabric and stepped through.

It was a large space filled with rolls of fabric, shelves of boxes, and an old-fashioned desk positioned along one wall.

'Mr Harlow? Hello? Is there—' She broke off and stared at the outstretched body of a man.

He was lying face down on the wooden floorboards, a large pair of sewing scissors protruding from his back.

'No.' Ginny let out an involuntary gasp. The blades had sheared through the thick wool of his old-fashioned suit and the fabric glistened in a way that suggested it was soaked with blood.

Nausea roiled in her belly and she dropped to her knees. Was he still alive? She reached for his wrist, not daring to move him. His skin was soft and warm but there was no sign of a pulse.

'Please, can you hear me?' she asked, voice urgent as her heart hammered in her chest. But there was no reply. Swallowing hard, she leaned closer, but he was as lifeless as the photograph of him on the wall.

Ginny fumbled for her phone. Her hands shook as the metallic scent of blood clogged her nostrils. She had to get out of there. Numbly, she got to her feet and hurried out to the front of the shop. Her chest was heaving, and she leaned against the counter. She was still trying to catch her breath when the doorbell tinkled and Tuppence burst in, eyes focused on the phone Ginny was clutching.

'Don't tell me it went badly? Does this mean we have to call JM? I was hoping we could avoid a scene. Maybe I should speak to him again?' Tuppence demanded, stepping towards the backroom. 'On a scale of one to ten, how angry is he?'

'Stop, you can't go in there.' Ginny lunged for her friend's arm, and Tuppence came to a halt. Ginny swallowed. 'I'm afraid he's not angry... he's dead. I need to call the police.'

'Dead?' Tuppence parroted. 'But I spoke with him

yesterday and he seemed fine. Are... are you quite sure? What if he's just having a nap?'

Ginny's throat ached, and she took a step back, trying not to think of the scissors protruding from Timothy Harlow's back.

'He isn't asleep.' She forced the words out as the temperature in the shop seemed to drop. Goosebumps prickled her skin. 'I-I think he's been murdered.'

Tuppence's eyes bulged, but she didn't speak as Ginny made the call.

It didn't take long, and the operator assured her that the police would be there soon. Ginny just hoped it would give her enough time to come up with an explanation of how, once again, she'd managed to stumble across a very dead body.

TWO

'Are you sure we shouldn't let them in?' Tuppence said ten minutes later, as a woman in her forties pressed her nose up to the haberdashery shop window. 'That's Tyla. She's probably after more wool for the crotchet rug she's entering in the fete. I could help her.'

'We can't let anyone touch the crime scene.' Ginny gently nudged Tuppence away from the display of sewing patterns her friend was thumbing through. 'Including us. The police will be here soon.'

Bang. Bang. Bang. Tyla pounded against the glass, the sound ricocheting around the room like a gunshot.

'Sorry.' Tuppence shook her head. 'It's just so hard to sit still when there's a dead body in the next room. I can't believe he's been murdered. And stabbed in the back.'

Neither could Ginny. While the initial nausea had gone, her rapid pulse was still ringing in her ears. 'How well did you know him?' she asked, by way of distraction.

'We were friendly enough when we were young, but while most of us went to the local high school, he attended some fancy boarding school in York. After that he kept to himself when he came home for holidays. Then he moved to London to study fashion design, which is where he met his wife. He released a collection of menswear that did very well, and people thought he was going to be the next big thing. He hosted a television sewing show, back in the late eighties, and became as well known for his Victorian dress sense and moustache as for his quick temper. It made him a minor celebrity, but the show was cancelled after a couple of seasons. His wife died not long after, and he moved back to Little Shaw when Megan was about seven.'

'Oh, how sad,' Ginny gasped.

'Yes, poor wee thing. No mother and him as a father. Sorry, that seems like a terrible thing to say now. But he was always at pains to remind people about his time in the spotlight.'

'That explains the poster in the window. I was trying to work out why it said "celebrity judge".'

'Oh, yes, he always liked to lord it up this time of the year.' Tuppence nodded, allowing several of her curls to spring free from under her hat. 'Though apart from at the fete, our paths haven't crossed much... until I tried to return my fabric, that is.'

'You said that he was bad-tempered. Does that mean he had enemies?'

Tuppence snorted. 'Probably dozens. He often got into arguments at the town meetings and once refused to speak to poor Rose for a week because she wanted him to order in a polyester-blend fabric. The only reason people tolerated him was because he had exquisite taste and often got in exclusive prints. But I know Elsie refused to buy her fabric from him, and so did several other people.' She paused. 'Do you think that's why he was killed?'

Bang. Bang. Bang.

'Let me in, Tuppence Wilde.' Tyla's face was pressed up against the glass. 'You have no right to keep me standing out here. It's not your shop. Where is Timothy? Don't think I won't tell Megan about this.'

At the mention of Megan, Tuppence's cheeks drained of colour and Ginny's shoulders sagged, as they both realised what this meant. Harlow's daughter would have to be told that her father was dead.

'Were they close?'

'Not that I ever saw. Harlow seemed happy to let Megan work in the shop from when she was ten. Poor thing has never done anything else. I always got the feeling he thought of her as cheap labour rather than a daughter.'

'What a shame.' Ginny peered over to the photograph on the wall, and Megan's tired smile. It was as if her father's charisma had come at her expense.

'Do you think we should call her?'

'No, we had better leave it to the police,' Ginny said, not feeling up to telling someone their father was dead. Or trying to speculate on what had happened.

Bang. Bang. Bang. Tyla thumped on the door again.

Tuppence harrumphed. 'She must really want to win that ribbon. I wish the police would hurry up. Do you think they'll be cross that we locked ourselves in here?'

Oh yes. Ginny swallowed. She was almost certain of it.

The operator had expressly told them to wait outside the shop. But they hadn't reckoned with several determined shoppers who kept trying to shoulder their way in. Since neither Ginny nor Tuppence wanted to mention the dead body, they'd opted to barricade themselves inside instead.

It was a choice she was now regretting. The pounding at the door continued and Ginny checked the time. It was quarter to two in the afternoon, which meant Connor would be getting ready to lock up the library. If only she hadn't agreed to finish early. If only—

'Finally,' Tuppence said, as an all-too-familiar white electric vehicle pulled up outside. Detective Inspector James Wallace. His arrival was closely followed by sirens as a marked police car and an ambulance both came to a screeching halt.

Thank goodness.

Ginny hurried to the front door and slid back the deadbolt. Tyla, who was still standing on the doorstep, didn't seem in a hurry to move, but after a sharp glare from Wallace, she scuttled away.

The DI was in his late thirties with short dark hair and a permanent scowl, which hardened as he locked eyes with them.

Ginny couldn't blame him after what happened the last time. And while they *had* helped solve the case, Wallace hadn't been best pleased with Ginny and her friends' interference.

But he and Ginny were also neighbours, and slowly becoming friends.

Though judging by his frown now, this might set our friend-ship back a few steps.

'Seriously?' he growled, making Ginny suspect that no one had told him who had called it in. His usual uniform of dark slacks and an equally dark leather jacket was hidden beneath the all-in-one paper suit.

'We didn't do it.' Tuppence stepped forward, hands high in the air. 'I swear we didn't. It was just a big misunderstanding. But not a fight. There weren't any harsh words. And, yes, tech-nically Harlow banned me from coming back, but like I said, it was just a mis—'

'I think DI Wallace wants to know why we didn't wait outside the shop.' Ginny touched her friend's arm and Tuppence lowered her hands down by her side as relief flooded her face.

'Oh... of course. I knew that. But we had no choice. The

spring fete is in three weeks, which means there are a few desperate crafters in the village. They wouldn't take no for an answer. It was like a zombie movie. You know the kind where they won't stop once they've smelled brains. In fact—'

'Where's the body?' Wallace cut in as a tiny muscle at the side of his neck began to twitch.

'It's behind there.' Ginny gestured to the velvet curtain dividing the two spaces, before Tuppence could inadvertently make him angrier. 'We didn't go near it. I promise.'

'Small mercies,' he muttered, as the doorbell chimed again and PC Anita Singh walked in, wearing a similar crime scene suit. Wallace grunted a greeting to his colleague and said, 'Singh, come with me.' He then pointed with his finger. 'You two can wait over there until we're ready to get a statement. Don't touch anything.'

Ginny and Tuppence silently made their way past a display table of buttons, ribbons and a fanned-out collection of boxes, all containing sewing scissors. Ginny shuddered, once again thinking of the lifeless body. Is that where the weapon had come from? She knew better than to open any of the boxes to see if the contents were missing. The police would do it themselves.

Over by the counter, Wallace and PC Singh were having a whispered conversation that was only interrupted by the door chimes as two paramedics came through. They weren't pushing a trolley but did have large packs on their shoulders.

Wallace waved them over and they all disappeared into the other room. The curtain was tugged firmly back into place.

Ginny stared out of the window. A crowd had gathered on the other side of the road, held back by two uniformed officers and a stretch of police tape that had been set up to cordon off the area. In a strange way it did seem to resemble the zombie movie Tuppence had alluded to. In the distance, more sirens sounded.

'How long do you think we'll have to stay here?'

'Until they've taken our statements,' Ginny guessed. 'I'm sure they'll be as eager for us to be gone as we are.'

'Wallace didn't look pleased. Though I'm not sure why. Last week he was stuck investigating who stole William's ham sandwiches from the packed lunch he'd taken to lawn bowls. A murder is a bit more exciting.'

'I don't think he'll see it that way.'

'You're probably right.' Tuppence wandered over to the rolls of fabric leaning against the wall. Her hand drifted out to a bright floral print and she let out a pained sigh. 'This is the one I'd decided to use instead. If only we had arrived earlier. *"Better three hours too soon than a minute too late."'*

'I didn't know you were a Shakespeare fan.' Ginny raised a surprised eyebrow and turned to her friend.

'Oh, is that who said it?' Tuppence stepped away from the fabric, as if not wanting to tempt herself to touch it. 'I only know the quote because Taron used to say it sometimes when he was working on a commission.'

Out of her three friends, Tuppence talked the least about her husband. All Ginny knew was he'd died ten years ago and had been a successful artist who'd done several murals in the area, and had a small studio at the back of their cottage. Tuppence didn't offer up any more information, and instead wrapped her arms around her waist.

'It's from *The Merry Wives of Windsor*,' Ginny said, steering the conversation in a different direction. Not that she was a Shakespeare expert, but Eric had been fond of amateur dramatics and had been involved in several productions over the years, even going so far as to—

Her skin prickled as something tugged at her mind, but before she could follow the thought the front door opened again and a woman in her mid-thirties walked in.

She had red hair pulled back at the nape of her neck, large

brown eyes and was wearing the same white paper suit. Frowning, she looked around before PC Singh appeared through the curtain and beckoned the woman over.

'That must be Imogen Smith, the new pathologist based in Preston. I heard she was lovely. Much nicer than the old one,' Tuppence whispered as Wallace and Anita returned. 'Oh dear. He doesn't seem happy. Look at his furrowed brow and clenched jaw. All classic signs of anger. Remember what Doctor Judy said?'

Ginny nodded. Tuppence had made them all watch several YouTube videos about how older women could use body language to make them feel more confident and visible. Ginny wasn't sure it had helped her stand out more, but it had been interesting to learn about visceral reactions and tell-tale signs. And Tuppence was right.

Wallace looked angry.

He stalked over, while the paramedics headed back to their ambulance. 'The pathologist is examining the body, so we'll get your statements. Tuppence, please go with PC Singh. Ginny, you're with me,' Wallace announced.

'That's a relief,' Tuppence said, before wincing. 'Er, I mean that you're talking with Ginny. After all, she was first on the scene and you know how observant she is.'

'I'm well aware of her powers of observation,' he retorted in a grim voice as he beckoned Ginny over to the far side of the shop. He pulled out a notebook and fixed her a levelling stare. 'Tell me what time you arrived and exactly how you managed to find the body.'

'We left the library at ten minutes past one, so it must have been at least twenty past one when we arrived,' Ginny said, then calmly took him through everything that had happened up to when they decided to lock themselves in the shop. She also gave him a list of surfaces that she remembered touching, as well as the parcel of fabric that she'd put down, and what Tuppence had told her about the fight she'd had with Harlow earlier in the week. She even mentioned the several skeins of fallen tapestry thread she'd picked up from the floor before going into the backroom.

Wallace jotted it all down, then scanned his notes. 'Was there anyone else in the shop when you came in?'

'No. Well, not out the front,' she amended. 'If there was anyone out the back, I didn't hear them.'

'And what about when you stepped outside to find Tuppence? Did anyone go in or out while you were talking?'

She shook her head. 'With the weather being so lovely, the high street was almost deserted. It was the same at the library. If there had been anyone else around, we would have noticed. Though I don't know if there is a back exit.'

'There isn't. Now, tell me again what happened when you found the body. Did you touch or move anything?'

'I didn't move the body, but I did check for a pulse.' Ginny frowned, not sure why he was asking her when she'd already gone over it with him. She talked him through it once more, but his lips were still tight as he studied her.

'Would you be so good as to pass me your handbag?'

'My handbag? Whatever for?' Her grip tightened on the sensible black bag hanging over her shoulder. Then she stiffened, remembering that the last time she'd found a body, she'd inadvertently taken home a piece of evidence. Heat prickled her skin, but she passed it over to him.

Without a word he slipped on plastic gloves and went through the contents.

After what seemed like an eternity, he replaced her library book, wallet, keys, and various other items back in the bag and folded his arms. 'That's it for now, unless you have anything else to tell me.'

Again, the niggle pressed at her mind, but it dissipated like a puff of smoke when she tried to grasp it.

'No.'

'Okay. We still have your prints on file *from the last time.* And we might require you to come down to the station if we need more information.'

'Do you have any idea who killed him?' Ginny said, but was met with a flat stare.

'Nothing that I would like to share with a member of the public. And while I don't believe in coincidence, I'm choosing to give you the benefit of the doubt about being first on the scene. Again. However, if I find out you've been—' He broke off as the pathologist appeared on the threshold and made a gesturing motion at him. Wallace rubbed the back of his neck. 'Just stay out of it. Please.'

'I will,' Ginny assured him as he disappeared through to the backroom. And she meant it. From the little Tuppence had told her, Timothy Harlow had been a bad-tempered eccentric shop owner who'd gone out of his way to make enemies. And while it didn't make his death any less shocking, she had no wish to get involved in police business.

All she wanted to do was go home, put on her slippers and pretend the whole afternoon had never happened.

She was joined by Tuppence and PC Singh.

'How are you holding up, Mrs Cole? I hope DI Wallace wasn't too hard on you. I think he forgets that most of us aren't used to... well... *that*. Did he offer you any support?'

'I'm fine. Just ready to go home.'

'Of course, but if there's something you didn't want to tell the guv...' The PC trailed off, no doubt remembering it had been Ginny who first suggested her old library manager might have been poisoned. And while Ginny didn't doubt the body would've been sent to the pathologist anyway, it meant Anita, who was hoping to become a detective, stood in awe of her.

It was woefully misplaced.

And besides, even if she had noticed something – which she hadn't – she was hardly going to break her promise to Wallace.

She shook her head. 'Sorry. I told him everything I know.'

'Oh.' Anita swallowed a look of disappointment and even Tuppence seemed surprised. As if they'd both expected Ginny to pull an obscure clue out of her sensible leather handbag. 'Okay, well, PC Bent will drive you both home.'

By the time they stepped outside, the high street was a hive of activity and several library regulars tried to wave them over.

Ginny gave them a weak smile and kept walking towards the squad car parked further down the street. But Tuppence grinned and strode off in their direction.

The PC's face turned puce and he let out a yelp of alarm. 'Whoa. No, Mrs Wilde, I've got strict orders to drive you straight home.' He sprinted across and managed to insert himself between Tuppence and the many onlookers.

'It's okay, I was just going to give them a quick update,' Tuppence assured him in a cheerful voice. 'I'm sure Wallace wouldn't mind.'

'Then you don't know Wallace,' the PC retorted, now raising his arms to block the onlookers from getting closer as he attempted to herd Tuppence away.

Ginny walked past Wallace's electric vehicle and over to the squad car. A man with dark hair was hovering nearby. He was lean and probably not much taller than she was, but there was a tightness to his jaw that made her think he wasn't someone to back down from a fight.

Was he another detective? On seeing her, he spun on his heel and slipped under the protective barrier of the police tape. She blinked, but by the time a harassed-looking PC Bent and Tuppence appeared, the man had gone.

Should she say something? But what? Besides, he might very well have been a police officer. Or a paramedic? More importantly, she'd promised to stay out of it. Sighing, she climbed into the car while Tuppence got in next to her, still beaming.

'Well, I bet now JM and Hen are sorry they didn't come with us. They've missed out on all the fun.'

THREE

Unlike Tuppence, Ginny didn't want to tell anyone about the afternoon's events, especially the part that involved Timothy Harlow's lifeless body lying inert in the backroom of his shop. Thankfully, her friend accepted Ginny's refusal of company in favour of a long bath and a quiet night.

'Call me if you change your mind. I can come back in a flash.' Tuppence squeezed her hand before PC Bent drove away, leaving Ginny alone outside Middle Cottage.

Despite its name, Ginny's home was in fact a quaint semi-detached house with a pastel-pink door, and a newly laid front garden full of daffodils and jonquils. But for once she didn't stop to gently tug at the weeds or admire the new growth. She unlocked the door and slipped inside before any of her neighbours could see her.

Her first instincts were to tell Eric about what had happened, but she'd been trying to break herself of that habit, and her new year's resolution had been to only talk to her dead husband once a day. Instead, she turned to the black cat who

had padded through from the sitting room, his amber eyes
bright with curiosity. Or indifference. Sometimes it was hard to
tell.

She'd adopted Edgar six months ago after he'd been abandoned, and she liked to think they were helping each other. So,
now she tended to address her conversations to the cat instead.
Though if Eric wants to listen then surely that's okay.

She toed off her sneakers in exchange for her slippers and
headed into the kitchen. Edgar darted past and sat by his bowl
as Ginny recited the afternoon's events. But when she had
finished, he merely nudged her ankle to remind her he was
waiting to be fed.

'Glad to see the news hasn't made you lose your appetite.'
She shook out some dry food and made herself a cup of tea
before retreating to the small conservatory that ran down the
side of the house.

Edgar busied himself with one of the many pot plants,
swiping at something with his front paw. Ginny settled into a
chair and closed her eyes. She hadn't intended to have a nap,
but like many things these days, her body seemed to have other
ideas, and it wasn't until she woke up, her neck stiff and her
mouth slightly open, that she realised she'd been asleep. Grog-
gily, she looked at the clock on the wall. An hour had passed.

She was just contemplating whether to eat or have another
cup of tea when her phone rang. It was her sister-in-law's ring-
tone – Connor had shown Ginny how to set that up – and it
meant she couldn't ignore it.

Sighing, she retrieved her phone from the kitchen counter.

Nancy was in Provence on holiday, but Ginny had sent her
a quick text message from the police car, giving her an update
and telling her not to worry.

Clearly it hadn't worked.

'Again? You found a dead body *again*?' Nancy demanded as
the sound of young children laughing and shrieking floated

around in the background. Ginny had been invited to join the whole family, including the grandchildren and two dogs, to stay in the French countryside, but had refused. It had only been ten weeks since she'd seen them for Christmas, and there was the small matter of her job.

'It's an honour I could've done without,' Ginny assured her, as Edgar stopped his playing and disappeared out through the cat door. Ginny wished she could do the same. 'I swear it's got nothing to do with me this time. I'd never even met the man before.'

'Yet you managed to find him stabbed in the back with scissors? Oh dear, I probably shouldn't have said that in front of the kids. Hang on.' Nancy stopped talking as the loud shrieks died away. 'There, I'm up in the bedroom. Now, where was—'

'You were about to lecture me on staying out of it?' Ginny suggested in a mild voice. 'Don't worry, Wallace has already done that. But it's unnecessary, I promise. The only reason I texted you was because I know Ian reads the English papers every morning and I didn't want you to find out second-hand.'

'I should think not,' Nancy retorted, and then let out a sigh. 'It's probably useless to suggest you fly out and spend the rest of the week with us. All this murder can't be good for you.'

It was worse for Timothy Harlow, but Nancy wouldn't appreciate the comment so Ginny spent the next ten minutes assuring her sister-in-law that there was nothing to worry about. She was just finishing when the cat door clunked open and Edgar reappeared, dragging along a single black shoe.

'Oh no. Edgar, how could you?' Ginny groaned as he deposited it in front of the pot plant. He blinked his amber eyes in answer, before walking up to the chair she'd just vacated and jumping up.

'What's he done? Chewed through a first edition?' Nancy demanded, in a dampening voice. 'I thought you broke him of that habit.'

'I did... well, at any event he stopped destroying my books,' Ginny said, not sure how much credit she could really take in the matter.

While Edgar was no longer interested in her books, he had found a new avenue of crime to explore. In the last two weeks he had presented her with a teddy bear, a perfume bottle and someone's mail.

'Has he brought in a mouse?'

'At least I'd know what to do if it was a mouse.' Ginny leaned forward. On closer inspection she discovered it was a child's football boot. And a very expensive brand at that. 'He's taken a shoe from one of the neighbours, which means I need to go door knocking. Again.'

'Well, you did insist on adopting a cat.' Nancy's sniff suggested that Ginny should have known this would happen. 'Any idea who it might belong to?'

'The woman who lives on the other side of Wallace has four young boys who are always kicking a ball around. I'll try her first.'

'I suppose it's a good way to meet the neighbours,' Nancy admitted, as the sound of crying rang out in the background. Her sister-in-law sighed. 'I'd better go. But promise me you'll take it easy this evening. You've experienced a shock and it's important to get plenty of rest. Eric would tell you the same thing.'

'I know.' Ginny swallowed, trying not to hear his voice in her mind. 'Give my love to everyone and I promise I'll come straight home without passing Go.'

She looked down at Edgar, who was now curled into a glossy black ball, one paw covering his nose. His low, even purr suggested he was sound asleep, and it was clear he felt no guilt for his latest crime.

Which meant it was up to her to return the boot.

Wallace's car wasn't there as she walked past his house,

though the sitting room light was on, as was the low buzz of the radio. That was strange. But before she could consider it, Hannah appeared at her front door, closely followed by two young boys, who tore out to the driveway, both brandishing kites.

Ginny hurried over to the fence line and ruefully held up the boot as the harassed mother joined her.

'Don't tell me that sodding kid of mine threw it into your yard. I have been searching for it all day. Forty quid they cost… and a fat lot of good it is to only have one.'

'My cat just brought it inside, but I'm not sure where it came from,' Ginny admitted, not certain whether Edgar deserved the benefit of the doubt.

'Oh, I've heard about him. Phyllis down the road said he made off with her Visa statement the other day,' Hannah replied, as Irene, who lived four houses down, bee-lined towards them, clutching two shopping bags.

'From what I could tell, her front door was open and he found the mail on the floor. I was mortified. And I'm so sorry you've spent all day looking for the boot.'

'Relax. Who knows where your cat found it. My boys have turned feral so they could have thrown it in there. They keep kicking their football into Wallace's back garden. His old man won't like it above half if he catches them doing it.'

'Old man?' Ginny shifted her gaze back to the light in her neighbour's window, as Irene came to a halt and dropped her shopping bags, puffing slightly from the walk. She seemed to have no problems picking up the thread of the conversation and turned to Ginny.

'Oh yes. Wallace's father arrived this morning. Not that you'd know it. I swear he never speaks. Then again, it's not like Wallace is a chatterbox. The apple didn't fall far from that bad-tempered tree, if you ask me. Did you meet him last time he was here?'

'Of course she didn't, you dope,' Hannah chided. 'Ginny went away over Christmas, when Ted was here the last time.'

'That's right.' Irene gave an understanding nod.

Ginny still wasn't used to how much her neighbours knew about each other, and about her, so she forced a placid smile.

'I didn't realise he was visiting again.'

'Got here at ten this morning then Wallace suddenly raced out the door and drove off in that car of his,' Irene elaborated.

'And right mad he looked about it,' Hannah added, as the two young boys ran back into the house, yelling and screaming. Their mother waved the single football boot after them. 'Don't you lot make a mess in there. I've just finished cleaning up. Anyway... where was I?'

'Talking about Wallace and that sour face of his.'

'Oh yes, that's right. You'd think he'd be pleased to have something exciting to do.'

Ginny bit down on her lip.

Exciting was the last thing she would call it. Flashes of the blood-soaked suit pressed into her mind and she shuddered.

Irene patted her arm. 'It's all right, love. No one liked Harlow. He was a smug git who thought his you-know-what didn't stink. I'm only surprised something like this didn't happen sooner.'

'It's true,' Hannah agreed. 'He yelled at my mate because she asked him if he had a pattern to knit a toilet-roll holder. Snooty old sod that he was.'

'Still... looks like this one is a clear-cut case.'

'What do you mean?' Ginny's body went stiff. She'd been bracing herself for the questions to start coming about her part in the discovery, but the two women seemed more interested in watching the elderly man from across the road shuffle towards them.

'You heard the news?' He joined them.

'Heard it before you, I bet,' Hannah retorted. 'My aunt was

the last one to see him alive, so I got it straight from the horse's mouth.'

Despite herself, Ginny let out a soft gasp. She'd been the one to find the body, which made her one part of the equation, but if Hannah's aunt had been last to see him alive, she was the other part. They were bookends to a murder. She wrapped her arms around her torso.

'Oh... that's lucky.' Irene brightened. 'What did she say?'

'It's all very exciting. She went into Harlow's at twelve-thirty to get some gingham for an apron she was making. He was on the phone arguing with Milos Petrovic, and after he finished the call, he was in a filthy temper. As soon as my aunt told the police about the call, they sent officers out to interview him.'

A suspect so quickly? It hardly seemed possible. And why did the name sound familiar? Then she remembered the beautiful chair she'd seen at the haberdashery. The craftsman had been Vanja Petrovic.

'Is he related to the upholsterer?'

'Yes, Vanja is his uncle and Milos worked for him since coming over from Serbia a couple of years back. Bit rough around the edges, but is a decent sort. I think he mainly does the deliveries and whatnot.'

'Still waters run deep,' the old man reminded them in a gloomy voice. 'Anyway, seems there was history between Timothy and Milos, so I guess it's case closed.'

'I don't think it works like that. Just because they were arguing on the phone, it doesn't mean it's related to the murder,' Ginny said, still not clear on how they knew so much. In all her dealings with Wallace so far, he'd been incredibly tight-lipped.

'Well, tell that to the police. The woman at the shop heard it from her son-in-law that they searched Milos's room and carried things away with them. Probably found his fingerprints everywhere.'

'What's the betting they don't want to pay double time on the weekends to get it done before Monday?' the old man complained. 'That's when they'll make the arrest. And a good thing too, if you ask me.'

'Definitely. Might improve Wallace's mood. I suppose he can take the old man out now. I hope so. I need to send my oldest back over the fence to retrieve his ball, once the coast is clear,' Hannah said, as a loud crash echoed from her open front door. She swore under her breath. 'Is it too much to ask for five minutes of peace?'

'Just wait until they get older. The bigger the kid, the bigger the problem,' Irene prophesied before picking up her shopping and nodding to the old man. 'Now come on, let's get you home. And next time you come out for a gossip, take your slippers off.'

'They're comfortable,' he grumbled as they both shuffled away, leaving Ginny to head back to her own house.

The sun was starting to sink in the sky and the living room curtains in Wallace's front room had already been closed, while the faint scent of fried onions drifted out. Her nose twitched. Wallace seemed to survive on takeaway food, so she wasn't used to any cooking smells. Still, she supposed it would be good for him to eat properly. Especially now that she had a better understanding of what went into a murder investigation and the strain the detective inspector was under.

She walked back inside and pulled her own curtains closed before retrieving her teacup from the conservatory. Edgar was still sleeping in the chair, but lying on the floor by the pot plant was a small plastic bag with a Ziplock running across it. In one corner were tiny teeth marks, as if a cat had dragged it in. It hadn't been there when she'd left to see Hannah, which meant he must have done it while she was out.

Seriously? Ginny let out an exasperated sigh and carried it over to the kitchen table. Inside were several old-fashioned index cards, but it wasn't until she spread them out in front of her that she realised what they were.

Recipe cards.

Each one had been typed out on a typewriter, with the titles underlined. She'd once had her own collection, but she'd discarded them years ago, tending to stick to her old favourites or just looking on the internet for inspiration.

She doubted they belonged to Hannah or Wallace. And even though his father was currently staying, she couldn't imagine he'd pack his recipe collection to visit his son. Which meant she'd have to once again go door knocking.

'Dreadful cat... you are determined to ruin my reputation, aren't you?'

Edgar didn't answer and Ginny rolled her neck. After everything that had happened, she didn't feel up to going out again right then.

'I'll try tomorrow, and let's hope whoever you took these from doesn't have a sudden craving for' – she broke off to study the top card – 'Upside Down Apple Cake with Almond Butter Mousse and Cinnamon Dusting.'

Edgar yawned and peered over at her, before licking his leg and going back to sleep. Ginny almost envied him. Not because of his crime spree or lack of remorse... but because of his ability, whatever the situation, to sleep.

Something she doubted she'd be getting much of that night.

FOUR

Sunday, 16th March

The following morning, Ginny finished washing and drying twelve glass jars and spread them out on a large metal tray, ready to be sterilised. As she worked, the preserving pan bubbled away on the stove.

The warm scent of simmering Seville oranges filled the kitchen and steamed up the windows. She'd managed a few hours of sleep but had woken up at five in the morning and hadn't been able to drift off again. It had been far too early to find the owner of the recipe cards, so she'd cleaned her house and made a start on the marmalade that she'd promised Cleo for the Friends of the Village stall.

The timer went off, and she removed the lid, waiting for the bubbling to subside before testing the rind with a fork. Perfect. Her face was clammy as she busied herself with the next steps, pleased to let herself get lost in the familiar rhythm of scooping, straining and stirring.

Once that was done, she set the liquid aside and turned to the orange skins that were waiting to be cut. Her brow was covered in a light sweat as she picked up her favourite pair of triple-bladed scissors. Tiny drops of condensation clung to the metal and Ginny quickly put them back down, too late remembering the sewing scissors embedded in Timothy Harlow's back.

Maybe not.

She took a shuddering breath and leaned against the counter. As a rule, she wasn't superstitious, but she didn't want to think about Harlow's death while making marmalade. She put the scissors away in the drawer and reached for her paring knife. It would take longer but was infinitely preferable.

'After all, it's not like I don't have enough time on my hands,' Ginny said, as she got to work.

Edgar, who was currently rolling around on yesterday's newspaper, didn't bother to answer and the next two hours were spent ensuring the marmalade was up to her usual standards. It was almost mid-morning by the time she'd finished, and she stepped into the garden to shake out her limbs.

Yesterday's sunshine had been replaced by an overcast sky, but the rain had held off. Perhaps she'd spend an hour in the two raised vegetable boxes she'd had built. The kale and spinach swayed in the growing breeze as a curious cabbage moth tried to settle down on them. Ginny waved it off then stiffened at the sharp buzz of a doorbell. It was coming from Wallace's house.

It rang out several more times and was followed by a *thump, thump, thump* of someone pounding against the wood. Ginny winced. If Wallace was at home, he would hardly be happy.

The noise continued as the back door opened and the shadow of a figure slipped outside. While she couldn't see the person clearly, it appeared to be a man in his mid-sixties. The back gate that led through to the fields behind their houses creaked open and then closed again.

Was Wallace's father running away from the visitors?

Before she could decide, her own doorbell buzzed, followed

by the all-too-familiar sound of JM's powerful voice coming from the front of the house. 'Ginny? Are you there? It's us.'

'Go away, Us,' boomed the discombobulated voice of Hannah's husband from the other side of Wallace's house. 'It's Sunday morning.'

'Nonsense, it's almost lunch time,' JM corrected, her voice getting louder as she spoke to the unseen neighbour.

Spurred into action, before a full-on shouting match developed, Ginny hurried through to the front of her house where her three friends were waiting. Seeing their familiar smiles helped shift the tightness that had been lodged in her chest since stumbling across Harlow's body.

JM was very tall with straight, silver hair and dressed like she was a World War One spy. Today she was wearing a pair of wide-legged men's trousers and a crisp white blouse. Next to her, only coming up to her shoulder, was Hen, who was wearing a long denim skirt and a blue and white polka dot T-shirt, while Tuppence had on her overalls and a pair of orange Crocs.

Parked on the street was a line of three small silver cars, almost identical to Ginny's own. She quickly ushered them inside before any more of the neighbours could complain.

'Thank goodness you're at home,' Tuppence said.

'I hope you don't mind us turning up unannounced.' Hen clutched at her knitting bag. 'Especially after what happened yesterday. You must still be in shock.'

'Mind? Why should she mind?' JM demanded, once the door was closed. 'It's only natural that we would want to make sure she's feeling okay.'

'I told them that you weren't up to having visitors last night,' Tuppence added, looking pleased with herself.

Ginny found herself being dragged into a chaotic hug by her three friends. Unexpected tears prickled her eyes. One of the hardest parts of losing Eric was the lack of physical contact. And while she'd never been a hugger before, her friends seemed determined to convert her. Not for the first time, she let out a grateful sigh that she had met the three other women.

They finally untangled themselves and Ginny led them through to the kitchen.

'I take it you've heard the news?' JM said.

'My neighbours told me yesterday that the police have a suspect. Do you know Milos? Have they made an arrest?' Ginny asked, the questions spilling out so quickly that she almost laughed. In the past she'd been content to let others do the talking, but the more time she spent with her friends, the more they seemed to rub off on her.

'Not very well, though we all know his uncle. Vanja has lived in the village for years. From what he said Milos had a checkered past and that's why the family sent him to England. He's only been here for a couple of years and, for the most part, keeps to himself,' Tuppence said. 'They haven't arrested him yet, but he is still being held.'

'Poor Vanja. We must bake a casserole for him. I'm sure he'll be upset.' Hen took out the knitting needles that were never far from her side and cast on with some bright fuchsia wool.

'Or relieved... if it is true,' JM retorted, before her sharp gaze fell on the numerous jars of marmalade. 'But I'm sure that's the last thing Ginny wants to talk about. I'm glad you've been keeping busy.'

'Indeed. It smells delightful in here,' Hen added, colour rising in her cheeks that she might have upset someone. 'I saw Sandra last week and she told me you'd agreed to make some jars for the stall. I'll have to make sure I buy at least two. Look at the colour.'

'I was planning to make another batch for you all. And it's very sweet of you to worry. But I'm feeling much better.' Ginny filled the kettle and set out a tray of cups and a jug of milk, along with a plate of biscuits. She carried them over to the table

and then returned to the counter so she could scoop tea leaves
into her largest pot. 'And was that you knocking on Wallace's
door?'

'We'll let Tuppence explain that to you,' JM announced in a
dry voice.

Tuppence? Ginny swivelled around, still clutching the tea
caddy. 'Is everything okay? Don't tell me Wallace wants to talk
to you again?'

'Not that I know of. Well... not yet. But Hen thinks he will.
So, we've come to see him.'

'A pre-emptive strike,' JM added.

'Except we didn't take into account that he might not be
home.' Hen sighed.

Ginny's brows knitted together as she poured boiling water
into the teapot, releasing a rich, earthy aroma. 'I don't follow.
What's happened?'

'When we were at Harlow's yesterday, it seemed a great
pity that I wouldn't be able to swap over my fabric. And even
worse that I wouldn't be able to get my old fabric back since PC
Singh told me it was considered evidence.'

'Which is ridiculous. Next, they'll be saying the fabric was a
witness.' JM waved a hand in the air.

Unease crept down Ginny's spine. 'You took your parcel of
fabric back? But I left it on the counter. I would have seen you
pick it up.'

'You and Wallace both,' Tuppence qualified, in a way that
suggested she had considered it. 'But while you were talking, I
did find a very nice button on the floor. It was silver and the
exact thing I needed for my winter coat. And I figured it's not
like Harlow would miss it. Plus, when you think of how much I
paid for that fabric...'

'You took something from the crime scene?' Ginny re-joined
them as Tuppence retrieved a net bag and put it on the table.

'Well, yes. It was a spur-of-the-moment decision, and when

I realised last night what it might mean, I felt simply *awful*. I didn't have one of those fancy evidence bags, but this is what I use to wash my bras in. I think it will still serve.'

'Now we have more experience in these things, we thought Tuppence should hand it in as soon as possible.' Hen knitted faster and faster, clearly worried. 'But Wallace wasn't at the station so we came here. His car isn't there, but we saw someone inside. Do you think he's avoiding us?'

'Not if he knows what's good for him.' JM's expression darkened.

'It could've been his father. He arrived yesterday,' Ginny explained, now understanding what had happened. Wallace's father must have slipped away from the house, not wanting to talk to anyone. 'Apparently he's quiet. Perhaps it will be best if you leave the button at the station, after all.'

'I suppose we'll have to.' JM picked up one of the jars of marmalade and toyed with it. 'But we should take a photograph of it first.'

'Oh, that's an excellent idea.' Hen opened the net bag and the button rolled onto the table. It was a dull silver and was embossed in the style of a Roman coin.

The hairs on the back of Ginny's neck prickled as something once again teased at the corner of her mind, but before she could follow the thread, Hen picked up the button and passed it to JM – which meant both their fingerprints were now on it.

JM then carefully placed it on the table and Tuppence took several shots of it, before returning it to the bag.

'There. I don't think Wallace could have anything to complain about.'

'Exactly,' JM agreed. 'It's called due diligence.'

Ginny was almost certain that it wasn't called that at all, but simply picked up the teapot and poured out four cups before handing around the biscuits. She hadn't had an appetite the previous night but now felt hungry and took one herself.

She had just bitten into it when a wailing sound came from somewhere outside the house. It was followed by a high-pitched screech: 'Wallace, I need to talk to you. Let me in. Let me in.'

The four of them exchanged glances and hurried outside to where a woman was pounding on Wallace's front door. She looked slim though her figure was largely hidden under a grubby raincoat, and her long dark hair was pulled back from her angular face.

'You have to let me in.' She cried, her voice tinged with hysteria.

'It's Megan, Timothy Harlow's daughter. Oh, the poor thing.' Hen's mouth quivered with worry as neighbours materialised on all sides to see what the commotion was. But Megan ignored the growing audience as she continued to ring the doorbell.

'And I thought it would be quiet living next to a copper.' Hannah emerged from her front door, wrapped up in a dressing gown, an irritated expression in her eyes. 'Don't bother, love. He's not at home. Just like I told the last lot.'

'Then I'll wait until he gets back, because I *must* speak to him. He's made a terrible mistake.' Megan pulled a phone out of the raincoat's pocket and stabbed in a number. 'I'll call him again and tell him so. He needs to know the real killer is still out there.'

A collective gasp went up from the neighbours.

'She's obviously in shock.' Hen's mouth trembled again.

'If she's not careful she'll end up in prison,' JM warned.

'I think we'd better save her from herself,' Tuppence decided, and hurried down Ginny's front path and around to Wallace's side. She put an arm around Megan and whispered something in her ear before leading her back towards Ginny's house. 'You don't mind, do you?'

'Of course not,' Ginny said, uncertainly. She'd promised Wallace not to get involved, but she couldn't imagine he would be pleased to come home to find a hysterical woman on his doorstep. Or that Tuppence had removed something from the crime scene.

They bustled Megan Harlow through to Ginny's kitchen and put a hot mug of tea into her hands, but it was several minutes before she finally stopped crying.

'There, are you feeling better?' Hen pressed another tissue towards her.

Megan took it and blew her nose. 'Th-thank you. It's very kind of you. But I need to speak to DI Wallace.'

'Of course you do. But not in front of everyone. You know how people talk around here,' Hen continued.

Megan's face darkened and she let out a bitter bark of laughter. 'Trust me, *no one* knows that better than I do. The only reason I'm still here is because I couldn't leave my father to run the business on his own. And now—' She broke off into a fresh flood of tears and it was several minutes before she finally looked up, her eyes red and bloodshot. 'I can't believe this has happened.'

'We're ever so sorry. But Hen's right, you can't wait outside Wallace's house. He wouldn't like it. And you've had a terrible shock. Why don't you let us drive you home?' Tuppence suggested.

Hen looked worried. 'She can't go back to her house alone. Megan, is there somewhere else you can stay? Do you have any relations? Or a friend?'

'No. There's no one who can help. And I don't have friends.'

'No friends or family? You poor thing.' Hen's worry increased.

'Can't miss what you don't have,' Megan said, before another tear leaked out from the corner of her eye. 'And it would be impossible to sleep while poor Milos is still being held.'

'What makes you so sure he's innocent?' JM held Megan's gaze, as if she was in court.

But Megan didn't seem to notice as she toyed with the handle of her teacup. 'Because Milos and his uncle, Vanja, are good friends of ours. My father helped Vanja set up his business almost twenty years ago, and now the classes are always sold out and everyone in the area uses him,' Megan said, before turning to face Tuppence. 'Well... almost everyone.'

'I'm on a budget,' Tuppence defended. 'But I'm sure he's a lovely man.'

'He is. And so is Milos. The only reason Wallace is holding him is because he's an immigrant.' Megan began to sob again. 'Someone has set him up.'

'How have they set him up? And why was he heard arguing on the phone with your father?' JM asked.

'They're saying they found my father's watch in Milos's room, and that his work boots had blood all over them. But it's not true. Milos's boots were stolen a week ago. He takes them off before he goes into anyone's house, and when he was delivering a sofa last week, he came outside and found them gone. Whoever did this must have taken them and planted them in his room, along with my father's watch. He is being set up. And if you think a trained upholsterer would *ever* let anyone in his workshop use sewing scissors to stab someone, it shows how little you know.'

'Excuse me? What are you implying?' JM bristled before Hen quickly patted her arm.

'It's okay. Megan just means that no self-respecting sewer would use their good scissors on anything but fabric.'

'Oh, I see.' JM rubbed her chin as if considering the information before giving a decisive nod. 'Well, that does change the case. I wonder that no one pointed it out to Wallace.'

'You know how busy police are. They might not have time

for a hobby,' Tuppence reasoned, as she chewed her lip. 'But it's a jolly good point. I can't believe I didn't think of it sooner.'

'There was a lot going on,' Hen reminded her.

Ginny wasn't sure that this fact alone would be enough to convince Wallace that Milos was innocent. She turned to Megan.

'Besides the scissors, do you have any other reason to think Milos didn't do it?'

Megan was silent for some time as her narrow fingers reached up to a gold locket hanging around her neck. She toyed with it for several moments before letting out a shuddering sigh. 'Yes... You see, we're in love. There's no way he would ever do anything to hurt me.'

And with a final twist of the necklace, she burst into tears again.

FIVE

Sunday, 16th March

Between sips of tea and crumpled tissues, Megan brought up a photo on her phone and held it out. Milos Petrovic looked younger than his thirty-eight years, with caramel hair, high cheekbones and warm eyes the colour of chocolate. He and Megan were standing at Blackpool Pleasure Beach. His arm was wrapped tightly around Megan's shoulder and his gaze was loving. Megan looked just as smitten, with one hand resting on his chest, just below a gold pendant hanging from his neck.

Ginny leaned closer, wondering if it was the same as the one Megan was now wearing. But it wasn't a locket; instead, it was flat and in the shape of something.

'It's lovely, isn't it?' Megan touched the screen, clearly following Ginny's gaze. She used her fingers to expand it. Up close the pendant was of a two-headed bird with a single crown on top. 'It's a Serbian eagle. He's had it since he was little.'

'Very nice. I'm not always a fan of too much jewellery but it suits him,' JM conceded.

'And you both look so happy together,' Hen added, as Megan reduced the size of the photo again and sighed.

'It was a magical day. This is when it first started. He had never been on a rollercoaster, you see. So, I offered to take him. We were friends, but I never thought for a minute he'd want more. I mean, look at me. I'm nothing compared to the kind of girls he could date. But he said he didn't want them. He wanted me.'

'Looks fade but character doesn't,' JM said, sternly. 'So, what happened? Why would the police think Milos killed your father?'

Megan let out an angry sob. 'Because my father was against us. He said it was beneath me to date someone like Milos. Which was such an irony, because he'd been making a fortune off Vanja's workshops and all the fabric he sold to the people who attended them. But he still thought he was better than Vanja and Milos. He didn't care that, for the first time, I had a life of my own. Someone who loved me. You'd think we were the royal family the way he carried on. But I refused to break up with Milos.'

'Rightly so,' Hen said warmly, and Tuppence nodded her head in approval.

'What happened then?' JM pressed before Megan could start crying again.

'My father threatened to stop supplying Vanja with exclusive fabrics, and to cancel all the future workshops. Milos went around to talk about it. To explain that there was no reason to punish Vanja. It didn't go well and they argued. And—' She gulped. 'My father called the police and said he'd been attacked, and that he wanted a restraining order against Milos.'

'A restraining order?' JM's brows rose up, and Megan miserably nodded.

'Milos isn't violent. I swear he's not. My father just doesn't like having his will crossed. I talked him out of filing for it, but it still looks bad.'

'So the police know about your relationship?' JM continued, and again Megan nodded.

Silence fell as they all considered the implications. It was easy to see why he was a suspect.

But even if he has a motive, it doesn't mean he had the opportunity.

Ginny pressed her lips together as she considered this. 'Where was Milos yesterday? Why are the police so certain he did it?'

Megan sighed. 'He had an argument with Vanja. I'm afraid his uncle was also against us being together. He wanted Milos to marry the daughter of an old family friend in Belgrade. Milos walked out on his uncle and went for a ride on his motorbike. He was on country lanes and even if there was CCTV footage, I doubt they'd try looking for it.'

'And where were you?' Ginny asked, partly to stop Megan from falling back into despair again.

It worked, and the other woman wiped away the fresh tears glistening in her lashes. 'I was with the accountant the whole time. It's all such a mess, and no one will believe me that Milos is being set up.'

'Yes, but *who* would do that? Is it someone who wanted to hurt your father... or Milos?' JM probed.

'My father, of course. Everyone loved Milos,' Megan immediately answered.

'What about the woman his uncle wanted him to marry?' Ginny wondered. 'If it's an arranged marriage, did she feel slighted? Or her family?'

'She's still in Serbia, and Milos swears she didn't want to marry either. Besides, I know who the killer is. It's Ants Mancini.'

'Mancini?' Hen dropped her knitting into her lap and

formed an "O" with her mouth. Tuppence and JM looked equally astonished. 'You think that Ants killed your father?'

'I don't think it, I know it.' Megan's tear-soaked eyes suddenly flashed. 'He's a terrible man who has hated my father for years. Wallace needs to arrest him before he flees the country. Otherwise, it will be too late.'

'Who is he?' Ginny ventured to ask.

Hen opened her mouth to answer, but Megan got in first: 'He's a tailor who works locally – he's popular as he makes all the costumes for the Little Shaw theatre. And then he decided to run us into the ground by setting up a rival business.'

'There's a second haberdashery shop in Little Shaw?'

'Yes,' Hen said, a frown between her eyes. 'Well, he's not in the town proper. He has a lovely barn about three miles out, and he's converted several other outbuildings, which he rents to local craftspeople. But Ants has been operating like this for several years. Why would he suddenly want to... hurt... your father?'

'He's jealous, you see, because my father is such a well-known celebrity, and we have the shop, which has always been a vital part of Little Shaw's heritage. He was desperate to be part of it, and tried to buy his way into the business, but my father told him we were family run and that's the way it would stay.'

'That's true,' Tuppence agreed. 'Megan's grandfather ran the business for many years before her father took over. My mother used to shop there.'

'And so did mine. It was the hub of the community,' Hen agreed.

'We have the reputation and legacy that Ants could never get on his own. It ate away at him. Plus, he believed that my father had gone back on his word about bringing him into the business. It's not true, of course. But it's why he decided to start upholstery courses in his old barn. He even held them at the

same time as Vanja's courses. He could offer more workshops –
a lot more than we could – because he had the space. Until
finally he set up his own haberdashery so he could sell directly
to people. We still have our loyal customers. But it's becoming
harder to convince them to support us.' Megan's hands
clenched together.

'What do you mean?' Ginny asked gently, and Megan
flushed and flexed her fingers, as if embarrassed to show how
she really felt.

'We have to charge more because of the cost of maintaining
the shop. And *that man* constantly undercuts our prices. Sometimes I'm sure he even sells at a loss. Financially, things have
been getting tough. My father went to see Ants a few weeks ago,
to broker a peace deal, and see if there was a way we could work
together, instead of against each other.'

'Well, I must say that it's an excellent idea.' Hen, who hated
any kind of conflict, looked relieved. 'What happened?'

'I'll tell you what happened.' Once again Megan's hands
clenched into two small fists. 'He agreed to the meeting, but on
the day, he laughed at my father. And said he would *never* work
with a... backstabber.'

'Backstabber?' Tuppence gasped, and all of the women
stared at each other.

Ginny tried to push away the unwanted image of Harlow's
dead body.

'That explains the sewing scissors. They were symbolic,'
Hen said.

'As far as metaphors go, it's nicely done,' JM admitted.

Ginny pressed her lips together as an elusive thought once
again danced around the corner of her mind. Was it to do with
backstabbing... or the scissors?

'Which is why I know he's behind it,' Megan declared, two
angry balls of colour staining her cheeks. 'Mancini swore to
make my father rue the day he refused to let him join the busi-

ness. And now he's done it. He's run us into the ground... humiliated my father by pretending to listen to the business proposal, and killed him into the bargain.'

'What did the police say when you told them this?' JM demanded. 'I mean, it's irrefutable proof, so I don't see how they could dismiss it.'

'They said they had several avenues of investigation, but I could tell they didn't believe me. Wallace said that just because my father was' – she choked on the words and it took several moments to collect herself – 'stabbed in the back, it didn't mean that was the motive.'

'Did he say he would look into it?' Hen asked.

'Yes, but an hour later they brought Milos in for questioning and refused to let him go. Vanja called me, begging for help. Language is a problem for him and he was worried Milos would be arrested. I went to the station, but Wallace wasn't there. And he didn't return any of my calls, which is why I came here. I know he's avoiding me, but he can't do it forever. I must make him listen before they make an arrest.'

Ginny bowed her head as she sifted through the information. Wallace was right. Just because Timothy Harlow was stabbed in the back, it didn't mean that was part of the motive.

And yet she also agreed with JM that as far as metaphors went, it was spot—

Oh.

Abruptly, Ginny stood up, her chair scraping against the wooden floor as the vague threads that had been trying to weave themselves together in her mind suddenly made sense.

The calendar.

Tuppence misquoting Shakespeare.

And even the button.

Her friends all looked at her, eyes wide.

'Is something wrong?' Hen frowned.

'I think something's right,' Tuppence corrected.

'Definitely. She's doing that thing with her mouth again,' JM agreed, before turning to Megan. 'Ginny's ever so clever when it comes to piecing things together.'

'What is it?' Megan leaned forward. 'Do you know something?'

'Yesterday was the fifteenth of March,' she said, but when no one commented, she elaborated. '"Beware the Ides of March."'

SIX

Ginny swallowed as everyone in the room stared at her. Megan's eyes were still fogged with grief, Hen's brow was wrinkled in confusion and Tuppence picked up her phone, as if pondering whether to ask YouTube what was going on.

She shouldn't have said anything. But before she could apologise for rambling, JM stood up and grinned. 'The ides of March. How could I have forgotten? It was the day that Caesar was stabbed in the back by the members of the Senate.' JM spread her arms out wide as if channelling the famous orator. 'Of course. The ides were a Roman concept for marking the middle of the month, and Caesar was warned something would happen on that day. "Beware the Ides of March."'

'That's right.' Ginny nodded. 'Though I believe it was Shakespeare's play about Caesar that made the quote famous.'

'Shakespeare?' Hen's eyes were wide with awe. 'Ginny, how clever you are to have remembered that.'

'It's utterly brilliant,' Tuppence agreed. 'Most of the time I don't even remember what day it is, yet alone the date.'

Heat stung Ginny's cheeks, and she tried to wave away the compliments. 'It's only a guess. And I had a bit of help... you see, someone had crossed off each day of the wall calendar. And the date itself is quite well known.'

'Not by me.' Hen shook her head. 'I've even seen the play a couple of times. But it's in one ear and out the other with me.'

'Are you saying my father was killed on the same day as Caesar?' Megan suddenly broke in, her angular face as green as the famous bronze *Statua di Giulio Cesare* in Rome.

Too late, Ginny realised her error. She should never have mentioned it when Megan was still so lost in grief. Or rage. Especially when it was only a theory at this point. 'Of course, it could be a coincidence. You heard Hen – she didn't know the quote despite having seen the play. I shouldn't have brought it up,' she quickly added, but it was too late.

Megan's long, narrow fingers clenched around the teacup as if she was trying to strangle it. 'It's not a coincidence. Mancini always made the costumes for the local theatre company and often performs in the productions. And he loves Shakespeare. And he's Italian. This proves he killed my father.'

'Oh, and don't forget the button.' Tuppence fumbled for her mesh bra bag and handed the tiny silver button over to Megan. 'Do you recognise this? Is it something you sell in your shop?'

'Absolutely not. We would never sell anything so garish.' Megan examined the button closely, turning it over several times in the process. Ginny winced. Yet more fingerprints on the evidence. 'But then Harlow's doesn't cater to costumes, which I assume this is for. It's more in line with what Mancini would sell. Why are you asking me this? Where did you find it?'

'In the shop, while we were waiting to give our statements,' Tuppence said, before suddenly seeming to remember she wasn't meant to have taken it. 'I, er... need to hand it in to Wallace.'

'It's proof he was there.' Megan sat bolt upright, her eyes far too large in her angular face. Her movements were jerky and filled with the kind of manic energy that came from sleep deprivation. 'Oh, thank you. This is exactly what I need to convince the police. Because the longer Milos is being held, the more time Mancini has to flee the country, like the backstabbing murderer he is.'

An uneasy sensation settled in Ginny's stomach. Wallace wouldn't be pleased if Megan charged into the station and accused someone of the murder. Or that she'd disturbed the neighbourhood pounding on his door.

'You can't publicly accuse him,' she said.

'I won't sit by and let him get away with it.' Megan got to her feet.

Ginny exchanged a quick glance with her friends, and they all seemed to recognise the need for restraint.

'That's not how this policing business works. We can certainly hand in the button and give them our theory. But that doesn't mean they will act on it.' JM put a hand on Megan's arm and guided her back into the chair.

'Are you telling me I should ignore this?'

'Of course not. She's just managing your expectations,' Tuppence said, soothingly. 'We learnt that from our last investigation. You see, it's vital that we don't give false hope to anyone. No one knows better than JM that the law works in mysterious ways.'

'*Very* mysterious,' Hen added, as she resumed her knitting. 'It really is much better to get a confession from him. That's what Ginny did last year, when she solved all those nasty murders.'

There was silence as Megan considered it, and Ginny sagged back in her chair. But her relief was short-lived.

'You're right.' Megan abruptly got to her feet again, this

time fumbling for her car keys. 'The police would never believe me. After all, they've already warned me to stop calling the station. But if I get Mancini to confess, it will prove he's guilty.'

'I don't think *that*'s a good idea.' Ginny's mouth dropped open in alarm. Their attempts at trying to stop Megan from charging into the police station had backfired. But how could they explain to the grief-stricken daughter that going to someone's house and accusing him of murder would only make things worse?

'What if we go to the police for you?' Tuppence suggested.

'No. I refuse to let my father's killer get away with this. I need to stop him from escaping. And to make him pay.' Megan's knuckles were white against the car keys, and Hen put down her knitting.

'Yes, love. But what if he doesn't want to speak with you? Or he might call the police and you'll find yourself in trouble?'

'Hen's right. You said yourself Mancini and your father were enemies. I doubt he'd let you in. Why don't you let us take you home and you can try to get some sleep?' Ginny suggested, wishing she'd never mentioned the ides of March.

'Sleep?' Megan's voice rose to a shriek and she bared her teeth. 'I won't know a moment's peace until my father's killer is caught. He's trying to ruin so many lives... all because of a stupid feud. Well, I won't let him.'

And then she was running to the front door.

'Damn. I should have known she'd be a flight risk.' JM hurried after her. 'I'll stop her. You come up with a plan.'

'I'd better help.' Hen scrambled up and followed JM out into the hallway.

'I think we've made a muddle of it,' Tuppence admitted. 'We can't let her visit Ants like this.'

'I should never have mentioned it. What if it's just a coincidence?'

'A coincidence? Of course it's not. I knew you'd find a clue the police had missed,' Tuppence said warmly, before picking up the bra bag. 'Though I suppose I helped by finding the button.'

'Still... it was silly to say anything when she's already grieving.'

'You weren't to know Ants was so involved in local theatre and was Italian. Or—'

Ginny was cut off by a kerfuffle from the hallway. They made their way through, to find JM leaning against the door, her arms spread wide.

'Let me out.' Megan clawed at JM's arm.

'I'm sorry but as your legal representative, it's my professional opinion that—'

'You're not my lawyer. And you need to let me out. Otherwise, he'll get away. Please, I must stop him.' Megan tugged at JM's arms before a huge sob racked her body. She was clearly exhausted.

'There, there. You cry it out, that's good. But JM's right. You can't talk to him. The police won't like it.' Tuppence put a comforting arm around the woman's shoulders.

'They don't care. They think the case is already solved. I can't believe my father's gone. And now they're trying to take Milos away from me.' With a low, guttural wail Megan slid to the floor and buried her head in her hands. It was followed by sobs that shook her entire body.

The four friends stared at each other, before Tuppence waved them to one side.

'There must be something we can do,' Hen whispered, her brown eyes filled with worry. Ginny's mouth went dry. It was bad enough finding the body and having to face Wallace yesterday. The last thing she wanted was to be on the wrong side of him again.

Megan continued to cry, and the uncontrollable flood of grief echoed through the hallway. The conflicting desire to soothe the devastated woman battled with Ginny's fear of the law.

'What if we talked to Mancini for her?' Tuppence suggested in a low voice, as Megan continued to cry. 'We could pretend to be buying wool.'

'You have to take the button to the police,' Ginny reminded her. 'And we need to get Megan home. She's clearly exhausted. And still trying to process her grief.'

'But if we take her home, what's the betting she'll hunt Mancini down as soon as we've gone. That's what I'd do.' JM rubbed her arm, where Megan had been tugging at it.

'Me, too,' Tuppence agreed. 'It's the only way to get any peace. What if Hen goes to speak with Mancini? She's the best knitter and sewer out of all of us, so he wouldn't think it was odd.'

'And I did want to ask him about quilting fabric,' Hen added, before glancing up at the clock on the wall. 'I could go there now.'

Ginny tried to catch her friend's eye, to silently convey that it was a bad idea. But it was too late, as Megan suddenly looked up, tears glistening on her lashes, her eyes red.

'R-really? You'd do that for me?'

'Of course,' Hen answered, before Ginny could open her mouth.

'Absolutely,' Tuppence agreed.

'It's the least we can do,' JM added.

It was only Ginny who was silent and they all turned to her, as if waiting for her answer.

It had to be no.

She tried to open her mouth, but indecision gnawed at her.

It had partly been her fault that Megan had another reason to suspect Ants Mancini. And Ginny knew the terrible abyss that grief could leave behind. The desperate need to have answers and hope. *But...* she'd promised Wallace that she'd stay out of it. And thanks to the last time she'd been involved in a murder case, she had a much stronger understanding of what it meant, and the dangers that went along with that.

The silence continued and Megan's mouth trembled.

Oh, dear. Ginny's own heart pounded in response. What if JM was right about Megan simply waiting until she was alone before confronting Mancini? And then what would happen? She might find herself arrested. Or worse. What if she got into a fight with the man? Visions of Megan wrestling with the unknown haberdashery owner danced in Ginny's mind.

She let her gaze travel past her three friends before settling on Megan, who was nervously chewing her lip. How could she say no to them all? Sighing, she rolled her shoulders.

'If we go and talk to Ants Mancini for you, it's on the understanding that whatever we find we will hand over to the police.'

Megan let out a grateful sob and flung herself into Ginny's arms. 'Thank you. Thank you. Thank you. I can't believe I didn't think of it sooner. After all, you were the ones who caught Louisa's killer, so you'll know just what to do.'

'That's right. Like I tell my clients, it's always best to leave it to the professionals.' JM stepped away from the door, her tone decisive. 'Now, how about I drive you home while Tuppence takes the button to the police station? And we'll let Hen and Ginny talk to Mancini.'

'Excellent.' Tuppence opened the door and guided Megan down the path towards where the three little silver cars were waiting. 'We will rendezvous at Megan's house once we're done.'

'Are you happy if I drive?' Hen asked.

'Of course.' Ginny collected her handbag and keys and, on seeing the rows of marmalade gleaming orange in the sunshine, she took a jar. Maybe between Hen's promise of buying wool, and the gift of the marmalade, they could at least get Mancini to answer a few questions.

Unless, of course, he was guilty.

She blanched, too late realising they hadn't thought it through. For all they knew Ants Mancini *had* stabbed Harlow to death, which meant they were on their way to visit a cold-blooded killer.

SEVEN

Hen took the sharp corner in one smooth motion, before accelerating up the hill, leaving the gentle green fields behind them. Ginny gripped the arm rest of the car door as the road narrowed into a single lane, flanked on either side by low stone walls and overhanging elm trees, with daffodils poking up between their ancient roots.

There was a tractor further ahead, but Hen flashed her lights and it pulled to one side to let them pass. Ginny was beginning to regret she'd agreed to let her friend drive. In most things Hen was the model of warmth and kindness, but when she was behind a steering wheel, she was more like a Formula One driver trying to deliver a pizza to hungry teenagers.

They hadn't talked much on the drive out of Little Shaw as Hen concentrated on the country lanes, and Ginny tried, again, not to think about the sewing scissors protruding from Timothy Harlow's body.

To think that this time yesterday her biggest worry had been when to plant her tomatoes. She shivered as the darkening skies gave the hills an ominous feel as the car swept past them. But finally, Hen turned down a long driveway that led to a collection of stone outbuildings, with a car park off to one side. The largest of the buildings had a slate roof and two long windows, and double doors painted in a soft pastel green. A sign hung above it, with *Green Hill Barn* hand-painted across it.

'Oh, this is lovely. I had no idea it was here.' Ginny released her grip on the arm rest and climbed out. Hen's eyes sparkled. She'd clearly enjoyed the drive. And suddenly some of Ginny's nerves dissolved. Maybe part of getting thrown into these strange situations was that she got to experience things in a different way.

Or, at the very least, leave her house.

'He's done an excellent job of restoring it.' Hen started to walk towards the double doors.

'Do you come here often?'

'Not really. You'll understand why once we go inside. There is so much beautiful wool that I'd have to sell my cottage to afford it all. Or a kidney.' Some of the brightness left Hen's eyes. Ginny swallowed and tucked her arm into Hen's. She knew her friend was worried about money, but because she'd never brought it up directly, Ginny didn't want to pry. So, she simply patted her hand as they walked along a cobbled path towards the barn.

Inside, the floors were polished concrete, and hewn wooden pillars ran parallel to the walls, stretching up to the supporting beams. Tiny fairy lights were wrapped around them, making it feel like Christmas, while wooden tables and shelves were filled with fabric and wool. Paintings and sketches hung from the walls and, at the far end, a group of women was gathered around a long worktable, all holding tapestry frames.

'That's Juliana Melville,' Hen whispered. 'She's a wonderful quilter and textile artist. She worked in London but moved back to Little Shaw five years ago. I've always wanted to do one of her workshops. And isn't that Cleo and Andrea from the library?'

Ginny immediately recognised two of her regular volunteers. As always, they were deep in conversation and didn't look up. Overseeing it all was a stunning woman with long blonde hair and smooth skin. She was dressed in a beautifully fitted pair of caramel trousers and white top that showed off a gym-honed body.

'She's very glamorous,' Ginny whispered.

'Isn't she just. It's hard to believe she's only a few years younger than we are. I really need to stop eating so many chocolates after dinner.'

'Nonsense, you have a lovely figure,' Ginny said firmly, but all the same did a double take at the youthful-looking woman before tugging at Hen's arm and turning away.

There was a counter across from them, and large doors that opened out to an internal courtyard. To the left was a noticeboard of all the upcoming events the centre was hosting.

Shoemaking. Crotchet. Beading. Tatting. Tooled leather. Basket weaving. It was a bewildering array that left Ginny feeling guilty about her habit of curling up on the sofa and reading a book.

They were interrupted by a tall, lean man in his mid-sixties, with thick grey hair and a deeply tanned complexion. He didn't look like a killer... but if Ginny had learnt anything in this life, it was that appearances could be deceiving.

He smiled broadly as he reached their side. 'Henrietta McArthur, what a lovely surprise to see you here. How can I help?'

'Oh, A-Ants,' Hen stammered, her face taking on a waxy hue as she gripped Ginny's arm. Her touch was clammy, and her startled eyes made Ginny think of a five-year-old child with very bad stage fright. Ginny, who had always avoided the spotlight, couldn't blame Hen for the sudden panic, and she patted her friend's hand again and took a deep breath.

'Wool,' Ginny supplied, pushing back her shoulders just as Doctor Judy, from the YouTube clip, had suggested. 'We're here to buy some wool.'

'Yes. That's right. Wool,' Hen echoed, sounding a bit more certain of herself again. She managed to give the man in front of them a smile. 'This is my friend, Ginny Cole.'

'Ah, the new librarian.' He smiled and held out his hand. 'I'm Ants Mancini.'

'Nice to meet you.' She shook his hand, still not entirely used to people knowing who she was. 'This is a lovely place.'

'Pleased you think so. I see it as a community endeavour. If you're a keen knitter, you might like the hand-dyed yarn from Wild Mountain in Scotland. We haven't even unpacked it yet.'

'Wild Mountain?' Hen's eyes glittered with excitement, and suddenly Ginny remembered her friend's self-imposed ban at being around craft supplies. 'I adore their products. Could we really see them?'

'Of course.' Ants led them out through the barn doors into a cobbled courtyard. Several of the smaller buildings had been turned into craft studios, as well as a tearoom with long glass windows. He came to a halt outside one of the buildings and pulled out a key. 'This is where we keep the stock. To be honest, I'm pleased to have an excuse to get away from the shop. We've been rushed off our feet all morning.'

Several boxes were set out on a trestle table and long skeins of pale pastel colours were everywhere. Hen let out a reverent squeal and hurried over.

The next ten minutes were spent with Hen and Mancini deep in conversation about techniques, colours and patterns. Ginny hoped Hen would bring up Harlow's murder as they chatted, but it was clear she'd underestimated the siren call of yarn.

Which meant she'd need to come up with a segue to discuss the murder. The jar of marmalade was still in her handbag, but she now realised that as far as icebreakers went, it was inadequate.

Did Wallace ever worry about such things? Or did he just show his warrant card and ask his questions directly? She suspected it was the latter. *What a tangle.* Somehow, in less than twenty-four hours, she'd managed to have her life thrown off-kilter again. She could almost hear Eric's gentle voice: *It's all right, Gin. Stranger things have happened at sea.*

Outside, people were walking across the courtyard to the tearoom, most of them holding shopping bags. Ginny frowned. Megan had accused Mancini of trying to run them out of business and it was clear that his own place was thriving. Was that proof he was behind it?

If so, she'd prefer not to be there, let alone stuck in a small stock room with the man. But they'd promised to find out what they could. She joined Ants and Hen at the table and took in a small breath for courage.

'It's wonderful to see how busy you are. Is it always like this?'

'I wish.' He put down the pale pink skein he'd been showing Hen. 'Even when we do get a big crowd, it doesn't mean they spend much money. That's why I started running classes and renting out the studio space. Speaking of which, Hen, I'd love for you to join us at some stage.'

'So would I. But I'm afraid it's not in the budget right now.' Hen glanced wistfully at the yarn in her hands and then back towards the barn where the current workshop was under way.

Mancini blinked and then chuckled. 'Sorry... I phrased that poorly. I meant that I'd love for you to teach some classes for us. Both your knitting and quilting are exquisite, and often get mentioned by our students. I think you'd make an excellent teacher.'

'Me? Teach other people?' Hen's hands fluttered to her mouth and her cheeks turned pink.

'I didn't mean to throw you. Why not think about it and we can touch base after the fete? In the meantime, let me show you some of the new patterns we have in.'

'Oh...' Hen put down the yarn and then picked it back up again, suggesting she was still distracted.

Ginny would have to try again herself. *Here goes nothing.* 'Speaking of the fete, do you think you're so busy because of what happened to Timothy Harlow? Maybe everyone's worried the shop won't open again in time for them to get all their supplies. I suppose you must have known him.'

A tiny flicker played along Mancini's jawline and he ran a hand across his chin, as if trying to smooth it away. Clearly her questions had thrown him.

Hen put down the yarn she'd been holding as he considered his answer.

He finally spoke. 'Yes, I knew him. But I won't pretend I liked him very much. Which is no doubt why the police were out here yesterday questioning me.'

The police had already spoken to him. Ginny's mouth went dry. Megan had led them to believe that Wallace didn't consider Mancini a suspect. It was the whole reason why she'd begged for their help.

'The police? Whatever for? Surely they don't think you were involved?' Hen squeaked. Then she winced, as if suddenly remembering that was the reason they were really there.

However, it seemed to finally break the ice and Mancini let out a rueful laugh. 'I would've been more surprised if they *hadn't* thought that. I heard Megan was hysterical and was screaming my name to anyone who would listen.'

'I'm sure she doesn't mean it,' Hen said, feebly.

'I'm sure she does. It's no secret that her father disliked me. I can only imagine what he's told her over the years,' he said,

though his voice was understanding and there was no anger
there.

Ginny leaned forward. 'Are you saying that you didn't reci-
procate it?'

'You mean did I hate him?' He pinched the bridge of his
nose and considered the question. 'I'd say I found him frus-
trating more than anything. Why do you want to know?'

'We promised Megan we would,' Hen blurted out. 'I'm so
sorry. You must think we're terrible to come here under false
pretences.' She stepped forward, head bowed.

Ginny felt just as bad. They really should have planned
things better. Come up with a way to talk to him, without trying
to imply he might have murdered anyone.

But Mancini just shrugged. 'I was half expecting
Megan to turn up in person. I should be grateful that she
sent an envoy. I take it she doesn't believe Milos killed her
father?'

'No. She is convinced he's innocent and that, er... someone
has set him up.'

'That someone being me?' He raised an eyebrow and then
glanced at his watch. 'Would you both like to join me for a pot
of tea? It would probably be more comfortable for us to sit
down.'

It wasn't the answer she'd been expecting, but Hen's eyes
brightened at the mention of tea, and Ginny supposed it would
be safer if they were in a public space, rather than in the
confines of the stock room, so they followed him across the
courtyard to the tearoom.

There were several empty tables inside, all covered in
vintage tablecloths, with mismatched floral teacups and silver-
ware. Mancini stopped one of the waitresses and after a brief
conversation led them to the far corner.

The girl returned not long after with a large pot and a three-
tiered tray of delicate sandwiches and cakes. But it wasn't until

the tea was poured and Ginny had nibbled a piece of sponge cake that their host finally spoke again.

'What did Megan tell you? That I'm an ogre who tried to run her father out of business?'

'Something like that,' Ginny admitted, forcing herself to not look away. It was the least he deserved. 'She said you were jealous of their shop's prestigious history, and of her father's reputation, and that you had tried to pressure him into becoming his business partner.'

'Well, that much is true.'

'Oh.' Hen put down her teacup so quickly that it rattled against the saucer. She put her hands on it to stop the noise. 'Sorry, I wasn't expecting you to say that. Does that mean you did want to own the shop?'

'Not at all. Being tied to a high street business in this economic climate isn't my idea of fun. But I was envious of the history of the place.'

'How so?'

'Even though I've never been friends with Harlow, our grandfathers were close. In fact, they were business partners.' He extracted a small photograph from his wallet and slid it across the table.

Ginny studied the black and white image. It was clearly very old and showed the front of Harlow's Haberdashery, with a horse and wagon off to one side of it. It was almost identical to one of the images hanging behind the counter in Harlow's shop. Except that in this photograph the name above the shop was *Harlow and Mancini*, and there were two men out the front, not one.

Ginny's shoulders stiffened and she looked up to discover Ants had been watching her. 'How long ago was this taken?'

'It's dated on the back – nineteen thirty-two. It was between the wars and my grandfather worked in one of the textile mills. Harlow's great-grandfather was a solicitor and hoped his son would follow in his footsteps, but instead he'd been kicked out of college and sent home in disgrace. Somehow, our two grandfathers met, and despite the class differences, began talking about the textile industry. It was dying at the time, but my grandfather believed there was still a way to make money. He had excellent taste and a real eye for design – just no education or capital to do anything about it. Harlow must've liked what he heard because they decided to go into partnership.'

'Why haven't I ever heard about this? Or seen it mentioned at any of the local history displays?' Hen said.

'One year after they leased a building and set up the business, they'd been so successful that they'd made enough money to buy the shop outright.' Mancini's dark eyes turned to stone and his nostrils flared. 'Except when the paperwork was signed, my grandfather's name wasn't on it and Harlow insisted that they'd never been partners. He took advantage of a brilliant but illiterate man. And stabbed him—'

He broke off but the unsaid words still hung between them, floating above the delicate clinks and chatter of the surrounding tables.

And stabbed him in the back.

'Surely people must have known?' Hen gasped.

'My grandfather could barely read or write, and he'd worked in the mill all his life. Unlike Harlow, who was well educated and entitled. He threatened to have my grandfather arrested for trespassing.'

'That's shocking,' Ginny whispered, and Mancini nodded.

'He married my grandmother not long after and they took over her family farm. But his heart was never in it. Over the years he tried several times to buy Harlow out, all unsuccessful. It broke him in the end. My own father also tried to buy the place back. And... and like my grandfather... it ate away at him.'

'Are you suggesting that you don't feel like that?' Hen, who was so rarely without her knitting needles, clutched at the table,

as if unsure what else to do with her hands. For the first time
Mancini laughed.

'Definitely not. Though I do seem to have inherited the
family love of textiles, so I like to think they'd both approve of
what I've done with the place. But as for wanting to own the
shop? No... I couldn't think of anything worse. Though I am
upset sometimes that my grandfather's contribution isn't
publicly recognised.'

'Why did Harlow try to broker peace with you then?
Megan said you've been undercutting them to run them out of
business.'

'Undercutting them? Hardly. I'm here to make money and
to provide a platform for local artisans. If anything, my prices
are higher than those they charge in the shop because I have
more space. And more staff to support.'

Ginny swallowed as unease prickled along her skin. So far
there wasn't much about Megan's story that was holding up.
Or... had it been her father's story?

Deep in thought, Hen had started tapping on her saucer
with her teaspoon. *Tee. Tee. Tee.* The sound rang in Ginny's
ears, and she shifted back in her chair.

'Then what was the meeting about? Megan said her father
visited.'

'He wanted to rent my second barn. And he offered me a
down-payment in cash to do so.'

Hen dropped the spoon with a clatter as they both stared
at him.

'Are you sure?' Ginny said. 'Megan said they were on the
verge of bankruptcy. Where did the money to do that come
from? And why rent a barn from someone he considered an
enemy?'

'Your guess is as good as mine. Not that I bothered to ask
him, since I had no intention of letting him anywhere near my
business. But he had a bag full of fifty-pound notes, as if he

thought we could do the deal then and there. It was like something out of the movies.'

'How did he take your refusal?'

'Not very well. Though it was hardly surprising. Harlow had a great deal of self-importance.' Mancini leaned back in his chair. 'Maybe I could have handled it better, but considering the family history, I wasn't interested in dragging out the conversation. So, after I refused him, I asked him to leave.'

'And did he?'

'Not at first. He started making all kinds of threats and then stormed out.'

Ginny's mind whirled. Mancini's manner was open and calm, which suggested he was telling the truth. Then again, Megan said he'd been involved with the local theatre group. Was he acting now?

'Was he with anyone?' Hen asked, and Ginny gave her an approving nod. Excellent question.

'No. He came in alone. Though there was someone in the car. I caught sight of them when Harlow was driving off.'

'Was it anyone you recognised?' Ginny asked.

'Sorry, it was too far away, and they had a hoodie pulled over their head. But they were large and broad-shouldered.'

'Could it have been Milos?' Hen asked, but Mancini shook his head.

'Definitely not. This person was bigger than Milos. Like a bodyguard.'

Ginny swallowed, trying to piece together all the parts. Why had Harlow approached someone he disliked? What did he want to do with the barn? Where had the money come from and who was the person in the car? But from the little Megan had told them, there was nothing that linked them together.

And then there was the date.

'How does the ides of March fit in?' she wondered, before

realising she'd spoken the words out loud. Her hand flew to her mouth, but it was too late to stop the question.

Mancini's dark brows drew together. *Oh dear. This is what comes from having so many one-sided conversations with Eric and the cat.*

'Ides of March?' Mancini studied her, and Ginny wondered what her chances were of digging a hole in the ground and letting it swallow her whole. But it was Hen who came to her rescue.

'Ginny's a librarian, remember, and is forever thinking about books and stories. I think she's currently reading *Julius Caesar*. I-isn't that where the quote came from?'

Ginny gave Hen a grateful nod for smoothing over the awkward bump in the conversation. 'That's right. I adore it. I saw it performed once in London. Are you familiar with it?'

'No... I'm not a fan of the tragedies,' he admitted, not seeming put out by the random switch in the conversation. 'I much prefer something lighter. You should come along to our next theatre production. We're doing *The Importance of Being Ernest*. I'm not acting, of course, just doing the costumes. Usually I design everything, but this time I'm using original patterns and vintage fabric. That's why I was in Leeds yesterday, attending an auction.'

Leeds? Ginny frowned. She'd found Harlow's body at twenty past one, and Hannah's aunt had seen him alive at twelve-thirty. Which meant whoever had killed him, had done so in a very small window of opportunity.

A window that didn't allow for someone to be in both Leeds and Little Shaw at the same time.

'Are you saying you have an alibi?' she asked, and he gave her a reluctant smile, as if sad to bring their conversation to a close.

Shame flooded Ginny that this whole interview had been based on faulty logic. Was that why he'd been so happy to answer all their questions? And how much time could they have saved if they had asked him that first... instead of trying to casually slide it in?

'I'm afraid so. As I told the police yesterday, I was at the auction from ten in the morning until two in the afternoon. There were plenty of people to confirm it.'

'Oh dear.' Hen's eyes widened in alarm, and it was clear Ginny wasn't the only one feeling terrible about this discovery.

'Do you know Milos or his uncle? Do you think he did it?' Ginny asked.

Mancini rubbed his chin, his fingers long and elegant like those of a piano player.

'It's no secret that I'd love to host Vanja Petrovic's upholstery classes here at Green Hill, and did try to discuss it with him several times. It doesn't take a financial genius to see that Harlow had been making far more out of the partnership than Vanja ever did. But for whatever reason, he was loyal to Harlow. And so was his nephew. As to whether he's guilty... it's not for me to say.'

'Can you think of anyone else who might have had a grudge against Harlow?'

'I would say everyone who ever met the man. Most of my customers come in with some story of complaint against him. Though I'm not sure that overcharging for darning needles is a strong enough motive.'

Ginny had to agree. Which only left the button that Tuppence had found. She brought it up on her phone. But if he recognised it, he hid it well.

'Sorry, it's not something we stock,' he said, as an alarm on his phone beeped. He studied the screen then sighed. 'You must excuse me. I've got to check up on the workshop. It's almost finished, and I like to hand out feedback forms.'

'Of course. We won't keep you any longer, a-and we're sorry that some of our questions might have been inappropriate.' Ginny got to her feet, trying to shake off the terrible guilt.

But Mancini let out a throaty chuckle. 'Don't look so upset. I doubt this will be the last conversation people want to have with me about Harlow. But if you speak to Megan, please tell her I'm truly sorry about her father.'

He made his goodbyes and went out to the courtyard.

Hen let out a groan as he disappeared from sight. 'That was terrible. We basically accused that poor man of murder.'

'It wasn't ideal. But he took it very well,' Ginny said as they thanked the staff and walked through the barn and out to Hen's car.

The wind had picked up, rustling the leaves of the surrounding trees, and they quickened their step.

'It's still mortifying.' Hen unlocked the car and they climbed in. 'No wonder he didn't mention anything else about wanting me to teach a class. Not that I would have said yes.'

'Really? Wouldn't you even consider it?'

'No.' Hen shook her head and fumbled with the keys in the ignition. 'I mean, the money would be lovely... but I'm not sure I'd make a good teacher, and I'm not remotely qualified.' She looked at Ginny. 'Now, don't you tell JM or Tuppence about it. What if they try to make me do it?'

Hen's foot began to tap against the floor of the car. Ginny understood only too well the suffocating fear of having to start something new at their age, no matter how much sense it might make on paper.

'They won't hear it from me. Now, we'd better go and see Megan and tell her about Mancini's alibi. I hope she isn't too upset.'

'It may help her accept what's happened. And it does suggest someone else might have had a reason to kill Harlow. The man in the car, maybe?' Hen frowned. 'Though why didn't she tell us that her father had a large bag of cash? If they were so broke, where did it come from?'

'I don't know. But if she didn't tell us about it, does that mean she hasn't told the police either?' Ginny shuddered. They had only agreed to help Megan because of how devastated she'd appeared. But what if there had been another motive behind it?

Had Ginny and her friends been too ready to take things at face value?

Too naive?

An uncomfortable tightness formed in her chest as she faced the possibility that it was true. But as Eric liked to say, the truth often *was* uncomfortable. Which was why so many people avoided it.

Hen slipped on her driving gloves before firing up the engine and heading back in the direction of Little Shaw. As they drove, Ginny closed her eyes. Oh, how she wished her sweet, wise husband was with her. It had been over a year since his death, but still she felt his loss. For so much of her life he had been there, like an anchor holding her in place. Without him she kept seeming to drift back and forth with the current.

Still, as soon as they had talked to Megan, they could stop pretending they were anything other than four women who should have known better. Then the tightness in her chest would disappear and she could get on with her new life.

EIGHT

The house where Megan Harlow grew up was nestled above Little Shaw on a steep slope that eventually flattened out to display a collection of old stone cottages. Number five was set back, with an overgrown garden held in by a rusted metal fence.

The gate creaked as Ginny pushed it open, and Tuppence, who was dead-heading last year's growth from an old-fashioned yellow rose bush, looked up. JM appeared from behind a lavender bush, wielding her own secateurs.

The two women ushered them down the overgrown garden path to a gravelled space by the front door. A dog barked from the other side of the fence. It was followed by a sharp hiss as a woman with bright gold hair appeared from the neighbouring house.

If she thought it was strange that four women were standing in Timothy Harlow's garden the day after his murder, she didn't show it. She just snapped her fingers at the dog. 'Come here, Verona. Now.'

The dog barked again, before disappearing back inside,

along with the woman. Once she'd gone, Hen peered behind a lovely magnolia tree. 'Where's Megan? How is she?'

'A mess.' Tuppence peeled off her gloves and dropped them in JM's gardening basket that was near the path. 'First, she wanted to go to the police station and then out to Mancini's farm, but we convinced her to lie down. I'm not sure if she's asleep though.'

'We didn't want to leave her on her own in case she did anything she might later regret. Which is why we thought we'd make ourselves useful,' JM explained. 'It's a pity to see such a lovely garden so neglected.'

'I'm pleased you convinced her to stay at home.' Hen heaved a worried sigh and brushed off the dead leaves clinging to JM's sleeve. 'It was bad enough that we practically accused Ants of murder. Imagine if Megan tried to see him.'

Once Hen and Ginny had finished going over what they'd learnt, Tuppence frowned. 'I don't understand why she didn't tell us the truth about the feud. Or the money.'

As the others muttered in agreement, the front door opened, and a groggy-looking Megan stepped out. She blinked several times and gripped the door frame.

'You're back? Wh-what happened? Did you speak to him? What did he tell you?'

'Maybe it's best if we go inside?' Ginny suggested, as several neighbours appeared at their fences. Despite how awkward their meeting with Mancini had been, they couldn't forget that Megan had just lost her father and was still in shock.

Megan swallowed hard, her neck muscles visible, but ushered them in and closed the door.

The cottage was tiny, with a small living room that ran onto a kitchen at the back and a stairway leading up to the bedrooms. It was sparsely decorated with no paintings, no television or knickknacks scattered around. Only a single photograph was on the wall. Harlow had his arm around a woman with dark hair, and a tiny Megan was cradled between them. To the left was another woman, who looked similar to Megan's mother. A sister, maybe?

There was only one leather sofa and a wooden coffee table as well as a small dining table pressed against the wall. Megan dropped into the only chair, leaving Ginny and her friends to cram onto the sofa.

It was poorly sprung and they all sank down, leaving their knees uncomfortably high in the air, almost in line with their chests. Suddenly Ginny felt like a naughty schoolgirl.

She shifted awkwardly, trying to get more comfortable before going over everything they'd discovered, minus Mancini's offer to Hen. But it wasn't until they reached the part about the auction in Leeds that Megan showed any reaction.

'He could be lying, right?' Despair was etched across her features and Ginny's heart ached for her.

'The police would have confirmed it by now. There's no way he could have come back to Little Shaw in time, to—' Hen broke off.

'Drat. An alibi.' Tuppence frowned while JM leaned forward and got herself out the sinking sofa, with far more ease than Ginny could have mustered. She really must start going to exercise classes to work on her core.

'Let's put the alibi to one side for now.' JM walked to the window and leaned against the sill so she could take in the room, as if it was a court of law. 'Why would your father try to lease one of Mancini's barns? And where did the extra money come from? I thought you said things were tight.'

'They are. We're completely broke. Do you think we'd live like this if we didn't have to?' Two circles of colour appeared on Megan's cheeks and she waved her hand around the sparse room, before dropping her gaze.

Tuppence let out a squeak and mouthed the words: *Doctor Judy.*

They all looked at each other. Thanks to the YouTube clips on body language, they could now all recognise the gesture for what it was.

Megan was lying.

Again, Ginny's chest constricted. What else had Megan lied about? What had she dragged them into? But if her friends shared her concern, they didn't show it.

'We can't help if you don't tell us the truth.' It was JM who spoke, sounding a lot gentler than she usually did. Had she also recognised Megan's despair and thought of her own late wife, Rebecca? The pain of not wanting to let go of what you loved.

The low hum of the fridge in the kitchen was the only thing filling the silence and Megan's fingers once again toyed with the gold locket that was resting on her gaunt collar bones. Finally, she looked up.

'My father was a gambler. It's not something many people know. He likes – liked – people to think that our money comes from the business... and from his heyday as a television presenter and fashion designer. But it's not true. Most of the time we manage to stay afloat, but it hasn't been easy.'

So *that* was why Megan hadn't been completely truthful. Because her father was a gambling addict. Some of the discomfort and foolishness Ginny had been feeling dissipated. After all, she doubted she'd want to tell relative strangers something so personal.

'You poor love.' Hen leaned forward, as if to stand up, but like Ginny, seemed to be stuck in the sofa.

'When my mother was alive, I don't think it was such a problem. But she died when I was seven and since then it's been a rollercoaster. That's why I do the accounts and pay the bills. And stop him selling everything we own.' Megan studied her fingers, shame clearly making it difficult for her to look up.

She might have been lying before, but this felt genuine, and painful.

'Couldn't you tell someone? Ask for help?' Tuppence's normally bright eyes were full of sympathy.

'What could anyone do?' Megan let out a bitter laugh. 'Make my father become less of an arsehole? Nail down the television so he wouldn't sell it? The only thing he really cared about was the shop and his reputation.'

'Why didn't you tell the police about the gambling? It would have given them another avenue to go down,' Ginny asked, and Megan's face drained of colour.

'It's complicated. As difficult as my father could be at times... at least he didn't desert me. After my mum died, her sister wanted to raise me. But he refused. Said he owed it to my mother to look after me. Plus, it's hard to break old habits.'

There was a pause, and Ginny got the feeling that they were all thinking about old habits that were hard to shake. She had numerous ones. From talking to her dead husband through to not using her cell phone in public spaces. But none of them seemed quite as overwhelming as what Megan had been up against.

Yet it wasn't something she should be hiding from the police. Not if she wanted to prove Milos was innocent. But before Ginny could say this, JM broke in.

'Why would Mancini say that your father wanted the barn, if it wasn't true?'

'I don't know. I swear he never mentioned anything to me. As for the money, if there was anything extra... I've never seen it.'

'Is it possible that he could have won it gambling?' Tuppence wondered.

'Yes, I suppose so. He could be very secretive when he wanted to be.'

'Would he have left any information about it in the house... or on his phone?' JM began to prowl the empty room as if hoping to trip over a hidden bank account.

'I don't think so. The police did a thorough search here and at the shop. Plus, they took his phone. Oh God. I'm never going to see Milos again.'

'Nonsense. If anything, we now have more to go on. What about the large man in the car with your father? Do you know who that might be?' Tuppence also stood up, and Ginny found herself slipping deeper into the bowels of the terrible sofa.

'I have no idea.' Megan gestured around the sparse cottage. 'My father never brought anyone back here, for obvious reasons, and no one like that ever came into the shop, and – oh, it could have been Harry Redfern.'

'Who is he?' JM demanded.

'He's a pawnbroker. And a fence. He runs a poker game every Thursday night. My father often went.'

'So he could have owed someone money?' Tuppence's eyes were bright with excitement that Ginny couldn't share. Her concern that Megan might've had an ulterior motive when she requested their help had abated, but that didn't mean she wanted to solve the murder. This was where their part ended. It's what they'd agreed on.

Well... it's what *Ginny* had agreed on.

And while part of her mind was with her friends, trying to weave together the threads to find an answer, the churning unease that came with being out of her comfort zone made her limbs feel heavy.

'When did your father last go to a game?' JM asked.

'I don't know,' Megan admitted, a flush running up her neck. 'Thursdays were when Milos and I went to our ballroom dancing lessons over in Walton-on-Marsh. I should never have agreed to go. I should have stayed home and made sure my father didn't attend.'

'Did your father ever argue with Harry? Or owe him money?' JM folded her arms.

'I don't think so. At least, nothing that hasn't been long settled.'

'What about Vanja? How did he feel about your father threatening to take a restraining order out on his nephew? Could he have wanted revenge?' Tuppence walked across the room, before suddenly pivoting. Her curls sprang out in all directions.

'I'm not sure. I always thought he was nice, even though he wasn't happy about us being together either. But why would he kill my father? They'd worked together for years.'

'He could be a slow burn. And Mancini seemed to think that your father was taking advantage of Vanja. Maybe he got tired of it?' JM walked in the opposite direction before also pivoting. 'Where was Vanja when your father was killed?'

'I suppose he was at his workshop. He tends to spend most weekends there.'

'What about customers? Do they ever try to bring things back... or complain?' Tuppence suddenly demanded. 'Because based on my experience, your father didn't do well in that department. Especially when it came to French toile.'

Megan's colour deepened. 'Yes, there were often complaints. Though mainly it was because they had found something cheaper online. My father had no patience for that. And I'm sorry about what happened with your fabric. He over-ordered the rolls and ended up with a significant amount. The supplier wouldn't let us return it, so my father did what he did best – convinced a lot of people to buy it.'

'He told me it was a textile worthy of someone with excep-tional taste,' Tuppence complained. 'But he forgot to add that he told twenty other people the same rubbish. Sorry, Megan, I shouldn't speak ill of the dead.'

'It's true. But that's just what he was like. He had lots of charisma and didn't mind using it to get what he wanted. Which was usually for people to give him money.'

'Which means plenty of potential suspects. We need to start keeping track, at least until we can assemble our new murder board.' JM extracted a small notebook from her pocket and jotted something down.

'Oh, good idea. Our last one got confiscated by the police,' Tuppence added.

Ginny bit her lip, starting to feel like she was trying to hold back the tide. They weren't meant to be getting involved. Especially since it was clear the police were doing more than Megan had thought.

But the words stayed lodged in her throat. She'd never been good at speaking up, and the people-pleaser in her couldn't find a solution.

She was trapped between three dear friends and a grumpy detective. All while sinking further into the leathery abyss of a sofa. *But if I don't say something now, then it might get worse.*

Ginny coughed. 'I hate to be the voice of reason, but I think Megan needs to tell the police about her father's gambling. How can they find the real killer if they don't know everything? It's the best way to prove Milos didn't do it.'

'But what if they don't listen?' Megan looked up, tears still glistening in her eyes. 'Or I say the wrong thing and make things worse?'

'I... I'm not sure things can get any worse.' Ginny gave her friends an apologetic look. Hen, who was still stuck in the sofa with her, reached out and squeezed Ginny's hand. The warm touch eased some of the anxiety that had been building in Ginny's chest.

'Ginny's right, love.' Hen fixed her gaze on Megan. 'As much as we want to help, we need to leave it to the police. The pair of us made a mess of it when we visited Ants. We virtually accused him of murder.'

'And now we've got all this information, they'll have to

agree that Milos isn't a suspect,' Tuppence added, in an encouraging voice.

'But what if they don't listen?'

'Then they'll have me to deal with,' JM growled.

Megan bowed her head, but soon looked up. Dark lines of fatigue and despair ran across her face and her shoulders were slumped as if the weight of her grief had finally caught up with her. 'You're right. But I'm not sure I'm up to it tonight. Could you talk to them first and then if they need to question me again... well, I'll cross that bridge when I get to it.'

'Of course,' Tuppence immediately said, before producing the bra bag from her pocket. 'We'll go there now. Plus, it will mean I can finally give him the button.'

Ginny's jaw dropped as the mesh bag dangled between Tuppence's fingers. 'I thought you were going to drop it off before you came here?'

Tuppence wrinkled her nose. 'Did I forget to mention that I had a small problem at the station? PC Singh wasn't there, and Wallace was on the phone with the new pathologist. The woman at the desk wanted me to leave it with her, but I was worried it would get *misplaced*.' Tuppence made air quotes and Ginny's surprise turned to concern.

'Why would you think that?'

'Because I could see by her face that she didn't believe me. It might have been when I tried to tell her about the ides of March. I got myself into a muddle and started thinking about the *March of the Penguins*.'

'It's a simple enough mistake. I'm sure Wallace will understand.' JM patted Tuppence on the shoulder before turning to Ginny. 'Though maybe it would be best if just one of us went. You know how twitchy he gets when we're all together.'

Ginny knew only too well. Though she wouldn't call it 'twitchy'. She would go for 'exasperated', 'irritated', and possibly on the brink of 'furious'. But she could hardly refuse to speak with Wallace, since she'd been the one to insist on it.

'What if Tuppence stays with Megan, and JM and I drive you to the station and wait outside in the car? That way you won't feel totally alone,' Hen suggested, her huge brown eyes filled with understanding. 'I know how much you hate talking to the police.'

Ginny gave her friends a grateful smile for understanding her decision to tell the police about Harlow's gambling, and his mysterious business.

'Thank you. I suppose there's no time like the present.' She gripped at the armrest of the sofa and managed to haul herself up to her feet. Hen followed suit and they headed outside into the fading light, as she prepared to face Wallace.

It wasn't something she was looking forward to.

NINE

Little Shaw police station was a plain single-storey brick bungalow with a wheelchair ramp running up the side. It was almost dark by the time Ginny stood outside the door. She swallowed and tried to convince her pounding heart to slow down. Capiophobia was the fear of being arrested, and Ginny couldn't remember a time when she hadn't turned to stone at the sound of a police siren. Eric had always assured her, in that quiet way of his, that the chances of her ever getting arrested were zero, and perhaps in the past he'd been right. But these days, Ginny wasn't so sure.

Still, it was too late to turn back now.

Despite yesterday's murder, the station seemed quiet, and Ginny turned to where Hen's car was parked across the road. JM gave her a thumbs-up and Hen nodded in an encouraging way.

Feeling buoyed by their support, Ginny pushed the door open and stepped over the threshold. She was doing the right thing. And despite his temper, Wallace was a reasonable man.

The reception area was a depressing room with plastic chairs screwed to the wall and a general air of neglect. The only occupants were a couple of women sitting in one corner, heads bowed together. They didn't look up as Ginny crossed to the counter. It wasn't manned, but she could hear a rumble of voices from further back, and then a phone began to ring.

PC Bent emerged from behind a door several moments later and answered the call. He was closely followed by two more uniformed police, and a woman who Ginny recognised from her last visit to the police station. And, finally, out stepped Wallace.

He was wearing the same clothes as yesterday and, judging by the stubble on his chin, he hadn't slept. His eyes locked on her and for a moment Ginny thought he would keep walking, but something flickered across his face and he strode to the counter.

Her stomach sank. Maybe 'reasonable' hadn't been the right choice of word?

'Mrs Cole, why are you here?'

'Oh, um—' Ginny broke off and clutched at the bra bag in her hand. Did she begin with the button that Tuppence had taken? Or the conversation with Ants Mancini? Or... Megan herself?

Ginny was saved from answering by the appearance of a tiny woman with white hair, in a tweed skirt and bright white trainers on her feet.

At the sight of her Wallace muttered something under his breath and he brusquely swung open the reception-counter door and waved Ginny through. 'You'd better come with me.' Without waiting for an answer, he disappeared down the corridor, not bothering to check if she was following.

Ginny reluctantly trailed after him, into a narrow interview room. There was an old table with a tape recorder on top, and two chairs. Cameras blinked from the corner of the ceiling. Her breathing quickened as the walls seemed to press in on her. This was a bad idea. Why hadn't she just let her friends continue what they were doing? Why hadn't she—

Brrring.

Her thoughts were cut off by the buzz of Wallace's phone. He glanced at it and then swiped the screen. But before he could put it back in his jacket pocket it rang again. Whoever was calling, they clearly hadn't improved his mood.

'I don't mind if you answer that,' she said, hoping she could buy some time. She doubted it would help her have a cohesive conversation, but it might let her control her pounding heart.

Wallace glared at her. 'I take it this is about Megan Harlow turning up on my doorstep, before going into your cottage for an hour.'

'Y-you heard about that?' Ginny sank into the closest chair, not really surprised. Of course he'd heard. After all, there was nothing their neighbours liked to do more than gossip and speculate. 'We only invited her into the house because she was waking up half the neighbourhood, screaming for you to come out. We thought we were doing the right thing.'

'If you really wanted to help her, you would have encouraged her to accept the support from one of our family liaison officers, who is actually trained for that sort of thing.'

Ginny winced. She knew about the special officers but hadn't thought to ask Megan if she'd spoken to one. Somehow, she had the feeling Megan would've refused their help.

'At the time it seemed like the right thing to do,' she said, aware how feeble her voice sounded.

'I see.' He sat down opposite her and folded his arms. 'And what did she tell you?'

'She was very upset – for obvious reasons – and we couldn't get much sense out of her. Then she admitted that she and Milos were dating and that her father threatened to take out a restraining order on Milos. She's convinced the real killer is

Ants Mancini. She wanted you to arrest him, and because you were out, she was determined to accuse Ants herself. Poor thing was hysterical... and in dire need of sleep. We convinced her to go home on the promise that Hen and I would talk to Mancini.'

'You also promised that you would stay out of it,' Wallace growled as his phone buzzed again. He glanced at the screen and then rejected the call.

Ginny winced. Someone was eager to get through to him. Was it about Harlow's murder? If so, why wasn't he answering it?

Wallace narrowed his eyes at her, as if guessing her thought process, and turned the phone so that it lay with the screen facedown.

'Like I said, she was grieving and exhausted. And I might have made it worse when I told her about the ides of March.' Ginny stared down at the chipped veneer of the table as heat stung her cheeks.

'Ides of March?' Wallace echoed, his face flickering from annoyance to confusion. Sighing, she quickly explained the significance of the date, and the calendar that had been crossed off in the shop.

He didn't bother to write anything down, but by the way his lips tightened, Ginny suspected the police hadn't made that connection. Though at this point she wasn't sure if that was a good or bad thing.

'It might not mean anything, but, when I mentioned it to Megan, she became more convinced it was Mancini. Because he has a background in theatre and his family is Italian. And then there's the button...' Ginny trailed off as Wallace's face darkened, like a storm cloud ready to break. 'Tuppence accidentally picked it up at the crime scene yesterday.'

'Of course she did. I take it this is why I had a convoluted message about penguins.' He held out his hand for her to pass it over.

Heat stung Ginny's cheeks again as she retrieved the net bag and slid it across the table to him. Wallace picked it up and gave it a shake, then frowned as the small replica coin button rolled across the table.

'Sh-she got a bit muddled up,' Ginny admitted as he inspected the button. 'Megan Harlow said it's not something they sell, but that Mancini might have stocked them. As you will see, it's a Roman coin replica.'

A series of emotions flashed across the DI's face, before it settled back down to his usual, impassive mask. 'What happened when you went to see Mancini? Did he mention we'd already spoken to him?'

'Yes, I'm sorry about that. Megan was under the impression that you weren't looking into the case properly. That's why I'm here, to explain what happened and pass on what we know.'

'I see. And what exactly *do* you know?'

Ginny swallowed, and focused on the wall behind his left shoulder, not feeling up to returning his impenetrable gaze.

It didn't take her long to tell him about Harlow's gambling addiction, his visit to Mancini's farm, the large bag of cash and the mysterious person in the car. Or that Megan believed the evidence at Milos's apartment had been planted.

'I'm not sure how it all fits together, but it does suggest that someone else might have had a reason to murder Harlow. So... will you look into it?'

'I take it you've never considered that if Milos is innocent, then *you* might be our prime suspect. After all, you were the one to find the body.'

'Me? But I didn't even know the man.' Ginny blinked, too surprised to feel anything other than confusion. So much for being the voice of reason.

'And yet you seem to be going out of your way to steer the investigation in a certain direction, with buttons and Shakespeare quotes. Not to mention your sudden friendship with Megan Harlow.'

Ginny's limbs turned to lead as she stared at him, trying to consider his perspective. She'd been the first on the scene and now here she was with new evidence and theories. Then she remembered the way he'd interviewed her yesterday. *And* insisted on checking her handbag. Maybe he really did think she was a suspect?

Before she could reply, his phone buzzed yet again. He snatched it up and studied the screen before getting to his feet.

'We're done here. Please inform your friends to let us conduct the investigation the way we see fit. Oh, and we'll be visiting Megan Harlow tomorrow morning, so she'd better not think about leaving the village.'

Ginny's mouth dropped open in protest, but Wallace had already stalked out of the door, the phone clamped to his ear.

Her mind spun as she made her way out of the police station, and she almost crashed into a reporter who was standing at the bottom of the stairs. They were followed by a woman with a large camera over her shoulder. Across the road was a line-up of cars and vans that hadn't been there earlier.

'What's going on?' Ginny asked the reporter, but they'd already brushed past her. She turned to the woman with the camera, who grimaced.

'Milos Petrovic has just been arrested. We're hoping to get an interview with the lead detective,' she said, then disappeared into the station after their colleague, leaving Ginny alone on the stairs. Guilt caught in her throat. Megan Harlow had been right to mistrust the police.

Why hadn't Ginny listened? Because now not only was Milos in serious trouble, but there was a good chance Ginny might be as well.

'What happened? Are you okay?' Hen appeared at her side, closely followed by JM. 'No one will tell us what's going on.'

'They've arrested Milos.'

'What?' Hen squeaked. 'What did Wallace say? Did he tell you why?'

'No. All he said was that apart from Milos they only had one other suspect. Me.'

'That's ridiculous.' JM scowled and went to march up the stairs, but Ginny pulled her back.

'I don't think talking to him will do any good.'

'But we can't let poor Milos take the blame. And as for them suspecting you...' Hen trailed off. 'Oh dear. What a mess. What should we do?'

Ginny agreed. It was a mess. But it was clearly one that wasn't going to solve itself. She squared her shoulders. 'There's only one thing we can do. A real killer is out there and if the police aren't going to find out who it is, we will need to do it ourselves.'

TEN

Monday, 17th March

The Monday morning sky was gun-metal grey, and a sharp breeze caught at the long navy skirt Ginny had recently bought from the charity shop. The scent of lavender drifted over from the large pots by the library door as she stepped inside and switched off the newly installed alarm. But before she turned on the bank of lights, she let the cool dimness of the space wash over her.

This was when she usually collected her thoughts and mentally went through all the tasks she needed to get done for the day. But now all she could think about was the chaos of the weekend and the terrible interview with Wallace.

After they'd left the station, Hen had driven straight back to Megan's house so they could discuss what had happened.

Megan hadn't been surprised at Wallace's refusal to listen, which had only made Ginny feel silly for trusting her own instincts. And when the grieving woman had finally fallen asleep, Ginny and her friends had stayed up late into the night, discussing the best way forward.

After much toing and froing, they'd decided that JM would track down Harry the pawnbroker, Tuppence would speak with Megan's accountant to confirm her alibi and see what else she could glean, and Hen would talk to Hannah's aunt, who had been the last person to see Harlow alive. It was Ginny's job to call all of Harlow's disgruntled customers, and use her lunch break to visit Vanja Petrovic at his workshop.

All without attracting Wallace's attention.

Her skin prickled with unease. That part could be a problem, considering the detective lived in the house next door. Her concern had also increased after she'd spent an hour on the internet reading up on Timothy Harlow.

His reputation didn't seem to be exaggerated. After not showing a particular talent for design while doing his A-Levels, he'd suddenly decided to go to fashion school in London and his portfolio had been so compelling that he'd been accepted on the spot. It had never happened before and had set his reputation as the next big thing.

He'd launched his first collection while in his final year, and his girlfriend at the time, Jessica Firth, a talented seamstress and designer in her own right, had dropped out of the course to run the workroom for him. They'd eventually married, and she'd continued to sew for him until her early death.

Ginny had spent quite some time watching clips of Harlow's first collection. One journalist had described his style as 'electric elegance', and another had dubbed it as 'Oscar Wilde goes on a date with Vivian Westwood'. There were also numerous episodes from the infamous television show, and she'd soon been able to memorise all the cruel put downs he'd given to the contestants, despite being younger than most of them.

My eyes are bleeding... take it away.

If you can't show me perfection, don't show me anything at all.

This is an insult to the fabric.

'Why are you standing in the dark?' Cleo's voice came from over by the door and the lights flickered on.

Ginny jumped in response and pushed aside all thoughts of Harlow.

'Probably gathering her strength to deal with you,' Connor retorted, before appearing at Ginny's side. The grey shadows under his eyes had increased, which made her think he'd either stayed up all weekend, or that his flatmates had. She suspected the latter, since despite his young age, Connor didn't seem to socialise much. 'You okay, Mrs C? We heard about what happened.'

'It's all anyone is talking about.' Cleo joined them. She was clutching a large sewing bag that had the corner of a quilt poking out. 'I was at Green Hill Barn yesterday doing a workshop and we were all ever so upset. There's talk they might cancel the spring fete now that our head judge is dead.'

'How inconvenient for you all.' Connor disappeared behind the counter and flicked on the computer. 'It's almost like he did it on purpose.'

'Just because you don't have any interest in arts and craft, doesn't mean you need to be rude. Some of us have been working on our entries for months,' Cleo retorted, before turning to Ginny, her mouth in a flat line. 'That boy has no respect.'

'We all process things differently.' Ginny walked towards the staffroom and her office, hoping to convince Cleo to follow her.

'Hmmmm.' Cleo didn't sound convinced, but did at least hurry to catch up with her.

'I didn't realise they might cancel the fete. Can't they just get another head judge?'

'Get another head judge?' Cleo's look suggested that Ginny

had asked her to juggle flaming batons. 'Do you realise how difficult that would be? Harlow was one of a kind.'

'It was my understanding that he wasn't well-liked, and had a temper.' Ginny stopped at her office door and frowned. So far no one had talked about him in a positive light.

'Exactly. He was a terrible man. But it meant that no one could bribe him... or try to get on his good side. Mainly because he didn't have one. He was the one constant that we could all rely on to ensure that no one had an unfair advantage. But now everything is up in the air. Poor Sandra and Peter. They've worked so hard.'

Ginny pondered. Did that mean an ex-contestant might have had something against Harlow? It seemed a bit extreme to kill someone because of a local fete. But before she could ask Cleo any more questions, Andrea appeared, an almost identical sewing bag over her own shoulder.

'I hardly slept a wink, worrying that our category would be cancelled,' the other volunteer exclaimed before turning to Ginny. 'And you poor thing. You must have been all over the place about the marmalade. We must hope and pray that it goes ahead.'

'If it does, then Milos Petrovic will have even more to answer for,' Cleo prophesied darkly. 'I never liked him above half.'

'Neither did I,' Andrea agreed, much like she always did. It had led Connor to dubbing her 'the bridesmaid' because of the way she trailed after the much more opinionated Cleo.

Ginny swallowed. While she didn't like to encourage them to gossip, she realised this was her first chance to find out more about Megan's boyfriend. 'Did either of you know him well?'

'Well enough to not like his attitude,' Cleo retorted. 'We both did Vanja's course last year, and that nephew of his did nothing but moan and complain. I could tell straightaway that he was a bad apple. It was the eyes. Far too close set.'

Ginny opened her mouth, wanting to correct such a false stereotype, but Andrea broke in before she could say anything.

'It's still dreadful to think that he purposefully took those scissors from his uncle's workshop and stormed down the high street to stab Harlow. I heard it was one hundred times.'

'How do you know the scissors came from Vanja's workshop? There were plenty for sale at the haberdashery shop.' Ginny stiffened, forgetting about the stereotype and the exaggeration about the crime.

'Not this brand.' Cleo shook her head. 'Vanja imported them from the US. Said they were better. My sister-in-law's cousin knows someone who knows someone, who confirmed that's where they came from. Like I said... it's no surprise to me. He was very rude to us at that workshop.'

'Very rude,' Andrea echoed. 'You'd think he had better things to do than recut fabric for me... just because I forgot to match up the flowers on one of my seams and had to redo it.'

'Who knows? Maybe he did.' Connor appeared, holding a printout list of book reservations.

Cleo made a snorting noise and dragged Andrea out to the staffroom.

Ginny studied Connor, suddenly wondering if his lack of sleep was about more than noisy flatmates. Though Milos was thirty-eight, it was possible their paths had crossed.

'Do you know Milos?'

'Nah, not really. Though I've bumped into him a couple of times. He seemed okay.'

Ginny raised an eyebrow, since 'okay' was high praise indeed coming from Connor. 'You liked him?'

'I didn't dislike him. He mainly kept to himself, which for this village is difficult to do.' He narrowed his eyes. 'Don't tell me you and your detective club are looking into this.'

'Detective club?' Ginny coughed, but he just offered up one of his rare half-smiles.

'All that's missing are the matching deerstalkers and magni-fying glasses.' He shrugged and waved the piece of paper at her. 'I'm going to start on this list before the doors open. I reckon it's going to be flat out.'

Connor was right. Unlike Saturday, when it had been almost deserted, that day the library was flooded with locals, curious tourists and a handful of news reporters, all wanting to discuss the case and use the free WI-FI. At least word hadn't spread that Ginny had been the one to find the body, but she'd still been dragged into far too many conversations about Harlow and Milos. It also meant she'd worked through her lunch break and hadn't been able to visit Vanja. But she had started ringing the long list of customers that Megan had given her. Most of them had been only too happy to complain about Harlow and his aggressive sales techniques, but there was nothing to suggest they had murdered him in a blind rage.

Finally, the day was over, and Ginny let out a sigh as she flicked off the lights and locked the front door. Connor had finished earlier, and Cleo and Andrea were already halfway down the road, moaning about the buses, which meant Ginny was alone.

JM had insisted they meet at The Lost Goat for the two-for-the-price-of-one meal specials, but Ginny still had an hour before she was meant to be there. She could either walk home, feed Edgar, and call a few more of Harlow's customers... or she could visit Vanja's workshop and see if he'd talk to her. She checked the address and discovered it was only a five-minute walk away. She'd recently bought a dry food dispenser – so at least Edgar wouldn't starve.

Pale pink cherry blossoms floated through the air as she crossed the bridge. From there she went left and followed the road until she came to an old brick warehouse. It had once been a mill but unlike some of the other buildings in the village, it hadn't received any heritage status, or funding for repairs.

There were several businesses operating out of it, each having portioned off part of the building. At the far end was a sign reading *Vanja Petrovic Upholstery Services*.

There was no shop front or glass window to display any of the products, and if it wasn't for the small sign on the roller door, Ginny might've missed it all together. There was a door to the left, which was cracked open. *He must still be working.*

That was the first hurdle out of the way.

Ginny took a quick breath and tried to settle her nerves. Doctor Judy had advised that the best way to stop people suspecting you were lying was by sticking to the truth as much as possible. Was that why Tuppence had insisted they watch the videos? Still, if it meant that this interview went better than the one with Mancini, she would be happy.

She stepped inside to a charming showroom, which was filled with several mid-century sofas and chairs. They really were lovely and once again Ginny toyed with the idea of replacing her own one. She ran a hand across the rich golden velvet of a tub chair as the last of the daylight flooded in from a side window – probably the same one Tuppence had climbed through last week.

'What you want?' a sharp voice asked, and she turned to face a short, lean man with lined skin and wide brown eyes.

Vanja. There wasn't much of a resemblance to his nephew, and he didn't look pleased to see her. Ginny couldn't blame him for that.

'I'm so sorry to disturb you.' She cautiously moved towards where he stood in the doorway that separated the showroom from the workshop. He folded his arms across his chest and didn't move. He must have been in his seventies but despite his age, his muscles were corded from years of lifting furniture. Again, she thought of her own fitness. Soon. She'd do something about it soon.

'I'm Ginny, I'm a friend of Megan's. She said you might be able to help me. It's about Milos.'

His expression didn't change, and too late Ginny wondered if instead of being a loving and concerned uncle, he was angry at his nephew. Or angry at Harlow and his daughter.

'How you help?' he asked in a heavy accent, and for the first time she could see the strain around his mouth and the exhaustion in his eyes. 'Are you police?'

'No.' Ginny quickly shook her head. 'I'm not anyone important. But I promised Megan I'd try. She believes Milos is innocent.'

He continued to study her, before suddenly lowering his arms and beckoning her through the door.

Wooden workbenches lined one wall while two longer ones ran down the middle of the room. There were several sofas and armchairs in various states of disrepair and at the far end were rolls of fabric, carefully covered over with sheets of clear plastic, as well as two industrial sewing machines and an overlocker. The floor was immaculately clean, and so were the benches.

Vanja leaned against one of them and studied her. 'Ask your questions.'

'Do you believe Milos is guilty?' she said, deciding to match his blunt conversation style.

'No. He's not a killer.' Vanja gave an adamant shake of his head.

'But did he get on with Timothy Harlow?'

This time there was a pause and Vanja rolled his shoulders, as if considering. 'He thought Harlow was a liar. And that we could make more money without him.'

'If that was true, then why did you keep working with him? Did Harlow have something on you? Ants Mancini told me he'd approached you several times and offered you a more favourable deal, but you always refused.'

'I say no to Mr Mancini because I'm loyal.' Vanja patted his chest. 'When I arrived here, I had nothing. No one would come to Vanja until Mr Harlow told them to. He was a good man.'

Ginny's nostrils flared in surprise. She'd been expecting some kind of complicated reasoning. Or blackmail. But it was good, old-fashioned loyalty. Even if it was misplaced, if Mancini's guess at how much Harlow had been pocketing from the workshops was correct.

'What about when Harlow threatened to take out the restraining order on your nephew? Did you consider it then?'

He made a growling noise in the back of his throat. 'Mr Harlow did not want Milos to date his daughter. Neither did I. He must marry good Serbian girl and bring her here. It's much better.'

Ginny wasn't sure how to answer that so she peered around the workshop instead. It wasn't very large. Was that why Harlow had approached Mancini about leasing the barn?

She asked Vanja but he shook his head. 'I stay here. Harlow stay at his shop. No reason to have barn.'

'I see.' She rubbed her brow. So far, all she'd found out was that Vanja, far from being angry with Harlow, seemed to agree with him. And that he didn't believe his nephew was guilty. Except all the evidence said otherwise. The stolen pocket watch found in Milos's flat, the work boots covered in blood. Milos and Harlow having an argument on the phone. And the scissors that had been used to kill Harlow.

'Is it true the scissors came from here?' she asked, and for the first time something like pain rippled across the older man's face.

'Yes. Special ones.'

'But can anyone else touch them? Or is it just you and Milos?' she pressed, and his eyes flickered with interest.

Vanja strode over to a smaller workbench tucked in behind

the doorway leading back through to the showroom. He turned and impatiently beckoned for her to follow.

By the time she joined him, he'd lifted the lid of a wooden box. He held it out so she could see that it was full of sewing scissors, all identical to the ones that had been plunged into Harlow's back.

Her skin prickled and she gripped the bench, trying to push away the memory. Why was he showing them all to her?

'Milos cleans them after all the teaching. And sharpens them when they are blunt.' He nodded to a grinder attached to the bench and then pushed the box towards it.

Ginny turned to him in sudden understanding. Regardless of who had used the scissors during a workshop, Milos's fingerprints would be on them. *Was that part of the reason the police had arrested him? Because his fingerprints were on the scissors?* She looked over to the side window that Tuppence had climbed through. Had someone else done the same thing? Or simply walked through the door carrying a pair?

'Did you tell the police about this?'

'They don't listen to Vanja.' He put the box of scissors down, and Ginny wondered what else they hadn't listened to.

'If Milos is innocent, do you know where he was on Saturday afternoon?'

'No. Since he started dating Megan, he likes to keep secrets.' He sighed and glanced at his watch. It was a clear indication that their interview was over. Then she remembered the button they'd found. She retrieved her phone and brought up the photograph.

'One more question. Do you recognise this?'

He peered at the screen for several seconds then shook his head. 'No. I cover my own buttons.'

'Okay, thank you,' Ginny said, and made her way back outside.

At least she hadn't managed to accuse anyone of murder this time, but she also wasn't sure how useful it had been.

She glanced at her watch and hurried back down the street towards The Lost Goat. It was time to meet her friends. Then she thought of Connor's comment about them being a detective club. *Cheeky boy.*

All the same, she couldn't help but smile.

ELEVEN

Despite the blustery weather, the beer garden was filled with customers, all huddling into their jackets.

Ginny nodded to a couple of library patrons on her way to the door but stopped as the screech of an electric guitar rushed out – like a desperate genie who had finally been released from its bottle and had no intention of ever going back in.

The hairs on her arms prickled as a second wail followed, much as if the guitarist in question was standing too close to the amplifier.

'What a din. I don't care if the meals are half price, I'm not listening to this racket,' the couple behind her complained and marched away. She watched them leave as another dissonant shriek escaped.

'Don't do it, love,' someone from a nearby table called out and Ginny gave them an apologetic grimace, sorry that she couldn't take their advice. Bracing herself, she stepped inside.

The usual lighting had been changed, turning the once

friendly pub into a gloomy cavern of shadows. The taproom was only half full, and there was no one lining up at the bar.

Had her friends decided to meet somewhere else? Hope flared and she retrieved her phone to check for a message, but before she could unlock the screen, JM appeared from around the corner. Ginny slipped the phone away and joined her.

'Terrible, aren't they? Who would call themselves The Black Plague Revival?' JM's loud voice only just managed to rise above a drum solo that made the whole floor vibrate.

The noise was coming from a makeshift stage where three black-clad youths were bouncing up and down, clutching at guitars. At the back, a drummer was lost behind a sea of long, dark hair.

'They should be going on their break in a moment,' an old man shouted, from further down the bar.

'Let's hope they break their instruments at the same time.' JM scowled.

'Or we could unplug them,' Mitch, one of the regular bar staff, bellowed as he joined them. 'I told Neil not to hire them. The one on the bass only started lessons two months ago.'

'Neil? Is he the new manager?' JM glanced to the end of the bar where a scruffy-looking man was talking on the phone and scratching his belly. 'I stopped remembering their names after one chap tried to make me wear a glow stick on my head.'

'Griffin. What an idiot he was,' Heather, who also worked there, yelled as she touched Mitch's arm. The barman's whole face softened, and he planted a kiss on Heather's bright purple hair.

Despite the noise, Ginny smiled. The pair of them had started dating several months ago, and although Heather was ten years older than Mitch, they both seemed very happy. It was a sharp contrast to when Ginny had first met him. Back then he'd been lost in the endless grief of his fiancée's death four years earlier. It was part of the mystery that Ginny and her friends had helped solve. And since discovering the truth, Mitch had found peace.

And love.

Unfortunately, the brewery refused to let Mitch and Heather take over the pub management because of their lack of qualifications, and instead kept sending in a succession of replacement managers. There had been four in less than five months.

'This one's even worse. If it keeps up, we might get off,' Mitch bellowed, as the music came to an abrupt halt.

It was like stepping out of a storm – all around them, patrons blinked and rubbed their ears. Taking advantage of the lull, JM ordered drinks while the musicians crowded around a group of young girls who'd been cheering them on.

'Oh my God, it's Spider. He's so hot,' a girl screamed and pushed her way across to the drummer, whose face was still hidden under a nest of hair.

Was this Little Shaw's version of Beatlemania? Ginny shuddered at the idea as they carried the drinks back to the table, where Tuppence and Hen were studying an unappetising sandwich.

'Why is the ham frozen?' Hen used one of her knitting needles to give it a prod. 'And... is that a green pea?'

'No wonder the poor sods didn't stay to eat it.' Tuppence gathered up the plate along with two half-finished drinks and disappeared in the direction of the bar.

'The food and glasses were here when we arrived. But we wanted to get a table as far away from the noise as possible. Though after looking at the sandwich, I'm not sure if we should eat here.'

'Definitely not. Heather just told me that the new manager hired some student to do the cooking. Apparently, he also manages bands. Including this lot,' Tuppence explained once she'd returned.

'Sounds dodgy. Luckily, I have a backup plan.' JM passed around the drinks then opened a large bag that had been hanging from her chair. From it she produced a shallow glass container. Carefully she prised the lid off it to reveal a selection of delicate samosas, layered with thin strips of pastry.

They were still warm, and the faint waft of garlic and onions clung to them. In the centre was a small bowl of glistening chutney. 'I was worried this might happen so I brought these along. Just in case. It's a new recipe and I think it's got the right balance of fennel this time.'

'I'm not sure we're meant to eat outside food here,' Hen said, though her eyes were fixed on the container.

'They should have thought of that before putting green peas and frozen ham into a sandwich and trying to pass it off as a pizza.' JM produced four white linen napkins and passed them around. Several patrons looked over with interest, but she waved them away. 'Can you believe how nosy people are?'

'Naught so queer as folk.' Tuppence plunged her samosa into the chutney then took a large bite before letting out a happy sigh. 'Very nice. Thank you.'

'I thought we could all do with a little treat. Though my mango chutney didn't turn out very well. Ginny, you'll have to show me how to make it.'

'Of course.' She nodded, still not sure on how appropriate it was to be eating their own food in the pub. But after Hen bit into one and let out an ecstatic sigh, Ginny relented.

The warm pastry flaked in her mouth, and she finished it in two bites, before taking a sip of the gin and tonic that had been put in front of her.

The next ten minutes were spent eating before JM cleared everything away and Hen produced a small, rolled-up piece of felt from her knitting bag. She flattened it out on the table and then opened an old metal tin full of exquisitely made miniature felt people, houses and objects – none bigger than a matchstick.

'It's our travelling murder board.' She spread out the tiny creations. 'They have Velcro on the back to make them stick. That way, I can just roll it away.'

'That's a jolly good idea. But how did you make them so small?' Tuppence wanted to know.

'It was easy enough. I was forever making felt toys for Alyson. And, of course, things for her dollhouse. Working to scale is fun.'

'To you, maybe,' JM retorted as Hen picked up a tiny figure with a piece of black wool stretching across his cheeks in lieu of a moustache.

'Oh, it's Harlow. Aren't you clever?' Ginny marvelled at the detail her friend had put into it.

'I'm glad you like it.' Hen pressed it into the centre of the board. 'I'll put Mancini in the top corner since we've ruled him out. I can also rule out Hannah's aunt. She might have been the last one to speak to Harlow before his death, but only cared about his refusal to stock Christmas decorations. It was a dead end.'

'Literally,' JM quipped.

'I wish I had something to report,' Tuppence said, once Hen had added the two extra figures in the top corner of the board. 'I visited Megan's accountant, who has the personality of a wet fish. I couldn't get a thing out of her except that Megan had been there from twelve to three on Saturday afternoon. I was hoping to find out that Harlow had a secret bank account. Following the money isn't as easy as I thought it would be. How did you go, JM?'

'Harry Redfern was as tight-lipped as the accountant by the sounds of it. He refused to tell me anything at first. But I got him to speak in the end. Unfortunately, Harlow hadn't been to a game in months and didn't owe money to any of the regulars. Nor had he won any substantial sums recently.'

'That is disappointing,' Hen sighed and reached for what looked like a tiny pack of cards and a gold coin made from an Easter egg wrapper. She stuck them with the other ruled-out theories. 'If he owed money to someone, they would have had a motive. Or, if he'd won, at least we'd know where the money had come from. Do you think he was telling you the truth?'

'Oh yes. I made sure of it.' JM's eyes gleamed in a way that Ginny almost pitied the man. 'There is one other thing I found out. While I was in the pawnbroker's, I discovered this.' JM extracted a brass pocket watch from her handbag and put it on the table.

It was old-fashioned, the kind a Victorian gentleman would use. And—

'Oh, JM. Please tell me you didn't break into the police station and steal evidence,' Hen said in alarm as she pointed at the watch. 'Because that's Harlow's. He wore it everywhere.'

'It is, too.' Tuppence leaned forward to examine it. 'But Hen's right. If Milos stole it from Harlow, the police really need to keep it as evidence.'

'Thank you for the lecture on the finer details of the law,' JM replied in a cool voice. 'However, I didn't steal anything. Harry Redfern had ten of them. They're replicas. He insists they fell off the back of a truck.'

'No, how extraordinary.' Hen's eyes widened and she stretched out her hand. 'And sorry for jumping to conclusions.'

'Don't be silly. Besides, I *like* that you think it's something I might do.' JM's face softened and she patted Hen's arm.

Ginny reached for her phone and skimmed through the photos that Megan Harlow had given them, until she found the watch. She held it out so they could compare the two. They really were identical.

She sucked in her breath. 'So, someone could have just

bought a replica watch from Harry Redfern and planted it in Milos's apartment, along with the stolen work boots.'

'Exactly,' JM agreed, and glanced over to Hen. 'Will it be difficult to make a miniature watch for the board? I think it's important.'

'Absolutely.' Hen rummaged around in the tin before producing a very small antique clock that belonged to a doll-house. She also retrieved a pair of red doll's shoes. 'Here we go. These will do for now. I don't suppose Harry Redfern gave you a list of who bought the watches?'

'No, unfortunately. But at least it's a clue. Now, how did you go, Ginny?'

'I called several of the people on the list, but like Hannah's aunt, they mainly complained about little issues. Cleo was worried the spring fete would be cancelled because of Harlow's death. It seems he was the only person everyone could rely on not to be biased.'

'That's correct. He hated everyone equally,' Tuppence agreed. 'I once heard him reduce Andrea to tears because she used a zigzag stitch. Said it smacked of an amateur.'

'Is it possible one of the past entrants had a grudge against him?' Ginny suggested.

'I suppose so, though surely someone would have topped him years ago if that was the case,' Tuppence said. 'And there would be plenty of contenders. He didn't just judge craft. He judged everything, because he thought he was the pinnacle of taste and refused to work with anyone else.'

'More like an arrogant so and so,' JM retorted. 'Still, it's worth following up.'

'I could ask Cleo and Andrea tomorrow,' Ginny said, as Hen took out a selection of tiny figures: one with a sewing needle, one with a saucepan, and one with a paintbrush, and put them next to Harlow's felt body.

'What about Vanja? Did you manage to talk with him?' Hen asked, adding a tiny felt sofa to the board.

Tuppence immediately leaned forward. 'Oh yes. Did he mention anything about how to add piping to cushions?' she demanded before catching JM's annoyed expression. 'Sorry, never mind.'

'It's okay.' Ginny bit back a reluctant smile. 'It seems he really did like Harlow. Said he was the only one to help him when he first arrived in the village, which is why he's stayed loyal. He didn't approve of Milos and Megan's relationship either. Though it's clear he loves his nephew and doesn't believe he's the killer.'

'I don't suppose he knows who is?' Hen moved the felt sofa up to the far corner with the other false leads.

Ginny shook her head. 'No. I showed him the photograph of the button, but he didn't recognise it. However, I did find out something useful. Cleo mentioned that the scissors at the crime scene belonged to Vanja's workshop. After every workshop, Milos collected all the sewing scissors to clean them. The box isn't too far from the window that Tuppence broke in through. So, it's possible someone else might have done the same thing.'

'It's at the side of the building, where there are no CCTV cameras. I was very careful to check,' Tuppence added with pride. 'Which means our killer could have easily stolen the scissors and used gloves, in order to frame Milos.'

'But how can we work out who they are?' Hen said, as she added what appeared to be a tiny house window onto the board.

'Easy. We create a profile,' JM said. 'Based on what we know. Let's see. They like knives, Shakespeare and murder. And possibly have a criminal record based on their knowledge of breaking into workshops.'

'Not everyone who breaks into workshops has a criminal record.' Tuppence scowled.

'Yes, but we can't assume that everyone is a lifelong learner like you are,' JM explained, which seemed to pacify her.

Ginny frowned as she turned back to the miniature clock and red shoes attached to the board. 'What about Milos's apartment? If someone did set him up, they would have needed to break in. Do we know where he lives?' she asked.

'He lives in a bedsit. It's in that lovely old building past the vet clinic, but is very run-down. I think that's why the rent is so cheap.' Hen reached for her phone. 'I'll text Megan and find out which number it is. She might even have a key so we could have a look around. Or, at the very least, one of the neighbours might have seen something.'

'Okay. Let us know when you hear back. I could go and visit tomorrow after work.' Ginny nodded and tried not to show her disappointment. She'd driven past the building numerous times and the inhabitants didn't strike her as the kind of people who would talk to the police... or four widows trying to solve a crime. Still, it had to be worth a try.

'In the meantime, what else are we meant to do? Even with our new profile of the killer, we still don't have a clue.' Hen stared at her phone, as if willing Megan to reply.

'Oh, I know.' Tuppence held up a hand, as if she was in a school room. 'We need to follow the money. We didn't get anywhere with the accountant or the pawnbroker, but we still have Harlow's solicitor.'

'Who happens to be my good friend, Edward Tait.' JM broke into a smile. 'I'll pay him a visit tomorrow. He's due to have his office cleaned anyway. I can do it at the same time. If Harlow was setting up a new business, Tait would have to know what it was.'

Edward Tait was JM's self-appointed nemesis and she'd taken to volunteering at his legal office several times a week. He usually looked pained at the arrangement but since she'd also managed to collect more of his outstanding debts than any of his past employees, Ginny had to suppose it worked equally well for him.

And if he could shed some light on where Harlow's money had come from, and what the business was, it might give them a new lead.

'I'll come with you. The bakery below his office does great cheese scones,' Tuppence said.

'I have my knitting group tomorrow so I will ask if anyone else had a grudge against Harlow, and I was going to visit Megan to make sure she's okay,' Hen said, just as the metallic wail of a bass guitar rang out. A large groan went up from the patrons, which was answered by a clash of a snare drum. The whole room seemed to vibrate from the noise and Ginny's brow pounded with the start of a headache.

'Look, there's Wallace.' Tuppence pointed towards the bar. 'Do you think he's going to arrest them for noise pollution?'

Ginny could just see the detective clutching a pint as he walked towards the band, but instead of going up to them, he sat down at a nearby table, where an older man was already nursing a drink. The other man had salt and pepper hair pushed back from his face, a light tan and a short silver beard and moustache. And was the only one in the pub who didn't seem perturbed by the strangled sounds coming from the nearby stage.

'That's his father.' Hen rose so she could better see. 'I'm surprised Wallace has managed to drag him out. Last time he visited, we hardly saw him.'

'Wouldn't even look at me when I bumped into him at the shop. I ran over his foot with my trolley and everything.' JM also pushed back her chair to get a better view. 'It's like he doesn't have any manners. Oh, and who is that woman going over to him? She's very beautiful.'

Tuppence's eyes widened. 'That's the new pathologist. Imogen Smith. We saw her at the crime scene, didn't we, Ginny?'

Ginny, who didn't feel up to standing and drawing attention to herself, peered over to where a woman with long red hair and huge brown eyes had joined Wallace and his father. The white crime scene suit from the other day had been replaced with a pair of wide-legged jeans and a white T-shirt, and she was holding a glass of wine as she sat down at the table. They exchanged several words and Wallace even managed to smile at something she said.

It was unexpected and Ginny suddenly wondered if they were on a date. But it was hard to imagine the grumpy detective dating while in the middle of a murder investigation. Or bringing his dad along.

Then again, if Wallace believed Milos was guilty, then the case was closed. So, perhaps it *was* a date. Or a celebration.

Wallace suddenly shifted and for the first time seemed to notice Ginny's friends. His face darkened, and he pushed away his drink and stalked over.

Ginny closed her eyes as the bass continued to pound away at her cranium. They really shouldn't have come here.

'Oh no.' Hen promptly sat down and rolled up the felt mat. 'I wonder what he wants?'

'Maybe he wants to apologise to Ginny.' JM gathered up a clump of tiny felt knives and what looked like a cartoon bomb and returned them to the tin.

'Or to see if we're okay after being first at a traumatic crime scene.' Tuppence opened Hen's knitting bag so that the impromptu murder board could be hidden away. But, as he got closer, the deep lines around his mouth suggested it wasn't any of those things. Ginny's palms went sweaty.

Did he know about their decision to investigate?

'I'd like a word.' He raised his voice, to combat the noise.

'That's all very well, but what about your father? You shouldn't let him sit so close to the band. Don't tell me he enjoys it,' JM challenged, oblivious to the potential danger.

'His hearing aids are turned off. He does it whenever he's not interested in something,' Wallace shouted, his tone almost jealous. As if he wished he could do the same right then. He swivelled to face Tuppence. 'Removing evidence from a crime scene is a serious offence... and if—'

A guitar solo kicked in and they all winced. Wallace folded his arms until it was over.

'Furthermore, why did I get a report that a woman walked into Harry Redfern's pawnshop today and threatened him?'

'*Threatened him?* I barely touched the man.' JM snorted before seeming to remember why she'd been there. She gave him a dazzling smile. 'Please expunge that statement from the record. What I meant to say was, "How fascinating."'

Wallace's jaw clenched as a murderous rift of 'Stairway to Heaven' started up, but before he could continue a woman in her fifties had stormed over to their table.

Her hair glowed bright magenta, even in the dull light, and perfectly matched her lipstick. She had a pair of reading glasses on top of her head, as well as a second pair dangling from a chain around her neck.

At the sight of her, Wallace threw up his hands and marched away. The woman hurried after him. She appeared to be yelling, but the words were lost underneath the wave of distortion flooding from the stage.

Ginny sank back into her chair, pleased the lecture had been cut short.

'Poor Wallace. Brenda should know better than to waste police time like that.' JM gave the woman a disapproving look and then finished her drink. 'This rivalry is getting out of control.'

'What rivalry?' Ginny asked, now that her heart rate had returned to normal.

'Brenda Larson and Lily Major are two amateur bakers who have been competing in the spring fete for the last thirty years.

They leave the rest of us in the dust. One of them always wins and the other always comes second. Though never twice in a row,' Hen explained.

'Lily won last year and for the last eleven months she's been boasting about her new recipe, and how it will finally break the stalemate,' Tuppence added. 'But last week she started telling anyone who would listen that Brenda had stolen it. I wouldn't put it past her to have asked Wallace to press charges.'

'That would explain why Brenda's talking to him now. She's probably pleading her side of the case,' Hen added.

'They wouldn't have dared do it while Harlow was alive,' JM pointed out. 'He would've disqualified them both on the spot.'

Ginny frowned, trying to follow the conversation. Since her move to Little Shaw, she'd grown accustomed to the main quirks that came with living in such a small place... but she hadn't come across an annual baking rivalry before.

'I hope that doesn't happen,' Tuppence admitted. 'Because when Lily was talking about her cake recipe that was stolen, it did sound rather delicious. I'd like to see it.'

Ginny sat forward as Brenda continued to wave her arms wildly at Wallace. With everything that had been going on, she'd completely forgotten about the collection of recipe cards that Edgar had brought in on Saturday afternoon.

'Tuppence, did Lily say what the cake was?'

'Oh yes, it sounded quite extraordinary. It was an upside-down apple cake with almond butter mousse and cinnamon dusting.'

'Very ambitious,' JM said, before studying Ginny's face. 'Why, is everything okay? I hope you're not involved in this. You don't want to get between two bakers. They play all kinds of dirty. I'm not sure even my legal skills could get you out of it.'

'I'm not involved, exactly.' Ginny sighed. 'But my cat is. I don't suppose any of you know where Lily Major lives? I think

I'd better pay her a visit in the morning, before Wallace loses what little patience he has left. Plus, if she's entered every year, then she must have known Harlow well. I might be able to find out if anyone had a grudge against him.'

'What if *she's* the one with a grudge?' Tuppence pointed out and Ginny swallowed. If that was the case, then it meant she could be playing Good Samaritan to a potential killer.

TWELVE

The following morning, Ginny walked into her conservatory to retrieve the recipe cards. They were exactly where she'd left them, along with a half-finished cup of tea. Everything had been so upside down since Saturday afternoon that she'd completely forgotten about both.

'I suppose I should be grateful that you didn't move them,' she said to Edgar, who was trying to herd her into the kitchen to give him a second breakfast. 'Would you at least like me to pass on your apologies?'

Edgar blinked and sat down.

'Or your deepest regrets and a sincere promise to never do it again?' she pressed, as she shook some dry food into the bowl. He snubbed it, and turned his head away, as if he couldn't even look at her. She reluctantly laughed. 'Yes, how dare I try and get you to show any remorse.'

She left the cat to stare at the wall while she put her teacup into the dishwasher along with her breakfast plate. She'd been half tempted to visit Lily Major last night and restore order, but by the time they'd left The Lost Goat, all she'd wanted to do was go home and hope that the ringing in her ears would eventually stop.

It had, and, despite the murder, she'd slept surprisingly well.

Once she was finished tidying up, she checked her reflection. In the last few months, she'd been trying to add some more excitement to her wardrobe, and today she had on a fuchsia cardigan over a white T-shirt, and a denim skirt. She'd never stand out the way her friends did, but at least she didn't feel quite as dowdy as she once had.

'What do you think, love?' she said, deciding to use up her single daily question to her dead husband. There was no answer, but a warmth filled her chest and she blew a kiss before opening the door.

The March morning was grey and overcast so she retreated inside to get a long raincoat before heading off by car. The rain had started in earnest by the time she reached Lily Major's house, and Ginny pulled her hood up before climbing out of the car.

Lily lived in a small brick bungalow with a tidy garden out the front. It didn't look the kind of house a killer might own, but Ginny supposed that was the point.

It was also five miles from her own house and, as she pushed open the gate, she wondered how Edgar had managed to go so far. Last night, after telling her friends what her cat had done, Tuppence had shown her several YouTube clips of other cats being filmed stealing things, and some even had tiny cameras attached to their collars.

Ginny wasn't sure she was ready for a catcam yet.

The door opened before she could knock and a woman in her seventies appeared with a halo of white curls and an old-fashioned housecoat. Ginny frowned. After seeing Brenda, with her magenta hair and bright lips, she'd been expecting Lily to be a similar foil. Instead, she was a good twenty years older and looked like she ironed her doilies. By the front door was a pair of bright white trainers, and Ginny blinked, remembering the appearance of the tiny woman who had been at the police station on Sunday night. Had Tuppence been right about Lily trying to press charges?

'Oh dear. Don't tell me I have a library book overdue. I try to be ever so careful,' Lily said, by way of greeting.

'No, it's nothing like that. And I'm sorry for turning up on your doorstep. We haven't properly met before, but my name is Ginny.'

'I remember reading all about you in the parish newsletter. You're our lovely new librarian. I'm Lily Major. How can I help?'

'I'm actually here to apologise on behalf of my cat.' Ginny extracted the small collection of handwritten recipe cards from her bag and held them out. 'He has been on a bit of a – er, crime spree – lately. And on Saturday he came home with these.'

Lily's hand flew to her mouth. 'My recipes. You found them. Oh, you are a dear, dear soul. I thought I'd never see them again. What a naughty puss. I had no idea you lived so close by. Where are you?'

'I'm in Middle Cottage on Ten Mile Lane,' Ginny replied.

Lily's gentle face hardened. 'Ten Mile Lane? I knew it. We need to go to the police station and press charges.'

'You want to press charges against my cat?'

Lily blinked and shook her head. 'Of course not. How absurd. Against Brenda Larson. She lives in number three, River Row, but her mother lives around the corner from you. I bet she hid them there to throw Wallace off the scent.'

'What are you saying? That Brenda stole your recipes, hid them at her mother's house, and that Edgar stole them from there?'

'Exactly,' Lily agreed, a flush of high colour spreading across her cheeks, turning her from sweet and smiling to a glowing spitfire. JM hadn't been joking about getting involved in the rivalry.

Suddenly Lily narrowed her eyes and tried to peer past Ginny's shoulder, out onto the street. But she was too small and had to make do with crouching down, to see past Ginny's handbag instead.

'Is everything okay?'

'It's not safe. Quickly, you'd better come in before anyone sees you.' Lily all but dragged her into the house and slammed the door shut.

Ginny wasn't certain who could possibly see them, or why it would matter, but she allowed herself to be ushered inside, trying not to notice the trail of raindrops coming off her coat. Lily was clearly upset, and since Edgar had been the cause, the least she could do was try and soothe her: 'I'm sorry about the distress you've been caused. But please don't make yourself anxious. It seems cats can cover long distances when they want to. Is it possible that you left your back door open and he wandered inside?'

'I only leave it open when I go into the garden. I would have seen a cat come in. No, it's clear that Brenda broke into my house and stole them. And I know exactly when she did it. On Saturday the eighth of March. There was a special committee meeting for the fete and then I went to the hairdresser. When I got home, they were gone.'

Lily led her into a sitting room. It had floral wallpaper but most of it was lost under a sea of red and blue rosettes. They were lined up in alternative colours, the ones at the top faded with age. Her friends had mentioned that Lily and Brenda were alternate winners, and they hadn't exaggerated.

There were also numerous framed newspaper articles and photographs, including one with Timothy Harlow standing between a younger-looking Lily and Brenda. His arm was around each of them, but his expression suggested it was less from happiness and more from trying to keep them apart.

The headline read: *Inaugural Spring Fete Marred by Butter Knives at Dawn.*

Butter knives? Ginny wasn't sure she wanted to know what it meant. But things had clearly escalated. She looked back at the photograph of Harlow. As usual he was wearing a Victorian-style suit, complete with a top hat and a silver-tipped cane in one hand. How well had Lily known him? At the very least the question might distract her from pressing charges against Brenda. Or, for that matter, Edgar.

'It must have been a shock to hear about Harlow's death.'

'It really was.' Lily's eyes lost their blaze as she sank into a comfortable armchair and nodded for Ginny to sit in the other one. 'Not that I didn't want to murder him myself, every second year, when he gave the red rosette to *that* woman. But when you've known someone for such a long time, you get used to them being part of your life. And of course, he was also our weather guru, who ensured we always had a sunny day, no matter what the forecast was.'

Weather guru? Ginny blinked. From what she gathered, Harlow had an inflated sense of himself, but to take credit for avoiding an April shower seemed a bit much.

'That is a remarkable record,' she said, diplomatically, before taking a deep breath and hoping she didn't appear too nosy. 'It still seems strange that someone would want to kill him. I can't think who would do something like that.'

'That's because you haven't lived here long enough. There's only one person capable of doing it.' Lily folded her arms and glared at the wall of rosettes. 'Brenda.'

'But why would she kill him? Especially if this was her year to—' Ginny broke off too late, realising her mistake. 'Er, compete.'

Lily's face darkened. 'It's because after she stole my recipe cards and saw the brilliance of my creation, she knew she couldn't win. So, she had to go one step further and murder Timothy Harlow.'

'That seems a bit extreme.'

'We're talking about Brenda Larson here. Her middle name *is* extreme. But the joke is on her because they still haven't decided whether to cancel the spring fete. I bet the waiting is killing her.'

'When will they decide?' Ginny asked, pleased to move the conversation away from Lily's assertions.

'Hopefully today. It would be dreadful if they do cancel. Poor Peter and Sandra. Before they took over, there hadn't been a village fete in Little Shaw for almost a decade, due to lack of interest. But thirty years ago, they had a dream, and now it's one of the most successful events in the county. And I got to play a small part in that history when I won the inaugural baking category. With a Madeira, would you believe?' She pointed to the top rosette. Then her eyes dropped to the most recent one, and she clasped the recipe cards tightly to her chest. 'This year is my time to finally put Brenda in her place.'

'If Brenda did steal the recipes, aren't you worried she might try and make the same cake?'

'Ha. She could try.' Lily's eyes darkened with malice. 'But it wouldn't taste very nice. I always code my ingredients, you see. Just in case.'

'Oh, I see.' Ginny sank back into the chair, not sure what to say next. It was clear the two women were locked in a private battle. 'Well, I'm sure it will be delicious. I must admit when I saw it, I had an urge to dust off my cake tins.'

'You bake?' Lily's eyes narrowed further, as if suddenly seeing her as competition.

Ginny quickly shook her head. 'Not nearly well enough to enter. I prefer making jam and marmalade,' she said, before suddenly wondering if that was another landmine in the waiting. 'Not that I plan on entering them either. I'm just donating some to the Friends of the Village stall.'

Lily's placid smile returned. 'Oh yes. Sandra mentioned it at the last meeting. That's very kind of you. We haven't had a good jam maker in the village since Tony passed away two years ago. He had a very light hand when it came to preserves. I must show you some of his recipes. He left them to me, you see – not Brenda. She can't boil a pot of water without—'

'I'd be interested to look at them,' Ginny cut in, not wanting Lily to get distracted again. It worked and the tiny woman gestured for Ginny to follow her out to the kitchen. She lifted an old shoebox down from the Welsh dresser and passed it over.

'Here you are. And while you do that, I'll make us a cup of tea.'

'Lovely,' Ginny lied. She needed to be at work in an hour but didn't feel up to upsetting Lily any more than necessary. So, she settled herself with looking through the collection of jam recipes.

There were also numerous chutney ones and when Lily brought over a tea tray loaded with two generous slices of lemon drizzle cake, Ginny was pleased she'd stayed.

'Thank you.' She took a bite. Delicate layers of crystallised sugar and citrus exploded on her tongue, followed by the combination of butter and sour cream that danced through the light-as-air cake. Now she understood exactly why Lily had won so many rosettes. 'Oh, this is extraordinary. You are a very talented baker.'

'Thank you. And unlike *some* people, I don't need to resort to stealing recipes to win. Of course, now we have proof, Brenda won't even be there to see me snatch victory.' A malicious gleam returned to the baker's eyes, and Ginny put down her fork. Surely there must be a way to fix this.

'I know it's not my business, but wouldn't it be better to not press charges? I keep thinking of that old saying – the proof is in the pudding. And this cake is wonderful. I can't imagine anyone could beat you.'

'Did Brenda tell you to say that?' Lily folded her arms, her mouth set in a petulant line.

'No. I've never met her, though I did see her at The Lost Goat last night. She looked very unhappy,' Ginny said, deciding not to mention who Brenda had been speaking to.

'Which proves my point. She's desperate. She knows that ridiculous angel cake with the meringue monstrosity on top, which she entered last year, wasn't up to scratch. She was lucky to come in second,' Lily said darkly, before rubbing her chin. 'Do you really think I should rise above it?'

'Your talent speaks for itself. And considering how busy the police are, I'm sure they'd be grateful.'

Lily let out a breath and, for the first time, the tension in her jaw seemed to fade. 'Thank you. Not just for returning my recipes but for reminding me about what matters.'

'You're welcome.' Ginny smiled and got to her feet. She hadn't managed to find out anything useful about Harlow's killer, but hopefully she'd stopped one feud from escalating.

THIRTEEN

Tuesday, 18th March

By the time Ginny locked up the library for the evening, she was feeling like she'd walked into a brick wall. The day had been spent casually probing Cleo, Andrea and half a dozen library-goers who had been on the receiving end of Harlow's harsh judgements. But they'd only offered up wild theories, much like Lily Major had done.

Her friends hadn't fared much better and had sent several text messages during the day with updates. Edward Tait hadn't been in the office, and Hen's knitting group had been full of gossip about the murder, but nothing substantial. The only positive was that while Megan didn't have a key to Milos's bedsit, she did have the room number.

Her friends had other obligations, so Ginny had agreed to visit on the way home. The rain had stopped and it didn't take long for her to drive to the other side of the village.

The building was indeed lovely, made from local sandstone with a slate roof and long sash windows. The date-stone above the door read 1829, but it was clear by the weeds growing out of the crumbling brickwork that the owner wasn't interested in restoring it.

The front door was covered in grime from the nearby road and despite the slot for letters, the top step was buried beneath a collection of weathered newspapers and advertising fliers.

Ginny's stomach twisted into a knot. Her plan had been to knock on the door and hope that one of the other occupants would let her in... and answer a few questions. What if it wasn't actually a bedsit? It could be a squat, and—

'What do you want?' a voice from behind her growled, and Ginny swung around to face a short man in his mid-fifties. He had a long face and greasy, grey hair that hung down to his collar, while his wide belly seemed at odds with his skinny legs. His eyes were narrowed, but on seeing her, he broke into a toothy grin. 'Hey, I recognise you. You're the library lady. The one who caught a murderer.'

'Er, yes. My name's Ginny Cole.' She held out her hand. He didn't take it, but now that he recognised her, his manner seemed curious rather than hostile.

'I'm Slim. And it's nice to meet you. I can't say I ever liked that Louisa much. She kicked me out of the library three times, just because my face didn't fit. Well, that and the fact I might have nicked a couple of DVDs here and there,' he amended with a rueful smile.

'I see.' Ginny blinked, not sure how to respond to the statement. Or the fact that Slim's nickname didn't quite fit his figure. Was that how he'd earned it? He seemed to read her mind and patted his belly.

'I'm packing a few extra pounds these days, but once upon a time I was like a stick. That's how I managed to fit through so many windows. Once I even got in through a cat door,' he said, before seeming to catch himself. 'In my previous profession, you understand. These days I stick to more stand-up jobs.'

'Oh-h, well, that's good,' Ginny stammered, floundering

with how one should reply to what she suspected was a confession he had once been a burglar before putting on too much weight.

'Yeah, well, I like to be practical.' He patted his belly again and then frowned. 'And I'm not sure who you're here to see, but we don't use that door. Landlord blocked it off last year because he was sick of it getting kicked in. So, now it's only the back door that gets kicked in.' He gave a raucous laugh and gestured for her to follow him along the side of the building.

He didn't seem to have any ulterior motive, and there was no small voice in her head telling her to run, so Ginny tightened her grip on her handbag and trailed after him.

The pathway was littered with broken glass and debris that crunched under her shoes as they reached the back. Several washing lines had been strung up and there were a couple of men sitting on overturned milk crates, clutching bottles of beer.

Slim ignored them and came to a halt on the concrete slab that stood in for the back garden. 'So, what's this about? Who are you here to see?'

'To be honest, I'm not sure,' she admitted, feeling too bewildered to come up with an excuse. And lying to someone who seemed happy to talk about his own illegal activities seemed a bit pointless. 'I'm a friend of Milos Petrovic's girlfriend. She's convinced he's innocent, but—'

'But she's too scared to come around here?' He arched an eyebrow then laughed. 'Yeah, Milos mentioned that his precious lady wasn't a fan of our palatial manor. Not that I can blame her. Place is a dump, and she seemed like a classy bird.'

'Something like that,' Ginny agreed, not sure if Megan would be flattered or horrified by the description. 'Did you know Milos very well?'

'Not really. He tended to keep to himself when he was here. Not that that was very often. He worked long hours and when he got home, he'd just go to his room. That's his one there.' Slim pointed to a second-floor window.

The second floor? Ginny swallowed down her disappointment as she peered up. There was no fire escape or trellis to make it easy to climb to, and the grimy window didn't look like it'd been opened in a long time. If someone had planted the evidence, then she doubted it was by going through the window.

'Is there any other way someone could access his room?' she asked.

Slim let out a bark of laughter. 'Easy as going for a piss... er, sorry, I mean yes. The back door has been kicked in so many times, we don't bother to lock it. And the bedroom doors aren't much better. Suppose it's lucky none of us have anything to steal.'

Except Milos didn't have anything stolen – it was the reverse. And, if Slim was correct, it meant someone *could* have planted the evidence. The question was, did anyone see them do it? She doubted there would be any security alarms or CCTV footage.

'If someone did break into Milos's room, would it be possible for them to do so without being seen?'

Slim raised an amused eyebrow. 'That depends on who was doing it. I, naturally, have the skill set to make it an easy task. But, like I said, I'm a reformed character these days.'

'Of course. I didn't mean to imply it was you.' Ginny's face heated up, but he just laughed again.

'I'd be offended if you *didn't* think I could do it,' he assured her. 'But as for who else might manage it, well, that's a different kettle of fish. The bedsit is only for males and most of us aren't exactly living the high life. So, someone like you, or Milos's bird, would stand out like a sore thumb. But there are always people coming and going from this place. I've been here for five years, but some only last a few weeks before buggering off.'

'Is it possible that one of the other tenants might have gone into his room?'

'Anything's possible. Though I doubt they would've done it unless someone had greased their palm, if you know what I'm saying.'

'You mean someone might have paid them to do it.' Ginny gasped, quickly realising that would be by far the most obvious scenario. 'Is there any way we could ask them?'

'Not unless you've got a death wish. Those two are okay.' He nodded to the men drinking in the garden. 'But some of the residents aren't what I would call gentlemen. Probably why they all scarpered the moment the coppers arrived.'

'The police didn't interview them then?' A ripple of irritation prickled Ginny's skin. Had Wallace just found the evidence without digging any deeper?

But Slim shrugged. 'No idea. Maybe they tracked them down later, but when they turned up with the warrant, I was the only sad sack left. I had a cake in the communal oven and didn't want it to burn. Like I said, I've mended my ways, and was thinking of entering the fete. If it's still going ahead,' he added, sheepishly, as if embarrassed to confess to using the kitchen.

'So, you gave a statement to the police? What did you tell them? And do you remember who you spoke to?' she asked, not sure if he would answer her. After all, he had no reason to tell her anything; however, he seemed to enjoy having someone to talk to, and she wondered if he was lonely. She made a mental note to see if he was a member of the library before she left. He might enjoy coming along to some of their community sessions.

'Can't say I'm a fan of the coppers. Not that I knew much. Like I said, Milos kept to himself. As for who they were, it was Wallace. Miserable bastard that he is. And some woman with a fancy title. I think she's the one who looks at the bodies.'

'The pathologist?' Ginny widened her eyes. She wasn't sure

on everything a pathologist did, but she didn't think it usually included searching a bedsit. Or that it was part of Wallace's job description, for that matter. From what Anita had let slip, that kind of thing was left to her and PC Bent. 'I'm surprised they were both here.'

'Apparently they were on their way back from some other case the pathologist woman was working on and stopped here on the way to the station,' Slim explained, before his face brightened. 'I might've overheard them talking while I was back in the kitchen. Old habits and all that...'

'Of course,' Ginny said, too busy processing the fact that Wallace and Imogen had more than one case to work on. The thought had never occurred to her, especially since at least one of those cases was a murder investigation. Was that why Wallace had been so angry with her on Sunday night? And why Imogen had been with him and his father at the pub?

More importantly, was it why he'd been so quick to arrest Milos? So that he could close the case? She frowned. James Wallace could be many things, but a corner-cutter wasn't one of them. Yet, it was hard not to think it.

'Have any police been back here since? To look for more evidence or to interview some of the other residents?'

'No. Though it's not surprising, since Milos was arrested that evening. I suppose they got everything they needed.'

Or they'd got everything that had been planted there. Ginny frowned, again thinking about Slim's suggestion that one of the tenants could have broken into Milos's room without anyone knowing. But she could hardly ask Slim to find out more if it wasn't safe.

Unless he happened to hear anything.

It had to be worth a try, and she reached into her handbag and extracted a card with the library address on it and her phone number. 'If the police do come back, or if you hear anything, would you mind calling me?' she said.

But Slim scrunched up his face and didn't take the card. 'The old phone doesn't have any credit. Turns out staying on the straight and narrow ain't as easy as it looks, and things have been a bit tight lately,' he admitted, colour rising along his neck, as if embarrassed.

Ginny winced, feeling terrible for putting him in that situation. Back when she'd run the surgery for Eric, she'd had many patients who refused to call mobile numbers because of the cost. Quickly, she extracted a ten-pound note from her purse and passed it over to him. 'I should have thought of that. You could use this to buy phone credit.'

His eyes lit up at the money. 'Sure. You got it.'

'Thank you, Slim. And if your library membership has lapsed, you should come down and sign up again.'

'Not much of a reader,' he said gruffly, as he pocketed the tenner. 'And I don't need DVDs anymore, but I'll think about it. Anyway, I'd better go. But if you want my advice, you should be careful about who you talk to. If someone did set Petrovic up, I doubt they'd appreciate anyone asking questions.'

Ginny shivered as Slim walked towards the two men drinking beer. What if he was right? If Milos didn't kill Harlow, then someone else did. And they might not take kindly to Ginny and her friends looking into it.

FOURTEEN

'It's not my place to criticise the police but there's one thing about this investigation I can't like.' William, one of the regular library patrons pushed a pile of books towards Connor the following afternoon.

Despite herself, Ginny leaned closer. Had someone else noticed the lack of police interest in looking further into the case?

'Is it because they wouldn't give you any reward money for telling them that Milos Petrovic once parked on a yellow line?' Esme, another regular, retorted. She'd been growing her bowl cut out and it was pulled off her face, making her look like a cherub.

'Double yellow,' William corrected. 'And if he can't respect a simple rule, it's a clear indication of sociopathic tendencies.'

'Pots and kettles. And what would you know about Harlow's death? Elsie was the one who knew Harlow best, on account of being a dressmaker. Refused to shop with him because of his shocking prices. What a pity she's in the Lake

District right now,' Esme retorted, before studying him with renewed interest. 'Oh... you mean the police should have travelled to Windermere to interview her? I did suggest it, but they refused.'

'Travel to Cumbria to interview your sister?' William scoffed in disgust. 'What a waste of time and money that would have been. Ten to one all she would have talked about is the cost of needles. No, Esme, what I'm referring to is the complete lack of a police press conference.'

'I will concede you have a point,' Esme said. 'They should never have set a precedent if they didn't mean to follow through with it.'

'Exactly. After the last murder, I went and bought a fancy fishing chair so that I could make a day of it next time. It has a cup holder and everything,' William explained.

Ginny sighed. So much for hoping she might hear something useful.

'It's funding cuts. Happening everywhere, it is.' Andrea appeared from the returns room, eyes bright. The only one not interested was Connor, who silently scanned William's books and printed out the receipt. He used an orange highlighter on the docket, so the due dates were visible. It was a lovely touch, and while none of the patrons had acknowledged it, there had been a lot fewer overdue books.

William and Esme drifted to the craft display, bickering over whether a fishing chair should have two cup holders or one, while Andrea, on the pretence of shelving, headed to a group of women weighing in on the likelihood of the fete being cancelled. Most of them were of the opinion it should still go ahead, apart from one, who suggested it would be disrespectful to celebrate before the funeral had even taken place.

The one thing they did agree on was that without Harlow's weather guru status to ensure sunshine, a ritual sacrifice would need to be performed.

'No doubt with blood.' Connor finally spoke as Ginny joined him at the issues counter. She wasn't sure how much more local feuding she could deal with in the one day. Did that make her a coward? Not to mention she'd promised to investigate why Harlow needed to rent a barn.

'Are you happy to stay here for an hour? I've got some paperwork to catch up on.' She had planned to start earlier but had instead spent the morning researching the other bedsit tenants, to see if one of them had planted the evidence. But after putting the address into the internet, the only names that had come up were ones who had previously committed crimes, and she'd concluded Slim was right about not approaching them.

'No problem.' Connor tipped his head to gesture at the half-empty library. 'Seems like things have gone back to normal. Well... as normal as this place can ever be.'

It was true. After the initial rush of journalists who'd descended at the weekend, the crowds had thinned away since Milos's arrest. Which made Ginny feel worse at their own lack of progress on the case.

What if there is no case?

The thought niggled at her. Despite Megan's insistence that Milos was innocent, they hadn't found anything substantial to prove it. Just a few vague avenues of enquiry, which weren't leading them anywhere.

Wallace's dark scowl flashed into her mind.

It was clear he viewed Ginny and her friends in the same category as Brenda and Lily: an irritation to be tolerated and managed. Then she swallowed and pushed the image away. If it was true the detective was stretched, evidence could've been missed. Which meant that just because Ginny and her friends hadn't found any answers yet, didn't mean they weren't there.

'Thank you. I won't be too long. I think you should finish early today and catch up on some sleep,' she said, as a man in his mid-sixties walked through the front door, clutching at a roll of posters.

He was smartly dressed in a beautiful navy jacket, a white checked shirt and heavy corduroy trousers, making him look like a gentleman farmer. Though if he was a farmer, then the strained set of his mouth suggested that he'd misplaced his sheep.

Ginny couldn't remember ever seeing him before, but his appearance had an extraordinary effect on everyone else, and an excited murmur went up around her.

'Peter Skye,' Connor said from next to her. 'Head of the Little Shaw spring fete and gala committee. And before you ask, I only know because my nan told me. I'm guessing that poster will have the fate of the... er... fete on it.'

'Of course,' Ginny replied, trying not to smile. Despite all Connor's efforts to pretend he didn't care about the library, the village or the local gossip, she'd long noticed how much attention he paid to everything. And now he was making puns. There was hope for him yet.

'Unless you want a riot, you might want to stop Cleo from getting to him first,' he added, as the woman in question darted from the children's section, clearly eager to find out what had been decided. Andrea seemed to have the same idea and was approaching from the other flank.

Peter Skye raised a neat eyebrow, as if discovering he was between a rock and a hard place, and had no way to get out of it.

Oh dear. Ginny, who was becoming an expert in running interference, slipped out from behind the counter and gave the man what she hoped was a kindly librarian sort of smile. 'Hello, would you like some help? Maybe we could talk in my office?' She steered him towards the back of the library as Connor appeared with the returns trolley and used it to block off Cleo, who was forced to come to an abrupt halt. He then thrust a stack of books into Andrea's arms, slowing her down as well.

Peter Skye nodded at her young assistant in gratitude and then smiled at Ginny. 'Thank you, you're very kind. And astute.'

'Not at all. I gather you've had a difficult few days,' she said, as they reached the small office and she ushered him in. 'My name's Ginny, by the way.'

'Peter Skye. And I'm sorry Sandra and I haven't come in sooner. The six-month run-up to the fete is always busy and it seems like the pair of us don't even have time to read a magazine. Though I promise I do like books. Mainly Tom Clancy.'

'He's very popular,' Ginny reassured him. She'd noticed how many people went to great lengths to explain their reading habits, as if worried that she'd judge them, or their choices. Which was silly, of course. There were enough books for everyone.

'It's nice to feel adventurous,' he admitted, while at the same time lifting up the collar of his jacket, as if trying to shake off the adrenaline of his close escape. Then he abruptly stopped and gave her a rueful grin. 'Oh dear. And now you've seen me run away from two of our most enthusiastic participants. You're probably thinking it's best if I leave the international spy stuff to Jack Ryan.'

'Cleo and Andrea can be quite determined,' Ginny said, trying to stay diplomatic.

He let out a bark of laughter. 'That's one way of putting it. Not that I'm complaining. I suppose where the fete is concerned, it's become a victim of its own success. But such is the reputation we've gained over the years, our whole community is invested in it.'

'So I've noticed. Everyone here seems to love it,' Ginny said truthfully, before realising it was the perfect opportunity to find out more about Harlow. 'It must have been such a shock to hear about Timothy's death.'

The smile faded from his lips and his eyes clouded over. 'It's been devastating. We've been friends for almost fifty years, not to mention how closely we've worked together ever since that very first fete. It's hard to imagine it without our head judge.'

'I'm so sorry for your loss.'

'Thank you. I won't deny that Timothy could be like Marmite – some people loved him and some... well... not so much. But to me he was the man who helped put Little Shaw on the map, and what he achieved for our community should never be forgotten. Which is the reason we've decided to go ahead with the fete. So we can honour his life in the only way we know how: through the power of sixty-five categories of local arts, craft, produce and baking.'

'Sixty-five?' Ginny blinked, suddenly having a newfound respect for Harlow if he judged all of them.

'Well, we do like to be inclusive of everyone's interests. We have a full list on our website. It's five pounds per entry.'

'I'm not really competitive,' Ginny said apologetically, and his frown returned. It seemed Lily wasn't the only one who took the fete seriously. 'B-but I know that Timothy Harlow appreciated competition.'

'You're so right. It was his vivacious appetite for excellence that helped make us so successful. Timothy treated it like it was on national television and everyone else rose to the occasion.'

Ginny nodded, not sure how to answer. Instead, she focused on her next question. Peter said they'd been friends for fifty years. Was it possible Harlow had talked about his desire to rent Mancini's barn? Or where the money had come from?

'I imagine it must have helped his own business as well. Do you think he ever considered expanding?'

'Expanding? No, why would he? The combination of the history of the shop... and his own personality... is what held that business together. If he expanded, he would have diluted his brand. And it would have pulled him away from his judging duties.'

'That makes sense,' Ginny said, wondering how Megan would feel about the suggestion her father had been the one holding the business together. 'And what about—'

She was cut off as the watch on his wrist beeped. He winced and tapped it off. 'Sorry, that's Sandra, reminding me we have a committee meeting in fifteen minutes.'

'No, it's my fault for being too talkative,' Ginny said, inwardly amused, since she'd never been accused of being chatty before her move to Little Shaw. But her smile quickly faded as she remembered the years of gentle evenings she and Eric had spent together. With him she'd always felt relaxed and happy to talk. So the change hadn't come from her move to the village: it had been forced on her by the long evenings without him.

Grief crept up her throat and Ginny stepped back as the room seemed to close in on her. It was like that now. Her pain had moved from being the constant nail in her foot, to something more mercurial. There one moment and then gone the next, sometimes for hours, or even a day, before suddenly sliding back in under her awareness.

'A-are you okay? Oh dear. I shouldn't have mentioned Timothy to you. I forgot you found the body.' There was true remorse in Peter's voice and his face was lined with worry. 'Should I call someone?'

'No, please don't.' Ginny resolutely pushed the memory away, relieved that the room shifted back into place. 'I'm fine. I just felt a bit faint. I should be apologising to you, since you're in a hurry.'

He let out a rueful laugh. 'How very English we sound, both trying to out-apologise each other. But if you're sure you're okay, I won't press.'

'Thank you. Now, how can I help?'

He looked down at the roll in his arms and gave her a reluctant smile. 'I wanted to get permission to put up some posters.

We'll be having an official press conference tomorrow, but I know how concerned our residents have been, so we decided to do what the young people call a soft launch—?'

'I'm sure it will be appreciated. We have two noticeboards and a locked one at the front of the library.'

'Thank you. Not everyone will be happy with the decision. Which is why we thought we'd give them a day's notice before the official announcement. To help them get over the shock.' He peered out of the office door to where a growing crowd of patrons awaited him.

A surge of sympathy ran through her and Ginny held out her hand. 'If you want to avoid questions before tomorrow, I'd be happy to put them up on your behalf.'

'That's very kind. Lily was right about you.'

'Lily Majors?'

'She called this morning to withdraw her official complaint about Brenda Larson. Then talked about your visit.' He closed his eyes and let out a wistful sigh. 'They wouldn't have dared behave like this if Timothy was still alive. But... still, I'm grateful for your help.'

Ginny wasn't sure she'd done much, apart from eat a delicious piece of lemon drizzle cake. All the same, she was pleased it had made a difference. 'You're welcome, and I'll put these posters up now. I'll start at the far wall, so you should be safe to slip away, assuming everyone follows me.'

Without another word, Ginny stepped out of the office, making sure the posters were visible as she threaded her way to the back of the library. From somewhere behind her Peter murmured a thank you, but it was lost as a rustle of excitement went through the crowd.

'She's putting the posters up.' Cleo rushed forward – despite Ginny's daily health and safety warnings about running in the library – the crowd fast on her heels.

'Is it still on?'

'Who is the new celebrity judge?'

'Why didn't I bring my fishing chair with me?' William complained, as he shouldered his way to the front. Ginny tried to ignore the yelps of the library patrons unfortunate enough to be in his path as she walked to the noticeboard.

Feeling a bit like a reality television host, she slowly unrolled the poster and pinned the top corners. She did the same at the bottom then stepped away to avoid being crushed by the large group. As they descended, she unrolled a second poster.

It was almost identical to the one that had been hanging in the window. But instead of Timothy Harlow's imposing glare and waxy moustache sitting above the title of 'head judge', a woman's face stared at the camera. She had smooth tanned skin, thick blonde hair and immaculate makeup.

And the name 'Juliana Melville' was written underneath.

Oh, it's the woman from Green Hill Barn. Ginny tried to recall what Hen had said. Something about her being utterly brilliant. She supposed it made sense. And she photographed beautifully.

'Well, if that don't beat all,' someone explained. 'It's Juliana Melville.'

'We were at her class on Sunday and she never said a word,' Andrea said, turning to Cleo. 'Did you know about this?'

'Of course I didn't,' Cleo told her sternly, though her eyes were wide and she chewed her lip. It was the first time Ginny had seen the other woman worried. Angry, yes. But worried, no.

'Is there a problem?'

'You bet there's a problem,' William interjected. 'And if this doesn't get Timothy Harlow turning in his grave, I don't know what will.'

'He's not even in his grave yet,' Cleo tartly replied, sounding a lot more like her usual self. 'But William's right. Harlow hated Juliana with a passion. And she hated him right back. They had

an affair many years ago. It ended badly and, later, he disqualified her quilt and accused her of cheating. She was furious and
called him a backstabber. Which is why it's such a controversial
choice.'

'Controversial?' William snorted. 'It will cause chaos. That
woman has never hidden what she thinks about woodturning.
Or pottery. What's the bet that she'll get them both down-
graded to a miscellaneous category by this time next year?'

'What's the world coming to?' someone else interjected, but
Ginny hardly heard. Her mind was fully focused on what Cleo
had said.

Backstabber.

FIFTEEN

'I remember when it happened. But it was almost thirty years ago.' Hen pulled out her knitting as they sat around one of the small study tables.

Most of the library-goers had left to spread the gossip, while Cleo and Andrea had raced home to finish their entries and make sure they included some of the stitchwork Juliana Melville was apparently so famous for.

'It's a long time to hold a grudge.' Tuppence picked up one of the old newspapers Ginny had retrieved from the makeshift stacks behind the library. The room had been damaged in a fire and was still being repaired, but an interim shipping container had been set up for some of the collection.

'Revenge is a dish best served chilly.' JM looked up from her laptop. 'I have been researching Juliana Melville on the internet. She is a fifty-five-year-old textile artist and designer who had a London studio for many years and has exhibited widely. She calls herself "an out and out... stabber".'

'A stabber? That's practically a written confession.'

Tuppence jumped to her feet, sending several newspapers fluttering to the ground.

Hen's eyes widened in alarm and she shook her head. 'It's not what you think. She's referring to an embroidery technique where you stab the needle through the fabric. There are two schools of thought. Stabbing and sewing.'

'Oh. What a nuisance.' Tuppence sank back into the chair.

'Sorry... but it is still a good lead. I only wish I remembered more of the details,' Hen said.

'What *do* you remember?' JM pushed her laptop to one side and picked up a newspaper from 1998. A shower of dust mites danced in the air, and Tuppence sneezed.

Ginny sighed and put aside the paper she'd been studying. They'd tried online searches, but the internet seemed so overloaded with modern scandals that there was no room for a village affair that happened thirty years ago. Was it suffering from the AI version of burnout and overwhelm? Or was it just because their internet skills were average at best?

'Let's see. There was a big fuss at the time. Harlow accused her of cheating and disqualified her. After that she refused to enter again. It was a shame because she was incredibly talented. She moved to London a couple of years later and – as JM mentioned – made a name for herself,' Hen said.

'What about the affair? Did they really have one?'

'I believe so. She was married but refused to leave her husband. Harlow was furious and it ended abruptly. He wasn't a man who liked playing second fiddle. Then came the fete and her disqualification.'

Ginny pressed her lips together. 'What about Juliana's husband? Is he still around? I wonder if we could talk to him?'

'I'm afraid not. They moved to London to save the marriage, but it didn't work. And she came back five years ago, with a fat divorce settlement and the body of a thirty-year-old. I hear she goes to the gym every morning. As for the husband, I think he lives in California.'

'So, he's no help then.' Tuppence picked up a tiny felt figure and pushed it into the top corner of the murder board Hen had spread out on the table. She picked up a second one with long blonde hair, and lipstick that looked remarkably like it had come from a red Sharpie. 'You made Juliana? That was fast.'

'It was no bother.' Hen's cheeks went pink as she pulled out a second metal tin. Inside was a collection of tapestry cottons, matchsticks, fuse wire and scraps of fabric. 'I thought it might help our process.'

'The wire in her hair is a nice touch. It looks like she's just visited the hairdresser.' Tuppence put the figure next to the one of Harlow. Ginny studied them, her mind trying to piece everything together.

'So, Juliana had an affair with Harlow and when she ended it, he disqualified her and accused her of cheating. Fast-forward two decades, and she's back in Little Shaw making a name for herself again.'

Tuppence took over. 'She also had means and opportunity. She just had to steal the scissors from Vanja's workshop, buy a replica pocket watch from Harry Redfern, and walk into the haberdashery shop.'

'And as the new head judge, she benefited from his death. The jury will need to know that,' JM added.

Ginny shuddered at the idea of going to such extreme lengths to get revenge. Though, after meeting Lily Major, it didn't seem outside the realm of possibility. She studied the murder board. In the bottom corner they'd set up a section of unanswered questions and Hen had made a felt bag of money, a tiny foil button and a little calendar square with the number '15' written in the middle.

'What about Tait? Did you have better luck finding him this morning?' Ginny asked.

'He wouldn't tell us anything about the will. Or Harlow's financial interests. But I've been sending him a reminder text every hour,' JM explained. 'He'll break soon.'

Ginny nodded, wishing she could move something to another part of the board. 'And we still have the button and the ides of March. Did Juliana have any connections with Shakespeare?'

'Not according to the internet,' JM said. 'She was disqualified on April the eighth, so wouldn't that have been a better day to have killed him? To give it a sense of closure.'

'Not if she wanted to become the next judge,' Ginny pointed out. 'She would've needed to allow time. Though it still feels like a tenuous connection.'

'We need to find a better one.' JM turned the page of the dusty newspaper, which signalled for them to get back to work.

Ginny had separated out each edition that had been published on the ides of March over the last forty years, and now had the task of going through them all. The first one had a woman with a Princess Leia hairstyle wearing a giant pumpkin costume on the cover. The next was dedicated to a tug of war between Little Shaw and the neighbouring village of Walton-on-Marsh. And on it went, until she picked up the 1993 edition which had a full-sized photograph of Timothy Harlow on the front page.

She mentally made the calculations – 1993 was the year he'd moved back to the village, and two years before the fete had been revitalised. His moustache wasn't as large back then, but his sneer was the same as he stared through a monocle. The headline read: *The Fashion Police Have Landed.*

Was this the connection they'd been looking for?

The entire front page was taken up by the photo, apart from a box at the bottom that directed readers to the rest of the news. *Everything you need to know about Britain's favourite bad gentleman of fashion on page three. Little Shaw's historical society on page eight. The truth about price fixing and why we're paying too much for petrol on page eleven. Blind date leads to wedding bells... more on page nine.*

Ginny wasn't quite sure why an article on Timothy Harlow was more important than the cost of petrol, but she dutifully turned to page three. All she found were more photographs of Harlow and a single quote that read: *If you can't show me perfection, don't show me anything at all.*

Frowning, she turned back to the front page, in case she'd missed something. Then she read through every other article, wondering if the typesetter had mislaid the real story. But there was no other reference to Harlow. Ginny sighed. Connor had explained to her about click-bait, where headlines only existed to make people click on the article, and she had to presume that that was what this was: a large photo and one of his over-used catchphrases from his time in television.

Her shoulders sagged with disappointment. What if the whole ides of March thing was a false lead? Or what if she was looking in the wrong places for answers?

If only her friend Harold Rowe was there. He'd originally been her manager at the library, before accepting a new role as the parish council chairperson. He was also an excellent historian who knew Little Shaw's past better than anyone. However, he and his husband, Myles, had gone on what they called an ABC tour of Ireland, as in Archives in the morning, Beer in the evenings and Castles every second day.

Which meant she'd have to keep wading through the waffle without his help. She picked up the following year's edition for the ides of March, which was filled with photographs of clouds that looked like alien faces.

The pained sighs from the rest of the table suggested her friends weren't faring much better. For the next ten minutes, there was only the rustle of paper as they all continued to search.

It was interrupted when Tuppence made a squeaking noise.

'Please tell me you found something.' JM looked up. There was a smudge of printer's ink on her nose and an impatient frown around her mouth.

'You'd better believe it. This is from five years ago. Here, listen: "*Locally born style maven, Juliana Melville, might have forged a successful career as a London textile star, but twenty-five years after her infamous disqualification from Lancashire's most famous village fete, head judge Timothy Harlow still refuses to apologise for the controversial decision. Melville has long claimed that he only did it out of spite after a love affair turned sour, but when asked by this humble reporter for more details, she refused to dish any of the dirt. Though she did say – on the record, I might add – that Harlow 'needs to stop trading on his fleeting brush with fame and accept his own inferiority'.*

"'Still, despite the drama, we're pleased to have Melville back in our village. She's just announced that she's running a series of sewing workshops out of Green Hill Barn. She's also available for custom orders. To find out more about her services, and when her next class is, please visit her website. And Harlow, if you're reading this, isn't it time to let sleeping dogs lie? Little Shaw might be small, but surely it's big enough for the both of you?"'

'What kind of nonsense journalism is that?' JM tilted her head sideways, as if trying to shake it out of her ear. 'I'm not sure how many walls they broke, but a crime was most definitely committed. And what was the point of it?'

'Well, it's giving us some useful backstory,' Hen suggested.

'And it's no worse than this article.' Tuppence held up a paper that had the headline: *Aliens Land in Tom Quiggley's Cabbage Patch.*

'I found three front pages with Harlow on the cover and not one of them even bothered with an article,' Ginny admitted. 'It's been pretty grim work.'

'I think it was from when they hired a new editor who had a drinking problem,' Hen admitted.

'*Or* the editor developed a drinking problem after being forced to write this garbage.' JM stood up and stretched her arms. 'Which is what might happen to us if we read any—'

She was cut off by the sound of a text message coming through, and she picked up her phone. A wide smile broke out on her face.

'What is it?' Tuppence demanded.

'It's from Edward Tait. I knew I'd break him.'

'Oh, well done.' Hen clapped her hands together. 'It just goes to show that persistence can pay off.'

'It wasn't just JM who did it. I helped,' Tuppence pointed out. 'I softened him up with a cheese scone.'

'Please. He can't be bought with a cheese scone. However, he *can* be bought with the code for the office internet. I've been withholding my volunteer services while he's been avoiding me, and it seems as if the place is falling down around him.'

'What does he say?' Ginny asked.

JM coughed, and adopted a petulant grimace, much like the one Edward Tait had the few times Ginny had met him. '"*I don't appreciate being blackmailed by anyone, JM.*"' As she read the text, she perfectly captured his tone. '"*And after we attend the client meeting next week and submit the draft you've been working on, we will be having a serious discussion. But... Harlow did ask me about setting up a separate company. One that he didn't want his daughter to know about.*"'

'Why wouldn't he tell Megan? I thought she ran his business,' Tuppence broke in, eyes like saucers.

'And what did the new company do?' Hen asked.

'He doesn't say. But listen to this.' JM once again seemed to channel the solicitor's posture. '"*There's a silent business partner. I never met them, and don't know their name. But I got the feeling Harlow feared them. So, don't go getting*'

involved. At least not until next week. Also, can you buy more
of that nice coffee? And those little cakes. You know the ones.
Now, stop bothering me. I'm very busy.'" She put down the
phone and leaned back in the chair as they all stared at each
other.

A business partner.

A secret one that Harlow feared.

'What should we do?' Hen whispered, as Ginny's jaw
ached with indecision. Did Wallace know? Would it be relevant
if they didn't have a name? Was it the same person who had
given Harlow the cash that Mancini had seen? It seemed likely.

'We need to speak to Megan. She should be closing the
shop soon. Let's go over there now,' JM decided, which sent
them all into action.

Hen rolled up the murder board, Tuppence folded the
newspapers and Ginny stacked them on the trolley before
walking them to the door.

'I'll come as soon as I've locked up for the night. I should
only be twenty minutes,' she promised.

Once they were gone, Ginny straightened the chairs and
walked around the library, checking everything was in order,
while Connor cashed up and shut down the computers.

She did a final inspection of the toilets to make sure they
didn't accidentally lock anyone in, and was walking towards the
front door when a teenage boy suddenly appeared in the
entrance way.

He was probably the same age as Connor, with long black
hair and ripped denim jeans. A large backpack was slung over
one arm, and his pale skin glowed, suggesting he didn't spend
much time outdoors. There was something familiar about him,
but she couldn't place what it was.

'Sorry, we're just about to close,' she told him. There was no
response, but as he walked past her, she caught the flash of
earbuds and the hum of loud music. His hands moved up and

THE WIDOWS' GUIDE TO BACKSTABBING

down, as if holding an invisible pair of drumsticks, and her eyes widened.

It was the drummer from the band. Spider.

On seeing him, Connor's irises darkened, and he all but jumped over the counter so that he could bar the way.

Ginny's mouth dropped open. It was the fastest she'd ever seen her young assistant move. And the angriest. Usually, he was unruffled despite the many provocations, but now his shoulders were straight and wide, while his arms were folded tightly in front of his chest.

The drummer came to an abrupt halt as Connor made a growling noise. Their eyes locked and the boy dropped the backpack at Connor's feet and slowly backed away.

'Relax, man. I'm just bringing you your stuff.'

'What about the rent you and Gaz owe me?'

'Can't give what I don't have. But, hey... when we hit it big in London, I'll make it square with you.' Then without another word he turned and disappeared outside.

Connor scooped up the backpack and crossed the floor. His shoulders had dropped, and the flash of anger was gone.

'Sorry about that. I told him not to come in while I'm working.' He tugged at the strap of the backpack. Whoever had packed it hadn't done a good job and the zip was half open, with several pairs of jeans dangling out the side.

'Connor, you don't need to apologise for anything. And of course your friends can visit you at work... that's if Spider *is* your friend.'

This threw him and his eyebrow shot up in surprise. 'How do you know Spider? And don't tell me it's from here, because he can barely read the cereal box.'

'We all had the... er... pleasure of being at The Lost Goat the other night,' she admitted.

He let out a long groan. 'My commiserations. That means you've met my flatmates. Or should I say ex-flatmates.' He nudged the backpack on his shoulder. 'We just got evicted for making too much noise at night.'

Oh. His lack of sleep suddenly made sense. If she'd had to listen to them practice each night, she wouldn't have been able to function at all. And they'd all but stolen his money.

'Such a terrible thing to happen. And with your first flat. What are you going to do?'

'Either move back home or go and live with Nan. At least until I save up some money. I stupidly covered everyone's rent for a few weeks, which means I'm skint.' It was clear that neither option appealed to him, and she wished there was something she could do. Unfortunately, some lessons had to be learnt the hard way. And at great cost.

'Could I give you a lift home? From what Cleo has been saying, the buses are worse than ever.'

'Nah. You've got your detective club business going on. Besides, my older brother has turned into a gym head. He'll give me a lift home once he's finished his workout.'

'If you're sure,' she said uncertainly, and then frowned. 'And you can't keep calling us a detective club because we're really not.'

'If you say so.' He gave an unconvincing shrug. 'Thanks for being cool.'

'I'm hardly cool.' She sighed before checking the time. 'Let's get everything locked up so we can leave.'

He gave her a glum nod and they spent the next five minutes in silence, before she set the alarm and closed the door. They crossed the bridge together, but Connor headed away from the high street and she made the short walk down to Harlow's Haberdashery on her own. She just hoped that the news about Juliana's appointment as head judge wouldn't cause Megan to do anything drastic.

SIXTEEN

From the outside Harlow's Haberdashery looked much the same, with the jaunty bunting hanging across the door and the rolls of fabric outside. The only thing missing was the large poster in the window that had announced Timothy Harlow as the celebrity judge for the fete. Ginny didn't think it was a coincidence that the new one with Juliana's face hadn't been put up.

Megan was tidying up a display table but looked up at the sound of the door chime. Her face was wan and her cheeks hollow. It was clear her first day back hadn't been easy. But at least she was there, which meant Ginny didn't have to worry about Megan accusing Juliana of murder.

'Sorry I'm late. Is there anything I can do to help?' Ginny stepped in, her skin prickling with the memory of her last visit.

'No, everything's done. Not hard when no one came in.'

No one? Ginny wasn't sure what to say. After there had been a murder in the library, they had been overrun with people, all wanting to be near the crime scene. Connor called them dark tourists. To have no one come in all day was a statement in itself.

'Maybe they were giving you space.'

'I'd rather they gave me money.' Megan mechanically walked to the door and flipped the Closed sign around, before twisting the lock. Then she picked up a heavy-looking roll of fabric, hoisted it over one shoulder and walked towards the back room.

'Would you like a hand with that?' Ginny said, surprised to see well-developed muscles in Megan's slim arms. But even so, it must be heavy.

However, Megan laughed. 'Don't worry, you can't work in a fabric shop without getting an upper body workout. This is nothing compared to some of the rolls. My father refused to lift a finger, but—' She broke off as grief swept across her face. 'Milos would always come by when we had a delivery, or if needed help. *I miss him.*'

A lump formed in Ginny's throat. She knew all about that kind of love. It was embedded in a hundred tiny actions that were only noticeable by their absence. She didn't try to promise Megan it would be okay. Instead, she waited until the younger woman had brushed away the tears running down her cheeks and pushed back her shoulders, as if she was slipping on a coat.

'Don't give up hope.' Ginny patted her arm.

'Thank you.' Megan managed a faint smile. 'Now, let's go out the back. The others are already there. Hen was worried she couldn't be trusted around our stock.'

Ginny nodded in understanding. After seeing Hen's eyes light up at Green Hill Barn, she could well imagine. Even if it did mean they were now sitting in the same room where a man had been murdered.

Ginny followed Megan through the heavy velvet curtain. Her nose twitched from the bleach fumes that hung in the air. Someone had cleaned up, and, despite herself, she looked down to the wooden floorboards. But there was no body there now. No blood. Just freshly polished wood that gleamed from a thorough scrub. Against the far wall were yet more rolls of the blue and white 'Woodland Delight' toile that had been at the root of Ginny's involvement in the case.

Her friends were huddled around a small table and Megan dragged two more chairs over from the wall. No one spoke, and the only sound was the *tick, tick, tick* from the antique carriage clock on the mantelpiece as the minute hand made its rotation. Finally, Megan looked up, the recent tears now replaced with a smouldering rage that made her tired eyes glow. 'I can't believe they made *her* the judge. He would have hated it.' The words were ground out.

The hairs on Ginny's arms prickled. It was the second time that Megan's meekness had become overshadowed by a Mr Hyde-type rage. Next to her Tuppence stiffened, while JM's eyes narrowed with distrust. Only Hen nodded, as if in understanding.

Then Ginny thought of the affair between Harlow and Juliana. It couldn't have been long after Megan's mother had died and the move back to Little Shaw. Had Megan been aware of the affair at the time? Or did she learn about it later on? Either way it must have been very painful.

'Did Peter or Sandra consult with you about the decision to make her the new head judge?' Ginny asked, not wanting to push Megan while she was so fragile.

'What do you think?' Megan retorted, before seeming to remember Ginny was new to the area. 'No, they didn't ask me. I'm not important enough to be involved in the fete.'

'It's a controversial choice,' Hen said diplomatically as she patted Megan's hand. 'A lot of people aren't happy.'

'Not according to Peter Skye. He told me this is what my father would have wanted.' Megan let out a bitter laugh. 'Which is a joke. All my father would want is for his killer to be found. And possibly drawn and quartered. He didn't have a forgiving nature.'

'Maybe he'll become less bloodthirsty now he's dead,' Hen said, in a hopeful voice. 'Is there anything else you can tell us about Juliana Melville? Does she ever come into the shop? Or speak to you or your father?'

Megan let out another bitter bark of laughter. 'Hardly. In the five years since she moved back, she hasn't exchanged a single word with either of us. Even last month, when we practically bumped into each other at the garden centre, she ducked behind a fiddle leaf fig and pretended she hadn't seen me.'

'That's terribly rude.' Tuppence folded her arms and leaned back in her chair so that the front legs lifted off the floor. 'The original affair and disqualification happened when you were a kid.'

'Maybe it's the guilt of having slept with my father so soon after his wife died,' Megan snapped. Her icy voice confirmed what Ginny had suspected. That the affair had taken its toll on the young, vulnerable girl who had not long lost her mother.

Hen's face filled with worry and she swallowed before taking a deep breath. 'I'm afraid there's something else. We have confirmed that your father was setting up another business. Apparently, he had a silent partner. Did he ever mention it to you?'

'Another business? That's not possible.'

'We heard it from a reliable source,' JM said. 'And it explains where the money came from, and the reason he was looking for a space to lease. Are you sure you don't know anything about it?'

'No, because it's not true. Someone's making it up. People are always gossiping in this village. The things they've said about us over the years—' Megan broke off and pinched the bridge of her nose. 'My father wouldn't hide that from me. He wouldn't.'

'We believe you,' Hen assured her. 'We just needed to check. Is there anything else you can tell us about Juliana?'

'Just that she's self-centred and vile, and doesn't care who she hurts along the way,' Megan snapped, her fists curling into two tight balls. 'And it's clear she wanted to be head judge, so she killed my father and framed Milos for it.'

'But why would she frame Milos? Wouldn't it make more sense to frame you?' Ginny said, trying to tease out an answer. But none was forthcoming.

What reason *would* Juliana have to frame an innocent man? Wait. That was the wrong question. It wasn't *why* Juliana framed Milos for the murder. It's *how* she knew about it.

Ginny turned to Megan. 'If your romance with Milos was a secret, how did Juliana know to frame Milos in the first place? Would your father have told her?'

'Absolutely not. My father might have been against the match, but he would *never* have told *that* woman anything.' The words were ground out before Megan broke into an angry sob. 'H-he would have changed his mind about Milos. I know he would have. I just needed more time to convince him.'

Her pain was primal and heart-breaking. Even if they did manage to prove Milos's innocence, there was no future where Megan would have her father's blessing. And despite the complicated relationship, it was obviously important to her. Again, they fell into silence broken only by the relentless *tick, tick, tick.*

Megan abruptly got to her feet and stalked towards a pinning board on the far wall. It was full of unframed certificates, photographs, handwritten letters and newspaper articles, much like the wall at the front of the shop. And Lily Major's living room. *What is it with all these walls of fame?*

'Do you know how much I hated him?' Megan's face once again contorted into a mask of anger.

'You don't mean that,' Hen protested, as Megan reached for

a letter and tore it into tiny shreds before throwing the pieces into the air, like confetti.

'Yes, I do.' She ripped away a newspaper article, which crumbled under her touch. She sobbed hysterically and tugged off a letter from Buckingham Palace. It was followed by a photograph which she screwed into a ball and launched across the room. 'Why couldn't he have been like a normal father?'

'No, love. I know you're upset now, but you don't want to destroy his legacy.' Hen wrapped her arms around Megan's shoulders in comfort.

Megan's sinewy muscles stood out against her thin frame and her eyes still glittered from the raw emotion that had swept over her. '*I* should've been his legacy. But he barely knew I existed,' she howled, trying to scramble free and pull another letter from the wall. Tuppence reached her other side and together they shepherded her back to her chair.

Ginny, not sure what else to do, retrieved the broom and swept up the mess. *Harlow's pride reduced to a pile of scraps.*

'What should we do now? Is there enough evidence for the police?' Hen asked, once Ginny returned.

Megan's head snapped up. 'They don't care. I still can't see Milos. Wallace doesn't even pretend to be interested. Which means we need to confront her directly.' Megan tried to get to her feet but seemed to sag under the effort.

'I don't think that's a good idea. You're still exhausted, and when was the last time you ate?' Hen asked gently.

'I'm not hungry.' Megan brushed away the concern, though her arms were shaking. 'What makes you think she'll tell you anything?'

'The same thing that made Harry Redfern spill the beans about the pocket watch to JM. She's a master negotiator.'

'I have a few tricks up my sleeve.' JM got to her feet.

Hen coughed and gave Ginny a pleading look that seemed

to say *I'm not sure JM should go on her own.* She had a point and so Ginny pushed back her chair and stood.

'Why don't we go together, and perhaps Hen and Tuppence could take Megan home?'

'I could pop to the supermarket on the way and get some ingredients. We could make a few meals for the freezer while we're there,' Tuppence suggested.

Megan's mouth set into a mulish line as if she wanted to protest, before her shoulders dropped with fatigue. 'Okay. Thank you.'

'Nonsense, there's nothing to thank us for. This is going to be fun.' JM cracked her knuckles and threw her car keys into the air, before catching them in one hand and marching out the door.

Ginny retrieved her handbag and gave her other friends a quick smile before trailing after JM. She just hoped that there wasn't too much *fun*.

SEVENTEEN

Wednesday, 19th March

Juliana Melville lived in a large, detached stone cottage not far from Green Hill Farm, and judging by the landscaped garden and late model car in the driveway, she'd done remarkably well for herself. The curtains weren't drawn yet, and light travelled out from one of the windows accompanied by the rallying notes of Tchaikovsky's 1812 Overture.

JM arched an eyebrow as they walked down the path. 'Sounds like someone is celebrating. Is it about her new role as head judge... or that she's got away with murder?'

'It's not what I'd listen to while cooking dinner,' Ginny admitted, reminding herself not to jump to any conclusions. 'I wonder if she'll even let us in?'

'We have a better chance than if Hen and Tuppence were here. Especially Hen, who adores her work. We're the least influenced by craft, so we should be safe from idolatry. Now, do you want to be good cop or bad cop?'

'I was thinking we could go for a more relaxed approach,' Ginny tentatively suggested, not sure how well she'd go in role play. Then she winced. What if JM thought Ginny was trying to tell her how to behave? It's the last thing she wanted to do. In fact, she often wished she had even a tenth of her friend's forthright nature. 'Or... we could just see what happens.'

JM abruptly came to a halt and fixed her sharp eyes on Ginny. *Oh dear. She* has *taken offence.* But instead of saying anything, JM just gave her a quick hug. 'Thank you.'

Ginny blinked. 'What for?'

'For not thinking I'm a silly old woman who likes to run around causing trouble,' JM said gruffly, for once looking uncertain.

It wasn't something Ginny had seen before, but it made her love her friend even more.

'But I *do* think that's what you are,' Ginny returned her gaze before grinning. 'Minus the old and silly part. And I hope you keep causing trouble for a long time.'

JM enveloped her in another hug and then winked at Ginny and marched up the path and knocked on the door.

Footsteps sounded from the other side and then the door opened. Up close, Juliana was just as stunning as her photo, despite her makeup being damp from the heat of the kitchen and most of her lipstick being on the wineglass in her hand. She was dressed casually in a loose linen shirt opened at the neck, and jeans. Diamond earrings peeked from her lobes and a gold pendant was pressed against her collarbone.

She looked at them both before waving a dismissive hand. 'Sorry. There's an embargo. No interviews until after tomorrow's press conference.' She began to swing the door shut but JM stuck her foot in front of it and pushed it back open.

'Excellent. Then we won't be disturbed by the press.'

'Who are you and what do you want?' Juliana's posture changed and she gave them a longer, more piercing look.

'I'm Ginny and this is JM. We're friends of M—' Ginny

broke off, suddenly realising that being a friend of Megan's might not be a great introduction.

'Mancini,' JM smoothly cut in. 'We're friends of Ants. He suggested we talk to you.'

It must have been the right thing to say because the hostility lessened and Juliana took a sip of her drink before waving them inside.

Ginny gave JM a grateful smile. It was an excellent recovery.

'I gather it's about running a private workshop. I have a flat fee and I do *not* negotiate it. In fact, after tomorrow, I will be putting it up significantly.' Without waiting for an answer Juliana led them through the hallway.

Several abstract paintings hung on the wall, and the only furniture was a bright pink sculpture of a sheep. Ginny had assumed a textile artist's cottage would be full of cosy quilts and cushions, but there wasn't a throw blanket in sight.

They finally reached the kitchen, and Ginny gasped. It appeared as if the entire back of the cottage had been removed and replaced with something three times the size.

JM, whose wife had been an architect and done something similar in their own home, studied it for several moments before nodding in approval. 'This is nicely done. Especially the Calacatta marble countertops.'

'You've got a good eye.' Juliana grabbed the wine bottle and waved it in their direction. 'Would you like a drink?' Since JM was driving and Ginny would probably fall asleep if she had alcohol, they both refused. Their hostess didn't seem bothered and just filled her glass. 'So, when do you want to run this workshop? I'll check my calendar.'

'We're not here about a workshop,' JM admitted. 'We wanted to ask you a couple of questions. About Timothy Harlow.'

There was silence as Juliana stared into the wineglass,

before holding it up to her lips and swallowing it in one long gulp. Then she carefully put it down on the striated marble counter and turned to them, eyes bright from the alcohol.

The record finished bringing the overture to an end. It seemed to shake Juliana from her trance and she burst out laughing. Her whole body convulsed and tears streamed from her lovely eyes. It was... unexpected.

'What's so funny?' JM demanded.

'You two, coming here to ask about Harlow. Clearly you think I killed him.'

'We didn't say that.' Ginny gave JM an alarmed look. Maybe they should come back when Juliana was sober?

'Oh, but that's the subtext.' She reached for a tissue and tried to dab at her eye makeup, before giving it up and tossing it to the ground. 'Let me guess... that "M" you started to say earlier... it wasn't Mancini, it was Megan. I heard that she'd been befriended by a group of old women.'

'Old?' JM took a step closer. 'You might want to rethink your use of that word. Especially considering that your date of birth is freely available on the internet.'

'Not that you don't look lovely. Or that we're ageist. Well, I hope we're not. Though sometimes it's easy to make assumptions,' Ginny said hastily, not wanting to make the situation worse.

JM bit her lip, suddenly contrite. 'Sorry, Ginny's correct. I shouldn't have mentioned your age.'

'And you really do look amazing. Do you go to the gym every day?' Ginny asked, her hand drifting to the slight roll around her stomach.

Juliana stalked to the fridge and produced another bottle. 'Thanks for killing my buzz.' She sloshed more wine into the glass and sat down on one of the stools at the breakfast bar, before waving to them both. 'Well, go on, sit down. It's bad

enough having my age thrown back in my face without you both
looming over me.'

'Oh... thank you.' Ginny took her seat, her mind trying to
piece everything together. Juliana wasn't reacting like someone
who had committed murder. And yet she wasn't reacting like
someone who *hadn't*. She tried to remember what else
Tuppence's video had told them about body language. It wasn't
always about a particular tell... it could be an anomaly. Something that was out of place.

If only she could work out what that was.

JM tapped the marble with her long fingers as Juliana just
gave them both an encouraging nod. 'So, come on, out with it.
Why do you think I killed Tim?'

Tim? It was the first time Ginny had ever heard him
referred to as anything but Harlow or Timothy. Well, apart
from a few more fruity epithets that some of the library patrons
had whispered to each other.

An anomaly.

'Because he called off your affair? Because he disqualified
you from the first spring fete and accused you of cheating,
despite never revealing the reason? Because you are about to be
officially announced as the new celebrity judge?' JM offered up.
'Take your pick.'

'You think I'd ruin a perfectly good pair of sewing scissors
over something that happened thirty years ago?'

'Well, I did until a moment ago,' JM admitted.

'Let me put your minds at ease. I didn't kill him.' Her
fingers fumbled for the gold chain at her neck and tightened
around the pendent at the end.

It was a habit Ginny had noticed that Megan did a lot,
though neither woman wore crosses, so it didn't seem to be for a
religious purpose.

'Why should we believe you?' JM narrowed her gaze, but
instead of wilting under it like most people did, Juliana leaned

forward and locked eyes with Ginny's formidable friend. That was also an anomaly. Or at least a talent.

'I had my revenge on him long ago. By going to London and having the kind of career he could only dream of. And—' She broke off and bowed her head. 'He was right to have disqualified me.'

'What?' JM demanded. 'Are you saying you cheated?'

A flash of pain flickered in Juliana's eyes, but she didn't look away. 'Yes, I did. It's taken a lot of therapy to even admit it, and it's not something I'm proud of.'

'But why?' Ginny asked, thinking of all the things Hen had told them about Juliana's considerable talent.

'I was young and naive, and while I had the vision and design, I didn't have the time or talent to get that quilt finished. So, I took my half-completed quilt to a woman in Preston. She was amazing. And so fast. But it wasn't my own work, and I knew it. Even if I couldn't admit it publicly.'

'How did Harlow find out?' Ginny asked. 'Do you think the woman told him?'

'I doubt it. She didn't seem interested in craft competitions and mostly worked as a dressmaker. Very talented. Later, after I set up my business, I considered hiring her, but she'd moved on by that time.'

'So how did Harlow know?' JM folded her arms, lips tight.

Juliana shrugged. 'Maybe he could tell the difference in style between the parts I did, and what Charlotte did. He was rather fond of using a magnifying glass. Which is not something I'll be adopting.'

JM's frown deepened. 'Which brings us to your new role... It does seem rather convenient that he died, and you are now taking his place.'

'I'm sure some people will think that, but it's nonsense. I'm far more qualified than he ever was. Our local creatives deserve better. They deserve to be supported and congratulated, not terrified and scared off. Trust me, it's a lesson I've learned the hard way.'

JM's annoyance softened. 'Learning the hard way can sometimes make the best teacher. Are you serious about supporting people's creativity?'

'Absolutely. The pressure I felt to win almost ruined me, and I don't want that to happen to anyone else.'

JM nodded. 'I ran an art gallery for many years and often lamented how many wonderful pieces of art we'd never see because some art teacher had terrified a ten-year-old child from ever painting outside the lines.'

'You're so right. That's why I love teaching workshops so much. I want to undo that damage and let everyone fall back in love with craft. It doesn't matter if you're sewing, stabbing or crocheting a crooked granny square. It only matters that you're there in the process. Enjoying it. Isn't that what life is about?' Juliana's entire face glowed with excitement and she let go of the pendant.

It swung back towards her chest, rather like a pendulum, and while the two women moved on to a discussion about the state of the arts, Ginny couldn't stop staring at the familiar shape of a two-headed bird with one set of wings, and a single crown perched on top. *The Serbian eagle.* Ginny's jaw dropped as two previously unconnected puzzle pieces forced their way together. She'd seen that pendant once before, in the photograph that Megan Harlow had shown them, when she and Milos were in Blackpool together.

So why did Juliana Melville now have it? Unless it was a coincidence. Except Ginny could almost hear Wallace's sharp voice in her mind. *I don't believe in coincidences.* She was starting to understand why.

There was a pause in the conversation and Juliana's fingers tightened once again around the pendant, as if trying to hide it from sight. But it was too late.

'That belongs to Milos Petrovic.' The words were out of Ginny's mouth before she could stop them. Further proof that she was learning to be a bit more forthcoming. Even if it was at times a little rude.

'What belongs to him?' JM was the first to break away from the conversation, a deep line between her brows. 'You know Milos?'

'No,' Juliana snapped and reached for the wine glass, before thinking better of it. Then she sighed. 'Yes. Damn. How did you know it's his?'

'Megan showed us a photo of him, and he was wearing it then.'

'I hadn't noticed,' JM admitted before once again frowning. 'Why do you have it?'

'I'd have thought it was obvious. I've been seeing him.' Juliana locked eyes with them defiantly.

Ginny sucked in a breath. An affair? Then she remembered what Slim had said about Milos's girlfriend.

Classy bird.

She had assumed he meant Megan, but had he been referring to Juliana?

'How long has it been going on for?' Ginny asked. 'And does Megan know?'

'Two months... and no. Megan didn't know. Milos wanted to break it off with her, so that we could be together, but I wasn't ready for that.'

Ginny frowned. 'It seems cruel to Megan to leave her in the dark like that. Especially when you also had an affair with her father, when she was a young girl still grieving for her mother.'

'That's *why* I didn't want him to rush into it.' Juliana's neck turned a mottled colour of red, and she dropped her head. 'I'm all too aware of what Megan must think of me. Can't say I even blame her.'

JM frowned. 'It still doesn't explain why Milos didn't end it with Megan, even if you didn't want to go public with the affair. After all, both Harlow and Vanja were against Milos being with Megan, and it was causing problems with their business relationship.'

Juliana didn't answer and Ginny's stomach dropped. It was a very good question. Why hadn't Milos done the right thing and broken it off with Megan? It would have been better for his own reputation and for his uncle's business. Unless he really did have a grudge against Harlow.

Have we been wrong this whole time?

'Why did Milos call Harlow last Saturday?' Ginny shifted in her chair and stared at Juliana.

'That's a very good question.' JM's brows pushed together again. 'They were overheard arguing, but if what you're saying is true, then it couldn't have been about Megan. Was it about the courses that Vanja ran?'

'You two really are persistent.' Juliana let out a long sigh and shook her head. 'There wasn't any argument. Milos didn't even know he'd made the call. You see, we were in Manchester together and were... *messing around.* All I can assume is that Milos had his phone in his jeans, and that it was an accidental pocket dial. If Harlow was angry, it was probably because he could hear us—'

There was silence as the three women stared at each other. Ginny's mind whirled. If that was true, then there hadn't been an argument. Just Harlow yelling into the phone. More importantly, how could Milos have made the accidental call and then travelled the thirty miles from Manchester to Little Shaw to kill Harlow?

Except she already knew the answer. He couldn't have done.

Milos had an alibi.

'Why is he still in prison?' JM's eyes flared bright. She'd clearly reached the same conclusion and wasn't happy about it.

Juliana shifted on her stool and turned away from them. Her side profile was still beautiful, but the soft lines of her neck gave a truer picture of her life's journey. It made her look human. And vulnerable.

'So much for all my talk about age just being a number. It's not that I don't want to believe it, but society makes it hard. Men like Harlow can get away with scandals and bad behaviour their entire life and no one bats an eyelid.'

'Apart from whoever murdered him,' JM interjected.

'I suppose there is that. But I knew I'd be judged for sleeping with a man seventeen years younger than me.'

'Nonsense.' JM snorted. 'Look at Mitch and Heather at The Lost Goat. The only people who are bothered aren't the ones that matter. It was wrong to let him sit in jail like that. Especially if you love him.'

'Well, that's the rub. It wasn't love. Just a delicious affair.' Juliana cast her eyes down to her fingers. 'What do you want me to do now?'

'I think you know the answer to that,' JM said, in a much softer voice as she extracted her own phone and slid it across the cool marble countertop.

Without a word, Juliana picked it up and brought up a number. 'Hello, can I please speak to Detective Inspector Wallace? Yes... it *is* important.'

EIGHTEEN

Thursday, 20th March

'Goodness, William has brought a chair.' Hen peered through the crowd to where William was comfortably ensconced in his new fishing chair. Esme was next to him, perched in a matching one, a large flask in her hand. They were both looking at the small rotunda that sat in the centre of the field where the spring fete was always held.

It was empty. Waiting only for Peter Skye to arrive. Ginny had seen him by the car park wearing the same jacket as yesterday – which only highlighted his ashen complexion. It had presumably come from the revelation that his celebrity judge, Juliana Melville, was in the news – for all the wrong reasons.

The police's own press conference had been held earlier in the day, to announce that Milos Petrovic was no longer a suspect and that all charges had been dropped.

There was no sign of Milos there. Or his uncle, Vanja. But the rest of the village had turned up, including Lily Major. She was sitting over on the left of the rotunda, clearly visible despite her tiny size. Balancing her out on the right was Brenda. Even Connor was there, after Ginny had decided they could close the library for half an hour over their lunch break.

A restless hum went through the crowd as Peter Skye appeared, with Juliana Melville trailing in his wake. She was wearing a black suit, much like she was attending a funeral, and her face was set in a stoic mask as she stopped at the bottom of the rotunda stairs, leaving Peter to climb them on his own.

He stepped up to the microphone. 'Thank you all for attending—' He was cut off by a high-pitched whine of feedback. He adjusted the mic's position, tapped it twice with his finger and then began again. 'It is with a heavy heart that we, the Little Shaw spring fete and gala committee, must announce that Juliana Melville has decided to step down from her newly appointed role as head judge. We have reluctantly accepted her resignation and wish her all the best...'

The speech continued but the crowd began to murmur, and JM made a snorting sound. 'What a pile of rubbish. I bet they forced her to step down. She deserves better.'

'Yes, but it was wrong of her to not come forward sooner.' Hen's brow wrinkled.

JM continued to frown. 'I agree. And I'm sure the police have pointed that out. But why should she get punished like this? I have no patience for it.'

'It is a pity,' Tuppence agreed, toying with the straps of her favourite denim overalls. 'And it means we'll have to wait longer to find out who the new judge is going to be. I wonder if they'll have to ask one of those footballers from Walton-on-Marsh. They're celebrities.'

'Just because they can kick a ball doesn't mean they can judge sixty-five categories of arts, craft, produce and baking,' a woman from nearby chipped in, before shrivelling under JM's glare.

It was hard for any of them to feel pleased, even though

they had managed to prove Milos was innocent. Because while justice had been upheld, someone's heart had also been broken. Which probably explained why Megan Harlow hadn't attended either of the press conferences.

'Have you spoken to her? How's she taking the news?' Ginny asked, once they were out of earshot of people.

Hen shook her head. 'I had a brief message this morning, thanking us. But she wasn't up to talking. And the shop is closed. There was a sign up saying it would be shut until further notice.'

'The poor thing. To think she was the one to stand by Milos all this time. To believe in his innocence... only to discover that while he didn't kill her father, he did kill her love.' Tuppence sighed.

It was something Ginny had spent the night thinking about. Even though Megan hadn't been the one in the wrong, she was probably feeling humiliated right now. Compounded by her father's death.

Hopefully she'd be up to seeing them all soon. In the meantime, what did the discovery mean about Harlow's murder? Or their involvement in it?

She checked her watch. It was time to head back to the library. Hen had to visit a sick neighbour, Tuppence had a dentist appointment and JM needed to wait for an electrician to arrive, so they made their goodbyes. It all felt rather ordinary compared to the past few days.

The crowd was starting to thin as she crossed the field, but Peter Skye was still by the rotunda, speaking earnestly to a small crowd who'd gathered.

On the fringe was a lean man with dark hair, eyes hidden behind sunglasses, speaking into his phone. Ginny's skin prickled with recognition as her memory flew back to the day of the murder.

It was the same man who had been outside Harlow's

Haberdashery, near the police car. He'd slipped away as soon as he'd seen she'd noticed him, and, despite adding him to the murder board, Ginny had forgotten all about him.

Until now.

He finished his call and looked out across the crowd as if searching for someone. She froze as his gaze swept past her before he turned away. She let out her breath. The plus side of being a sixty-year-old librarian was that even with her updated hairstyle and wardrobe, she was still invisible to the world.

It also meant he probably wouldn't notice if she took a photograph.

She retrieved her phone and focused the camera before taking several shots. If only he would take off his sunglasses and look directly at her.

But his face was turned to one side, meaning she could only get his profile as he continued to scan the crowd. He rolled his shoulders, thin lips set into a frown. He was clearly not happy. Who was he hoping to find there?

Ginny's stomach plummeted as she put her phone back into her handbag.

Megan? Oh dear.

Her panic rose as the man turned and stalked away, in the direction of the high street.

Ginny knew she was meant to be back at the library, but this was her chance to find out who he was. If only her friends were still there. Or the police. But there had been no sign of Wallace or Anita during the press conference, which hadn't really been a surprise, since they were now back to square one with their murder investigation. Which solidified her decision. She needed to find out who he was, and whether he was connected to the murder. Connor had a key and could reopen the library.

Despite being not much taller than she was, the man moved quickly and Ginny increased her pace. She squeezed past the last of the villagers, who were still talking about the press conference, and followed him over to the line of parked cars. Had he driven? At least she could get his registration. But he hurried past the cars and continued towards the high street.

Ginny's heart slammed against her ribs from the unexpected exercise, once again reminding her how unfit she was. The man didn't seem affected by his fast pace, and his phone was still clamped to his ear as he continued past The Lost Goat. He could walk and talk while she could barely catch her breath.

Please stop in there for a drink. She willed the thought towards him, hoping for a reprieve. Plus, she'd be able to ask Mitch or Heather if they recognised him. But he kept going, almost at a light jog now.

Several pedestrians moved out of his way as he reached the cobbled lane that led to the church, and the cemetery behind it. Sweat beaded Ginny's forehead and her vision blurred as she tried to keep up with him. He stalked past the church towards the old hall that was used for a range of community events.

Pounding music blared out from inside the stone walls, accompanied by the *thud, thud, thud* of feet. The man took the low stairs in one step and disappeared.

The music was accompanied by a series of *whoop*s and *oooo*s. Ginny came to a panting halt, unsure whether to go in.

What if he was waiting for her?

Except this was her chance to find out who he was. .

Ginny stepped inside the hall to discover at least twenty women all doing an exercise class to the tribal beat of the music. The sounds vibrated through her, and the class all moved, swaying and fist-pumping the air, making it hard to focus. But finally the music ended and the instructor began to bark out enthusiastic platitudes.

Ginny scanned the hall, but there was no sight of the man, just an open door at the far end of the building. Is that where he'd gone? She suspected it led directly to the cemetery, and through to the arterial road on the other side. Did he know she had been following him? If so, he must have led her there on purpose. The question was what she should do next. Should she try to continue after him?

The decision was taken out of her hands by a young woman in bright pink leggings who peered at Ginny and pursed her lips together.

'Oh, no offence, love, but I'm not sure you're ready for my class. It's advanced and you look like you're already done in. Probably best if you come on Mondays to Cheryl's session. She does the golden oldies.' With that she thrust a pamphlet into Ginny's hand.

'Did you see a man come through here?' Ginny gasped out.

'You mean Jordan?' The woman nodded towards a muscular man in his twenties with an orange tan and gleaming teeth. He waved at them in response.

'No. Someone else. He was wearing sunglasses.'

'Sunglasses?' she repeated as if it was a foreign word. But before she could answer, a group of women appeared in the doorway, their perfume and makeup competing as they talked in rapid fire at each other. The woman in pink rushed to greet them, leaving Ginny's question unanswered.

Ginny sighed and looked around at the previous class, but they were already disappearing towards what must be a changing room. She could either go in after them to ask them if they'd seen the man, or sit down and wait until they came out. She decided to sit. At least that way she'd be able to catch her breath.

But by the time the previous class emerged from the changing rooms, the next class had started and between the blaring music and the even louder grunts coming from the group, it was hard to tell if people could even hear what she was asking them.

'A man?' Ginny yelled to the woman who worked in the hardware shop on the high street.

'You mean Jordan?' The woman pointed to Jordan, who was lunging and twisting at the front of the class again.

'No.' Ginny shook her head and turned to the next woman, who she recognised from the fish and chip shop. 'Did you see a man come through?'

'Man?' the woman from the Codfather yelled back as the class let out another *whooop*.

Ginny nodded. 'That's right, he came through here five minutes ago. He was wearing sunglasses.'

'Wait... Jordan was wearing sunglasses?' The woman turned to her friend, brows lifted high. 'Did you hear that? Jordan had on sunglasses. Do you think he's had more surgery?'

The two women stared over to the advanced class, though their gaze soon seemed lost on Jordan's rippled muscles rather than wondering if he'd had plastic surgery.

Ginny thanked them before stepping out of the hall and away from the music. So much for her first attempt at trying to follow a suspect. All she'd managed to do was get out of breath and be called old.

The worst thing was that both were true.

'Oh, you poor thing. If only we had stayed a little longer,' Hen said, as they sat in the park next to the library. An overhanging oak tree creaked and groaned in the wind.

Apart from Ginny's aching muscles, she'd recovered from her fruitless chase. Her friends had been waiting for her once she'd closed the library, but instead of going to The Lost Goat to discuss her latest clue, they'd settled on the quaint park.

'We might have been so busy talking that he could have slipped by without me even noticing him,' Ginny pointed out as JM and Tuppence, who had been lining up at the ice-cream van alongside a crowd of children, returned with four 99 cones.

'No chocolate, sorry. Last time I got one it crumbled everywhere, and Ginny is wearing white.' JM licked her ice cream. 'But considering we all missed lunch, I think we deserve a treat.'

'It's just a pity, after all that, we still don't know who he is.' Hen ignored the ice cream and nibbled at the cone.

'But we can't feel too bad, because not even the internet recognises him.' Tuppence took a large bite, leaving a dairy moustache clinging to her top lip as she studied the photograph that Ginny had sent them all.

'I suspect that's because of my bad camera work.' Ginny absently took a small bite of her own ice cream. After she'd arrived back at the library, she'd spent the afternoon trying to identify the man on the internet. But the closest she'd got was an actor from the 1950s who had died several years earlier. 'I hate that I was so close, yet so far away.'

'Nonsense,' JM told her sternly. 'You learnt several things. It's clear he knew he was being followed, which makes me wonder if he did recognise you from Saturday outside Harlow's shop.'

'If that's the case, we can also assume that he didn't want to speak with Ginny.' Hen thoughtfully nibbled more of her cone. 'Otherwise, why run away like that? And risk going through a Zumba class. They don't take kindly to being interrupted. I think it's the endorphins.'

'The real question is, should I even have bothered?' Ginny said, and they all turned to her, mouths wide. She swallowed. Clearly, they hadn't considered the fact that now Milos was released, they didn't need to be involved. 'You think we should keep trying to solve the murder? But all we have is a blurry photo of a man we can't identify.'

'It's still a clue,' JM reminded her. 'And as well as our mystery man... we also have a mystery business partner. Is it possible that it's the same person? Perhaps that was why he turned up at Harlow's shop? Because he wanted to talk business?'

'Or he'd just killed Harlow and realised he'd left a button behind,' Tuppence exclaimed, before turning to Ginny. 'I don't suppose you noticed if he had on something with Roman coin buttons? Possibly missing one?'

'Sorry, I didn't see.' Ginny didn't want to admit she hadn't been fast enough to even see the colour of his shirt. 'But JM's right. What if the man was Harlow's business partner? The one he was scared of.'

'We could ask Megan.'

'She's still not answering her phone. And remember how angry she got when we suggested that her father had been setting up a business without her,' Hen said.

JM suddenly got to her feet. Her eyes were gleaming, either from sugar or from a good idea. It was hard to tell.

'Stop keeping us in suspense.' Tuppence also got to her feet, clearly eager to be doing something.

'Edward Tait,' JM declared. 'He's the one who told us about Harlow's partner in the first place. And I swear he's represented every dodgy, disreputable person in a twenty-mile radius. If anyone knows who our mystery man is, he will.'

They followed JM across the old stone bridge and towards the high street. Tait's office was above a bakery and an off-license and was accessed by a separate door.

'Will he still be at work?' Hen stared at it.

'Yes. He was at the golf course all afternoon so he'll be in there catching up.' JM retrieved her keys so they could all climb the narrow stairs to the first floor.

Despite the inauspicious entrance, the office was bright and inviting, with minimalist white walls and stunning artwork, which Ginny suspected came from JM. The reception desk was empty, and the door to an inner office was cracked open.

'JM... where's that file?' Edward Tait's voice boomed out, not bothering with any kind of greeting. Or qualifying noun. JM didn't seem unduly bothered as she skirted behind the reception desk, retrieved a clear folder and strode into the office.

'Here it is. Don't forget you still need signatures.'

'I'm not a moron,' he boomed, not bothering to look up. 'Now, go away.'

JM didn't move, but on discovering that the three of them were still frozen in the doorway, she waved them in. Like the reception, the office was tastefully furnished with a large bookcase, two leather reading chairs at the far end, and an expensive-looking coffee machine. The only thing out of place was Edward Tait. He was somewhere in his mid-forties but had the look of a man who hadn't slept in a decade, with brown tangled hair and a pizza stain down the front of his shirt.

Ginny's initial impressions of the man hadn't been good. He'd come across as rude, aggressive and full of self-interest, but recently he and JM had formed a strange symbiotic working relationship that left Ginny unsure whether to give him the benefit of the doubt.

The jury was still out.

'You're not going away, are you?' He finally looked up. His amber eyes were rimmed with red from too much time staring at a computer screen. Then he rolled his chair back from the desk and his gaze fixed on Ginny, Hen and Tuppence. 'Why are they here?'

'Why wouldn't they be here?' JM joined him at the desk and thrust her phone up to his face. 'Tell me who this man is.'

'No idea, and remind me to get Human Resources to talk to you about personal space.'

'You don't have Human Resources,' JM informed him. 'And

you haven't been wearing your blue light glasses, so I'm holding it up nice and close for you.'

He muttered something under his breath and studied it for a second before pushing away the phone. 'Never seen him before.'

'You sure about that?' Tuppence took a step closer. 'We think he might be Harlow's mysterious business partner.'

'Good for you. But that doesn't mean he is. None of the paperwork was done and he never gave me a name. So it could have been anyone.'

'Anyone he was scared of,' Hen reminded him. 'And this man looks scary. He ran straight through a Zumba class. That takes guts.'

'Did he just.' Tait raised an eyebrow. 'Better him than me. And it doesn't change anything. I've never seen him before.'

'What else did Harlow tell you about this person?' JM began to neatly stack a pile of papers, before pushing a tower of empty cups in front of him. 'And if these aren't in the dishwasher by the end of the evening, we will have words.'

'You're not the boss of me.' Tait growled but got to his feet and bundled the cups up, as well as several plates of half-eaten sandwiches. 'Go bother Megan. He was her father, she might know.'

'She's not answering her phone right now. The whole Milos thing has thrown her,' Hen admitted, as they followed him out into a small staff kitchen. 'We thought we'd give her some space.'

'Lucky her,' he muttered, as he loaded up the dishwasher and shut the door with a clatter. 'Now, go away and leave me alone.' He stomped back towards his office.

Ginny rubbed her chin. It had been a long day and it felt they were going backwards. Without the man's name, they had nothing to go on. And the only other path of enquiry was that Harlow had been trying to lease a property. She turned to JM.

'You said that Edward represented every dodgy estate agent in the area. If we could get a list of their names, maybe one of them would recognise our unknown man. Or remember having a visit from Harlow?'

'That's confidential information,' Tait said from behind them, though he was already tapping away on his computer's keyboard. 'At least promise you'll leave me alone once you have them.'

'Like you even have to ask,' JM assured him. 'Give us the names and we will be on our way.'

NINETEEN

'I hope JM and Tuppence had more success.' Hen cut the car engine outside Megan Harlow's house the following day. It was Ginny's afternoon off work and so they'd divided up the list of estate agents to visit. The first agent Ginny and Hen had met with had refused to give them a straight answer; instead, their entire conversation had involved cliches.

'*Harlow? No, the name doesn't ring a bell. But while you're here, let's talk about retirement. Imagine waking up each morning and looking out to a green field full of sheep, and then follow it up with a barista coffee made in your very own state-of-the-art kitchenette...*'

The spiel had continued in that vein for quite some time, and while Hen seemed to be dreaming about knitting, Ginny had felt duty bound to listen. And equally duty bound to never buy a unit at Summerville Sunset Vista retirement estate for fear of being turned into a Stepford widow.

The second agent had appeared more helpful and confirmed she'd shown Harlow a lovely industrial property on the edge of Little Shaw. She eagerly agreed to drive them there, but as she took them along a winding road behind the village, through a dense forest to an abandoned factory that was barely visible underneath a wall of gorse and self-seeded trees, she admitted she might have got the name wrong. *But while we're here it would be a good opportunity to look around this fabulous, once-in-a-lifetime investment opportunity...*

After they made their escape and crossed the agents off the small list attached to the murder board, Hen had suggested they check in on Megan, who still refused to answer their calls.

They climbed out of the car and opened the gate. The garden was much as they'd left it the other day, with half the roses still waiting to be dead-headed from the previous winter. They knocked several times, but there was no answer, and they were just deciding what to do when the next-door neighbour's dog appeared again at the fence, barking fiercely.

'It's okay, Verona. We're only visiting Megan,' Hen said in a sing-song voice.

Verona instantly stopped barking and sat on her haunches as if to say: *My apologies, I misread the situation. Please go ahead.*

The neighbour's door opened, but instead of calling Verona into the house, the woman with the golden hair cautiously stepped out. 'Poor lamb still won't see anyone. In the end all I could do was leave food on the doorstep. Still, it's gone now, so hopefully she's eating. You two were around the other day, weren't you?'

'That's right.' Hen held out her hand and made the introductions.

'Nice to meet you both. I'm Sherry. Sorry I was rude. I reckon I was in shock about the murder. Later, Megan told me how much you'd helped. Poor thing. I've always thought she could use a few more friends.'

'Have you known her long?' Ginny asked, wondering what

would happen if Megan was standing on the other side of the door, listening. Then again, they were only there to help her.

'About ten years. I wouldn't say we're friends, because she doesn't share much. But she's a good neighbour and always takes Verona for a walk while I drop the kids at school.'

'What about Timothy Harlow?' Ginny asked, deciding they might as well make the most of the opportunity. 'How well did you know him?'

'Well enough not to like him.' Sherry's smile faded. 'Still, I suppose that's no longer a problem. I just hope Megan can get the shop back up and going. She was worried that if things got too bad, she'd have to sell up.'

Ginny's heart ached. No wonder Megan didn't want to speak to anyone. She extracted her phone and brought up the photo of the man. 'Do you recognise this person? We think he might have been Harlow's business associate.'

'Business associate? He didn't have a business. Well, apart from the shop, and that was really Megan's baby. All he did was prance around in those stupid suits of his. Anyway, I've never seen that guy in my life.'

'Oh.' Hen's face radiated disappointment. 'Well, thank you. I suppose we'd better go, but if you do see Megan, could you tell her to call us.'

'Of course,' Sherry promised. 'And don't worry, I'll check on her again tonight. It's nothing a good neighbour wouldn't do.'

They were silent as Hen drove back to town. JM and Tuppence were still out working through their list and Hen had to go home to a huge pile of ironing that a neighbour was paying her to do.

'I don't even like ironing, and the money's rubbish, but it's better than nothing.'

'What about Mancini's offer to do the classes?' Ginny said, guilt creeping into her voice. She'd been so distracted by Harlow's murder that she hadn't paid much attention to Hen's dire financial situation. Or her fear of teaching. 'You'd be a wonderful instructor. Not only are you talented, but you're patient and kind.'

Hen coloured and wrinkled her nose. 'I'm completely self-taught. I can't imagine telling other people what to do. Besides, he probably changed his mind after we virtually accused him of being a murderer. It's not an ideal way to start a job interview.'

'Yes, that wasn't well done of us. What if we visit him once this is all over and apologise?'

'We'll see. Besides, there's always more ironing. Brandon likes it, because it means he gets the whole sofa to himself.' Ginny smiled at the memory of Hen's dog as they drew up outside Collin's Grocery Shop. 'Are you sure you don't want me to wait for you?'

Ginny shook her head. She needed cat food and milk, and after two days of frustration, she also needed a walk.

Once Hen had driven away, Ginny made her purchases before starting the short walk home. Her sister-in-law called just as Ginny reached the top of the street. She didn't like to walk and talk but knew Nancy would only worry.

'What's that noise I can hear?'

'It's the wind,' Ginny said, adjusting her handbag over her shoulder. 'I'm on my way home from the shop.'

'What? Walking? Why would you do something so dangerous?'

'Dangerous? I thought you'd be pleased that I've finally joined the twenty-first century and can talk to you on my phone while walking,' Ginny said. Her sister-in-law had teased her for years about Ginny's refusal to answer the phone while she was out and about.

'In theory I am, but I would prefer you not to be out walking while there is once again a killer on the loose. I knew you should have come to Provence.'

'I promise I'm safe,' Ginny said, as her house came into

view. A scooter had been left abandoned on the footpath, while the young owner was examining something in the gutter. He was one of Hannah's young sons and, further down the street, Ginny could see her neighbour holding court outside her house.

She gripped her phone, determined to stay on the call long enough to get inside, and that way avoid having to talk to the small crowd of neighbours in the street. She'd heard enough conversations floating around the library to know most of the popular opinions about Milos, Juliana and Megan.

'I still don't like it. What are the police doing about it? Do they have any other suspects?'

'I don't know,' Ginny said, truthfully. And if they did, it was more than she and her friends had. She pushed open her gate and quickly walked down the path. The metallic sound of power tools rang out from Wallace's house, though there was no sign of the detective's car, which meant his mysterious father must be inside working.

She hurried through and, with a sigh, leaned against the door.

'I hope they catch the killer soon.'

So did she. Ginny closed her eyes, and dropped her groceries to the ground, suddenly feeling exhausted. 'Nancy, would you mind if I call you back? It's been a long day and I have a headache.'

It was only a small lie and Ginny immediately felt guilty at the concern in her sister-in-law's voice. But while she didn't have a headache, she did feel tired from her unexpected run.

'Of course. Go and sit down and try to relax. But promise you'll ring later, so I know you're okay.'

Once the assurances had been made, Ginny ended the call. Taking a deep breath, she picked up her bag again, walked into the kitchen and flicked on the kettle.

Edgar was curled up on the kitchen table, his head wedged between the fruit bowl and the book Ginny had been reading. It didn't look comfortable, but judging by the purring sound, he seemed happy enough.

He didn't stir as she made her tea and carried it through to the conservatory. Next door the soft whir of power tools continued. Sinking into her chair, she leaned back before feeling the sharp press of something on her leg. She shifted and stared at a small plastic bag poking out from down the side of the cushion.

Tea forgotten, she let out a soft groan and tugged it out to reveal an all-too-familiar Ziplock bag, with a collection of recipe cards. *Again?* She peered through to the kitchen table, but Edgar was still fast asleep, as if not interested in seeing how his latest thievery was being received.

Maybe Nancy had been right about not trusting cats.

Ginny closed her eyes, in the desperate hope it was a mistake. But when she opened them again, the recipe cards were still there. She reluctantly pulled the first one out.

It was for madeleines, and was written in neat capital letters, spaced out with military precision. Ginny's stomach sank as she recalled Lily Major's recipe cards, which had all been typed. She flicked through the rest of them until she got to one labelled 'Brenda's Brandy Snap Torte' written across the top.

Of course.

She recalled Brenda Larson trailing after Wallace at The Lost Goat on Monday, furiously gesturing. They'd assumed it was because Lily had accused her of stealing recipes. But had she been reporting her own theft? And how could Ginny's cat possibly have stolen recipes from both their houses?

As much as she loved him, she didn't think he was *that* brilliant. Or motivated. Even with his own food, he spent half the time disdaining it. Yet, somehow, she still had the recipe cards in her hand.

Ginny closed her eyes, trying to recall what Lily had said about Brenda.

She lives at number three, River Row.

She glanced at her watch. It was 6.30 p.m., and the daylight had bled away leaving behind a dull grey sky. The last thing she felt like doing was facing the shame of returning stolen recipes for a second time. But it had to be done.

TWENTY

River Row was on a newish estate five miles out of the village, surrounded by moors. Light escaped from behind the drawn curtains at number three, and a car was parked in the driveway, which suggested Brenda was at home. Ginny knocked and the door opened only moments later.

Brenda's bright hair was pulled back from her face, and she was wearing a large apron that said, 'Kiss the Chef'. She'd been in the process of slipping it over her head, but at the sight of Ginny, she stopped mid-motion and her lip curled. 'What do you want?'

Ginny, who'd been going over in her head how to start the conversation, took a small step back. Brenda's reception was nothing like Lily's had been. 'I'm sorry to disturb you, but I hoped we could talk. I'm Ginny Cole.'

'Oh... I know exactly who you are, Mrs Cole. You're the one that visited Lily Major and implied that *I* had stolen her recipe cards. And then... to make matters worse... you ate her cake.'

The accusations were ground out with chilling menace.

Ginny gripped her handbag, trying not to think of all the other things she could be doing. At home finishing her cup of tea. Working through a crossword and hoping Eric might be looking over her shoulder. Even cleaning the oven suddenly seemed the more appealing option.

Though it did explain why Lily had been so quick to drag Ginny into the house. The neighbourhood really did have eyes. But it was too late to back away now.

'That's not what happened. My cat found her recipes and brought them into my house. I never implied you had taken them.'

'Yet it had the same result. It made her look like she was the victim. But it's my recipes that have been stolen, not hers.' Brenda's lip twitched but she folded her arms across her generous chest. 'What do you have to say about that?'

'Actually, I'm here to say sorry.' Ginny withdrew the bag of recipe cards and held them out to the angry woman on the doorstep. 'I found these in my house. I think my cat brought them inside.'

A series of emotions flashed across Brenda's face as she took the cards and cradled them in her arms like a child. Her emerald eyes were glistening with tears, but she hastily wiped them away and then peered over Ginny's shoulder, before clutching at her arm and dragging her over the threshold.

It was the second time in as many days that Ginny had been pulled into someone's house and she soon found herself in a bright sitting room with mustard walls and a large flat-screen television above the old fire recess. On the wall that separated the room from the kitchen were twenty-nine blue and red rosettes.

It was almost identical to Lily's wall, just in the reverse order, starting and ending with a blue rosette. There was even a copy of the same newspaper article, with Harlow trying to hold the two women apart, and the headline: *Inaugural Spring Fete Marred by Butter Knives at Dawn.*

'Tell me everything,' Brenda commanded in a steely tone.

It didn't take long, and while Ginny glossed over the conversation with Lily, she did go through the list of Edgar's thieveries, to convince Brenda it had been accidental. 'I have no idea where he got them from.'

'Clearly this cat of yours was in your car when you visited Lily, and he stole them from her. Maybe he knew that a great wrong had been done in the universe and was trying to restore order.'

Ginny, who had yet to see even a glimmer of remorse from her cat, shook her head. 'He didn't get them from Lily's house.'

'We'll see what the DNA results say about that.' Brenda waved the recipe cards in the air. 'I told Wallace I'd be back with proof. And now I have it. I'm going to call him right now.'

'I'm not sure it's a good time. They're in the middle of a murder investigation.'

'Are you saying this theft isn't important?'

'Of course not. But this is a victimless crime, compared to what happened to Timothy Harlow.'

'Victimless?' Brenda jabbed her hand in the direction of the trophy wall behind her chair. 'Do you call that victimless? I've been robbed of winning fifteen times. And still that woman won't rest. Besides, it's clear that the cases are linked. If the police just go and search Lily Major's house, I'm sure they'll find proof that she killed Harlow.'

Ginny sank deeper into the armchair. She hadn't held much hope that Brenda might have insight into Harlow's murder, and she'd clearly been right. But still, while they were on the topic, she might as well try. 'Do you think anyone else had a reason to kill him?'

'Of course not. For a start he was our weather guru. Never had so much as a drop of rain on the big day when Harlow was judging. It's not something anyone would risk. Anyone except Lily Major. Now... where's my phone? I need to call the police.'

'Wait, let's not be hasty,' Ginny yelped, not sure how to calm the baker down. She sifted through her conversation with Lily. What had she said about the theft? That they'd been taken the Saturday before Harlow's murder. 'When did you notice they were missing?'

'Why?' Brenda lowered her phone, eyes narrowed in suspicion.

'Well, it's the first question the police will ask you.'

Brenda considered it, before letting out a breath. 'It was the Saturday before last. Peter Skye called an emergency meeting about several regulation changes for twenty of the categories. I went to that and then to get my nails done, and when I got home, they were gone.'

'The same day that Lily's were taken.'

'So she'd have you believe,' Brenda said, but the anger had subsided. 'Why didn't she report it immediately?'

'Why didn't you?'

'I was waiting to see what kind of game she was playing. I still am.'

'It sounds exhausting,' Ginny ventured, and a ripple of emotion crossed Brenda's face. 'I wonder how much more baking you could do if you didn't have to worry about Lily.'

'I'd certainly sleep much better.'

'I'm not a great baker, but I do like making jam. One time I was in such a bad mood while making a batch of plum and ginger chutney, that I had to throw the whole lot out.'

'I hadn't thought of that before,' Brenda admitted. 'Though it explains why recently the only things that work is when I'm baking for the grandkids. It's hard to be cross when I think of them.'

'That's lovely. I bet if you thought about them and not Lily when you are preparing your entry... you'd be able to prove to everyone how good you are.'

Brenda was silent for a long time, before suddenly disappearing into the kitchen. She returned five minutes later with a large tray, laden with a brown teapot, cups, saucers and two slices of layered sponge cake. But instead of cream or a dusting of icing sugar, it had a sheen of pale blue icing.

Ginny's stomach rumbled and Brenda's mouth curled into a half smile.

'It's a duck-egg sponge. Glorious, isn't it?'

'It really is,' Ginny agreed, before studying Brenda's face. 'You did make it when the grandkids were with you, didn't you?'

'Relax, it tastes as good as it looks.' Brenda passed over a fork and Ginny cut off a small corner. The sponge was light as gossamer and seemed to float across the top of her tongue, before a delicate collection of flavours followed.

'Oh, my. It really is wonderful. If you want my advice, you don't need to go to the police... or give people a reason to doubt how good you are. This is proof enough.'

Brenda grudgingly nodded and poured out a fragrant cup of tea. 'You're right. I'll rise above it and be the bigger person.'

Ginny took another bite of cake and only wished that everything could be so easily resolved.

Half an hour – and two macaroons – later, Ginny finally waved goodbye to Brenda and climbed into her car. She no longer felt hungry, but she did long for a hot bath.

Ginny pulled onto the A-road leading back to the village. The night had faded to an inky black and the fields had given way to the moors. There were no streetlights on this stretch, only the looming shadows of the pylons. She pressed on the brake as one of the notoriously sharp corners approached, but instead of slowly releasing, the pedal went straight to the floor, with no resistance.

The car didn't slow down.

She pressed again but still nothing. Her heart hammered in her chest as the corner rushed towards her. Sweat prickled her palms and she gripped the steering wheel.

Breathe. She had to remember to breathe. Eric had been an excellent driver and had taught her many things over the years. What to do if you got a puncture. If you skidded on ice. But what was it for brakes?

Scrubby trees and tussocks flashed past, and headlights from an oncoming car shattered her vision. *Breathe.* She lifted her foot from the accelerator and fumbled with the automatic transmission, dragging it to Low. The speed decreased as the engine started screaming and she managed to take the corner, but the car was still going.

Her fingers gripped the handbrake. What had Eric said? Don't yank it up. Be slow and steady. Right. Her panic subsided and she slowly pulled up the hand brake. At first nothing changed, but then the car finally responded, and with one hand still on the wheel, she managed to pull over to the side of the road as she brought the handbrake up fully.

Shaking, Ginny put on her hazard lights before reaching for her phone and calling her breakdown service.

And then she leaned back in the chair and tried to steady her breathing. Had someone just tried to kill her?

TWENTY-ONE

Friday, 21st March

It was after ten in the evening when Ginny was helped up into the tow truck by Patrick, a burly man with a sleeve of tattoos and a gold tooth. He'd arrived ten minutes after she'd made the call and never had Ginny been so relieved for the prompt service.

But she was less so when he climbed into the driver's seat and started the engine, before turning to her and saying, 'I don't want to alarm you, but it looks like those brakes were cut on purpose.'

Her mouth went dry as she relived the terrible rush of speed. The darkness began to shimmer around her and Ginny leaned back into the truck seat, trying to calm down. Slim, who, now that she thought about it, had real insight into the criminal mind, had told her to be careful in case the killer started to see her and her friends as a threat. Why hadn't she taken him seriously?

'What does that mean?' she finally managed to croak. 'Should we call the police?'

'Not for a breakdown. No other car was involved. No property damaged and you managed to safely pull off the road. But... once Charlie gets his nose under the hood it might be a different story. Now, let's get you home. A cup of tea is what you need.'

Ginny leaned back into the passenger seat as Patrick headed towards Little Shaw. The night swept past them, but he didn't attempt to speak. She closed her eyes.

Intentional. It seemed too dreadful to contemplate. Who would do something like that? But she could only think of one person. Whoever had killed Harlow.

Were they angry that Milos was no longer there to take the fall? Her skin prickled, and she tried to calm her thoughts as Patrick pulled up outside Middle Cottage. He jumped out of the cab and came around to help her out.

'Thank you. It was very kind of you to give me a lift home.'

'Couldn't leave you sitting on the side of the road like that – my missus would have killed me. She says you're the one that got our oldest boy reading all those dragon books.'

'I suspect you and your wife are the ones who did all the hard work. I just gave him the book,' Ginny said, and he broke into a shy smile.

'Well, it's done the trick. Don't mind admitting I like those stories myself.' He walked her down the path and waited while she got out her house keys. She twisted them in the lock as headlights broke the darkness and Wallace's EV silently pulled into the house next door.

She froze as he climbed out and stared at her silver car sitting on the back of Patrick's tow truck. *Oh dear.* His face turned into a hard mask as he stalked down his path and through into Ginny's garden.

'Patrick... a word.'

'Seems you don't need to call the police. They come to you.' Patrick raised an eyebrow then joined Wallace at the gate. 'Alright, guv?'

She didn't hear the reply, but it had elicited interest from several of the neighbouring houses as lights suddenly appeared in the windows. Maybe she would've been better waiting by the side of the road for one of her friends to pick her up. Or for an Uber to arrive.

She looked at her front door.

It had been a long day and all Ginny wanted was to sleep. But while she could ignore any of her neighbours who might appear, she doubted it would be as easy to avoid Wallace. Not if he thought the brake failure was down to her involvement in the investigation.

She was right. After a short conversation, Patrick gave her a cheery wave goodbye and disappeared down the road, taking her car with him. But Wallace didn't retreat to his own house. Instead, he raised an eyebrow and gestured towards her front door. Clearly, he wasn't in the mood for wasting words.

Her usual fear of police was numbed by too much cake and adrenaline, so she led him through to the sitting room. Edgar was curled up at one end of the sofa but rose to his feet and jumped down at their arrival.

'I'll feed you in a minute,' she promised, before joining Wallace. Then she sighed. 'I'm sorry.'

'Don't be sorry. Be safe,' he said, as she realised the stark lines around his mouth and the sombre expression in his eyes weren't directed at her. 'Patrick thinks your brakes were cut on purpose.'

'He said the same to me. But it hardly seems possible.'

'Yet here we are. He also mentioned that you don't have a car alarm.'

'That's correct.' She'd meant to get one when she first purchased the car, but Eric's diagnosis had thrown all their plans into disarray and she'd never got around to it.

'I suggest you get one. My father can install it for you.'

'Your father? But he never speaks or leaves the house. I can't imagine he'd want to install a car alarm for a stranger.'

'He's a man of few words.' Wallace shrugged. 'But he'd be happy to do it. Now, let's assume that it *is* possible someone tampered with your brakes. What were you doing out on that road at night, alone? Because if it's about Harlow's murder, then—'

'It wasn't,' Ginny quickly cut him off. 'I was... visiting Brenda Larson.'

'Brenda Larson? Why?' A hint of incredulity flickered in Wallace's eyes.

Ginny chewed her lip and glanced over to where Edgar was carefully grooming himself, indifferent to their company. She let out a breath. 'It's a long story, but somehow my cat found her missing recipe cards. I was returning them.'

'Her recipe cards?' He repeated the words slowly, as if unsure he'd heard correctly. 'The ones she keeps accusing Lily Major of stealing?'

'Yes,' Ginny said, before admitting her role in returning Lily's recipes.

Wallace ran a hand through his dark hair once she was finished. 'I have absolutely no idea what to do with that information. Except to say thank you for solving that particular thorn in my side.'

'I hardly solved it, I just returned them.' Ginny felt a pang of sympathy for him at having to play judge between two feuding bakers, whilst in the middle of a murder investigation. Not to mention the other cases he was working on. 'You don't think someone cut the brakes while I was at Brenda's house?'

'It's more likely they did it earlier. But we won't know anything until the mechanic has looked at them.' He studied her. 'I've never met anyone who could go from the ridiculous to the macabre in the same night.'

Ginny flinched at how accurately he'd summed the situation up. One minute she'd been trying to soothe a woman over a thirty-year baking battle and the next she had been trying not to crash her car. 'It wasn't intentional.'

'I didn't say it was. Now, I'll save the lecture for another day, but considering Juliana mentioned your visit when we interviewed her about Milos's whereabouts on the day of the murder, I take it you and your friends are still involved. What suspects do you have?'

Ginny swallowed. They'd long moved past the time for pretending. 'Currently we don't have anyone, but we have ruled out several people.'

His jaw clenched, as if remembering his promise not to lecture her. But finally, he managed to speak. 'I'm going to need names.'

Of course he was. Ginny closed her eyes, going through their various theories. They all seemed ridiculous now, and not what she wanted to confess to a real detective. But she doubted he would go home until he had what he wanted.

'There was Ants Mancini, Vanja Petrovic, Juliana Melville, oh, and Harry Redfern. He's a pawnbroker.'

'Thank you, I know very well who Harry Redfern is,' he said in a dry voice, before shaking his head. 'And cutting brakes is very much in his playbook. Tell me exactly what JM accused him of.'

'Nothing. I promise. She only wanted to find out if Harlow owed money. Or had recently been to any poker games.'

'Oh, is *that* all? I swear you and your friends will be the death of me. Anything else?'

She told him about the replica pocket watches, and then her interview with Slim, at the bedsit, and his assertion that it would have been easy to plant the evidence. She then reached for her phone and explained about the man she had seen on the day of the murder, and at the press conference.

'I don't recognise him but send me the photo and I'll get the team to work on it.'

Somehow, she doubted he would pass on his results. She did as instructed and he checked it again before putting the phone down on her coffee table. Moments later, his phone buzzed and he snatched it up.

'What have you got?' he barked.

Ginny had no idea who was on the end of the line, but they were obviously just as concise with their words as Wallace was, as after mere seconds he ended the call and got to his feet. His anger had been replaced with something else and he locked eyes with Ginny.

'Tell me honestly, did you ever suspect Megan Harlow?'

'Megan?' Ginny's hands began to shake, and the room seemed to wobble. 'No... of course not. W-well, we did check her alibi with the accountant. But she was there the whole time. Why? What's happened?'

Silence danced around the room before he finally answered. 'She's missing.'

'Since when?' Ginny's breath caught in her throat as a thousand questions jostled to be asked. But she swallowed them down. Wallace would hardly tell her something like that if it wasn't true. 'What do you know?'

'Not much. A neighbour was worried about her. Said Megan usually knocked every morning like clockwork to walk her dog. Even the day after her father was murdered. But when she didn't show up this morning, she thought it was down to relief that Milos had been released. But an hour ago she finally decided to use her spare key to check. The place had been turned over, and some of her clothes were missing.'

Turned over? Ginny's hand flew to her mouth as Wallace gave her a level stare.

'When was the last time you saw her?'

'Two nights ago, after work. We went to the store to ask her about Juliana Melville.'

'What was her mood?'

'She was very low. The news about Juliana taking her father's place as judge had rattled her. So, while JM and I went to talk with Juliana, Hen and Tuppence took Megan home. I'm not sure how long they stayed, but I would guess until at least eight o'clock.'

'What about yesterday or today? Did any of you see her?'

Had they? Ginny had been at work, before closing the library to attend the spring fete press conference, but what had Hen said?

I had a brief message from her this morning, thanking us. But she wasn't up to talking. And the store is closed. There was a sign saying it would be shut until further notice.

'No.' Ginny told him about the message.

Wallace swore under his breath and pocketed his notebook and phone before stalking to the door. 'I'm needed at the station. We will be sending officers to check on Juliana Melville and Milos Petrovic. And to speak with Hen and Tuppence to establish a timeline.'

Why would officers need to check on Juliana and Milos? Shouldn't they concentrate their efforts on searching for Megan and whoever had taken her? Weren't the first twenty-four hours the most crucial when it came to a missing person?

As if reading her mind, Wallace faced her from the threshold. 'A pair of tin snips, which can be used to cut car brakes, were discovered in Megan Harlow's kitchen, along with a white rag covered in oil.' His voice was flat. 'We'll be sending a forensic investigator over to inspect your car and compare it with what we've found. This could be a case of attempted murder and we might need to take another statement from you tomorrow. In the meantime, I hope I don't need to remind you to stay out of it.'

Dread coiled in Ginny's stomach as the memory of her car racing towards the sharp corner slammed into her mind. She was spinning out of control, and everything was wrong.

She opened her mouth to speak but no words came out.

Wallace gave her a final glance then left the house.

Once he was gone, Ginny sank back into the sofa and recalled the venom in Megan's voice as she had ripped apart her father's letters and photographs.

I should have been his legacy.

What did it mean? Had she been implying that she had killed her father? Framed Milos? And cut Ginny's brakes? That seemed to be what Wallace thought. *Attempted murder.*

But what if Wallace was wrong? What if Megan really was missing and no one was doing anything about it?

Ginny closed her eyes and tried to work out which scenario was better, but it just made her brow pound with fatigue. In both cases, Megan Harlow was in a lot of trouble and Ginny had a terrible feeling that she and her friends had only made it worse.

TWENTY-TWO

Saturday, 22nd March

'What have you done?' Cleo pounced the moment Ginny walked into the library. It was fuller than usual for a Saturday morning, but Ginny supposed this was, as ever, to do with the murder, and Megan's disappearance.

It had been Connor's morning to open, and today Ginny had been grateful for the extra time to help ease the dreadful despair that had stayed in the pit of her stomach all night. It was now one week since Harlow had been murdered, and far from finding the killer, and helping his daughter with her grief, Ginny had ended up in a tangle. And not up to dealing with Cleo's abrasive questions.

'Done about what?' Ginny asked, hoping to deflect anything to do with Megan's disappearance. She'd had a phone call with PC Singh an hour ago and given another statement, as well as refused the offer of support.

The only thing the young constable hadn't offered was an update on the case, or whether they were treating Megan's disappearance as a crime or an escape.

'*Done about what?*' Cleo mimicked as her voice rose an octave, before waving a hand in the direction of the issues counter. Ginny reluctantly peered over, expecting to see a furious Wallace. Or, worse... some terrible sign that whoever had cut her brakes had done something else. Something directed at her. But instead, she saw cake.

Lots of cake.

Ginny blinked and allowed herself to be led over. Up close she realised there were only two cakes – both placed on identical cut glass stands and surrounded by stacks of empty plates and a large cutting knife.

'Well, can we start?' William stepped forward from the crowd of other patrons. He was brandishing a fork, while a large handkerchief was tucked into his collar. 'He said we could start as soon as you arrived.'

'No, *he* did not say that.' Connor shooed William back. His brows were gathered into a frown, but a look of relief flashed across his face as Ginny joined him.

'Why do we have two cakes on our issues counter, Connor?'

'Because everyone in this village has lost the plot,' he retorted, before pushing back his hoodie and running a hand through his long hair. 'Lily Rogers was waiting at the door when I arrived this morning. She insisted that I give you this cake. It has a French name.'

'Gâteaux. St Honoré,' someone offered up as Ginny took in the flaky layers of pastry and cream. They were surrounded by tiny choux balls and drizzled in a golden icing. 'It's what took first place in two thousand and eight.'

'Same year my cabbage swept the board,' came another voice.

Connor ignored the hecklers. 'No sooner did she make me promise on my life that no one touched it but you, than Brenda Larson stalked up and gave me *that*.' He waved at a towering, layered cake perfectly iced in rich dark chocolate.

'Her award-winning Doberge cake from three years ago,' a third person called out.

Ginny rubbed her brow as she turned back to Connor. 'But why? What's the point of it?'

'I thought that was obvious.' Cleo elbowed her way through the crowd so that she was leaning against the counter, an irritated expression on her face. 'For some reason they want you to adjudicate their baking skills.'

'It's never happened before.' Esme appeared next to William, holding on to her own fork. 'Harlow never let anyone else taste the entries, so this is our only chance.'

'But it makes no sense,' Cleo persisted. 'Why bring them to you? You're not even a baker, and don't try to tell me about the jam, because that doesn't count. Yet I've known the pair of them for years. Years, I tell you.'

'Maybe that's why they've given them to Mrs Cole,' Connor retorted. 'Because she doesn't go around acting like she knows everything.' Then he flushed, realising what he had just said. 'Not that you don't know things, Mrs C. I just meant you don't rub it in people's faces.'

'Are you implying that I *do* rub things in people's faces? And what about Sandra? The poor thing hasn't left the house since Harlow's death – who knows how she'll take this latest betrayal?'

'I'd hardly call two cakes a betrayal,' someone muttered.

'Of course it's a betrayal. Sandra's a jolly good baker in her own right. And as co-organiser of the fete, the least Lily and Brenda could've done is take this matter to her, instead of bringing in an outsider. Trust me, I know *just* how she feels,' Cleo snapped before flouncing off.

'Poor Cleo. She stayed up all night working on her quilt. And she really would make a terrific adjudicator between Lily and Brenda,' Andrea said and hurried after her.

Ginny sighed. She'd have to go and check on Cleo as soon as she'd sorted this out. Whatever *this* was.

There was silence as everyone looked on. And suddenly Wallace's words ran through her head. *From the ridiculous to the macabre.* Well... she couldn't do anything about the macabre, but she could certainly deal with the ridiculous. Without flinching, she picked up the knife and began to slice both cakes up into small, bite-sized pieces. Brenda and Lily had technically given the cakes to her, so surely it was okay to share them around.

It worked, and after putting enough pieces aside for her friends, who were due in for their book club meeting, the crowd dispersed and Ginny could get on with her morning tasks as well as spending fifteen minutes listening to Cleo explain just why Lily and Brenda had broken some mysterious spring fete protocol.

Of course, the cake couldn't distract everyone forever, and once the library patrons had stopped talking as if they were judges on the *Great British Bake Off*, they seemed to recall the murder investigation and the news that Megan Harlow was currently missing. Innocence or guilt unknown.

Ginny did her best to stay out of everyone's way and was relieved when her lunch break finally arrived.

Her friends were already sitting in the small reading nook they used for their book club meetings when she joined them. Three plates, each with a slice of Brenda and Lily's cakes, were sitting on the table, alongside three unopened copies of *Cranford*. Ginny winced. It seemed that not even the lure of sugar or Elizabeth Gaskell could lift their mood.

'I should have taught you how to slow down an automatic transmission. This is my fault,' Hen cried, as soon as Ginny reached them.

'Nonsense, it's nothing of the kind. What she really needed

was one of those mirror gadgets to check for tampering,' JM retorted.

'Yes, that's all well and good,' Tuppence broke in, 'but what was it like? Did your life flash before your eyes?'

Ginny was torn between laughter and tears as her friends suddenly descended on her and hugged her tight, before dragging her into the fourth chair, so she could answer their questions.

No, her life didn't flash before her eyes.

Yes, Eric had taught her how to use the emergency brake, but she would most definitely like more lessons from Hen.

And she wasn't sure about using a bomb detection mirror on her car every day.

Finally, they seemed satisfied, and Hen and Tuppence talked through their own interviews with PC Singh and PC Bent that morning.

Ginny brought out her notebook while Hen pulled the murder board out of her knitting bag and Tuppence and JM finally reached for the plates of cake.

'Oh, this is jolly good,' Tuppence mumbled through a mouthful of cream while reaching for a tiny felt figure in a sensible top and skirt. It was clearly meant to represent Megan Harlow.

Again with the ridiculous and the macabre.

'Where do we go from here?' Hen asked, once she'd finished her own cake and neatly stacked the plates and forks. 'Do we try to find Megan? Or the killer?'

'Unless they're one and the same,' JM said, in an ominous voice. 'What if she duped us from the beginning?'

'But why? If she did kill her father, the last thing she'd want is for anyone to investigate. Especially when the police already had a suspect,' Ginny said. It was the same question that had been going around in her mind all evening.

'Maybe she didn't think we'd find anything?' Tuppence

pondered before blinking. 'Oh, wait... that's just rude. We found plenty of things.'

'And it doesn't answer *why* she would want to kill her father,' Ginny reminded them, knowing she only had a half-hour break. She'd also promised Wallace not to do anything else involving the case. It wasn't something she intended to break, but, at the same time, what if someone *had* targeted her last night?

And tries to target my friends?

They could at least approach it from a theoretical point of view. 'What's her motive?' Ginny asked, refusing to think of Wallace.

'What if she blamed him for not approving of her relationship with Milos?' JM leaned across the murder board and found a tiny felt Milos figure. 'Then she found out about Milos's affair with Juliana, and decided to set him up for the murder.'

Tuppence's eyes brightened. 'Oh, that's good. Then she regretted setting him up because she discovered Juliana didn't really love him. So, she dragged us in to find the truth. Well... enough of the truth to prove that Milos was innocent, and they could start again.'

Ginny looked down at the murder board and picked up the tiny scissors that Hen had made, followed by the clock, and the window frame that represented breaking into Vanja's workshop. Then she moved them, one by one, next to Megan's figure.

'Harlow and Megan have known Vanja for years, so she could easily get scissors from his workshop. And she could have bought the replica pocket watch from Harry Redfern while on the pretext of asking about her father. As for planting the watch in Milos's bedsit – she'd been there before, so it wouldn't have been difficult.'

'And she had the strength to stab him, after years of lifting heavy rolls of fabric,' Hen said, a sob catching in her throat.

Silence fell as they stared at the tiny felt figures on the board. It could possibly work. And yet... what if they were wrong? What if Megan, far from being the killer, was a victim, just like her father had been? If her outburst had been grief. An orphan trying to navigate the new world she hadn't asked to be part of.

It was a feeling they'd all been through.

Their eyes met across the felt board and a wave of agreement passed. No matter what the police were thinking, there was a chance Megan was innocent. And, if she was... she could be in a lot of trouble. Or—

'I'll try her again,' Hen cut in, clearly wanting to stop the unspoken thoughts from escalating. Her hands shook as she held up her phone. But there was no answer. Her lip began to tremble. 'Do you think we should call Wallace?'

'No. Not unless we have information for him.' Ginny stretched out her hand to Hen. She was the one who worried and fussed the most. The one who felt everyone else's pain and who always saw the good in people.

'What about Milos? Do you think he'd talk to us?' Tuppence asked.

'I doubt it. From what I've heard he doesn't want to talk to anyone,' JM said. 'Tait tried to get hold of him, to look at starting a wrongful prosecution case. That man really must stop all this ambulance-chasing. He said Vanja's like a watchdog, not letting anyone through. Plus, the police might still be there if they're worried Megan is after revenge.'

'Doesn't mean we can't try Milos and Juliana. Anything's better than sitting around here, not doing anything,' Hen said. 'I feel so useless. Like we're letting Megan down.'

'Because we are.' JM scowled, while Tuppence began to pace around the table. 'Okay, let's try and talk with Milos and Juliana. And we still have a few more dodgy estate agents on the list. The ones yesterday were useless. If they weren't trying to flog a studio apartment full of mould, they were harping on about time shares.' JM sighed and got to her feet, quickly followed by Hen and Tuppence.

After they were gone, Ginny went back to her office and sat down, hugging her arms to her chest. Like the others, she wished she could help. But they'd hit a brick wall. They'd run out of clues. Not that they'd ever had many. A mysterious business partner that Harlow was afraid of, and that he wanted to rent a barn for some reason. And... if the police were right and Megan Harlow had killed her father, none of it would even be relevant.

Yet, what if it was?

The library had emptied of patrons and Cleo and Andrea were at the issues counter, holding court, while Connor prepared for the afternoon story time, which had become one of the biggest events of their week. Making the most of the lull, Ginny fired up the computer. But, despite trying numerous different search terms, she still couldn't find anything new on Harlow, or any mention of a business.

Instead, she transferred the photograph of the man she'd chased onto her computer, hoping it would reveal some kind of clue. Why had he been at the spring fete press conference? They'd assumed it was to see Megan, but what if it was someone else? JM had said that Juliana hadn't recognised the man.

Ginny was still frowning when Connor poked his head in. He'd exchanged his black hoodie for a checked shirt, like the one on the cover of the picture book in his hand.

'I'm about to start. Looks like quite a crowd.'

'That's because word keeps spreading. And I'm sorry I didn't help you set up for the event. I've been distracted today.'

'Relax. I know how busy you are with the detective club.'

'We're not a detective club,' she reminded him, yet again.

Though this time a stab of pain clung to her chest. If they were, they probably would have done a much better job.

'Sure,' he agreed, as if humouring one of the small children waiting for the story. Then he narrowed his eyes at the computer screen. 'You might want to tell your not-a-detective-club friends to stay away from that guy.'

'What guy?' Ginny swivelled around to follow his gaze. He was pointing to Harlow's mystery business partner. 'Y-you know him?'

'No.' He shook his head. 'I saw him at the gym while I was waiting for my brother. Jake said he was bad news. And my brother isn't known for his character judgement. So, if *he* thinks someone's bad news...' He trailed off, before checking the time on his phone. 'I'd better set up.'

Connor headed to the children's section leaving Ginny to stare at the photograph. Still no name, but they were one step closer. Maybe after work she could go to the gym and ask around. But that was still two hours away. What if he had Megan? What if she was still alive?

She reached for her phone and called Hen. It didn't take her long to tell her what she'd discovered.

'Oh, Ginny, well done. And just what we need. JM almost got into a fight with two estate agents and Tuppence keeps wanting to break into the offices after hours. They will be relieved to have something to do. We'll go to the gym now and see what we can find out.'

'Yes, but please be careful. For all we know, he's killed one person, and either abducted or killed a second. And possibly cut my brakes. I couldn't bear if anything happened.'

'Which is why we'll go together,' Hen promised.

'If we do find something, we will take it to the police immediately,' JM called out from somewhere in the background. 'Trust us.'

'I do.' Ginny swallowed and hurried back out to the library

floor, trying not to worry. But it was hard when she had no idea if it was good news or bad. Or how she would get through the next two hours of work.

TWENTY-THREE

Saturday, 22nd March

Ginny had never thought of herself as impatient. Or the type of person to pace the floor. But by the time her wall clock showed seven in the evening, she could barely bring herself to sit down as she refreshed her phone yet again. Nothing.

The last message she'd had from her friends was that they'd been to the gym and managed to get an address for the unknown man and were going to visit him. She'd replied asking for more details, and to be collected on the way. There had been no reply. And, with her car at the garage, she was stuck, unsure of what to do. She didn't even know the name of the man.

Should she go and visit the gym herself?

She checked her phone again. Still nothing.

Oh, how she wanted Eric with her. To ask him what to do. To have his gentle strength and support. But she'd foolishly wasted her one question that morning, when she'd asked how he'd slept. It had slipped out before she'd opened her eyes. The despair that followed was almost as bad as seeing the empty space next to her.

The cat chose that moment to pad into the room. Ginny bent down and ran her fingers through the velvet softness of his fur. 'Oh, Edgar, this is unbearable. I'm going to see Wallace. What if something's happened to them? Or there's been an update?'

He answered with a rare show of affection, pressing himself against her leg. His black coat glistened and his amber eyes met hers. The soft movement of his breath as she tickled the spot under his neck helped dissipate the tension in her chest. She stood up, a little calmer, despite her stiff muscles from her unexpected jog the other day.

'Thank you. Probably best that I always pat you before I visit the police.'

Edgar nodded his head, though she suspected it was more so he could get past her and onto the sofa, than in agreement. But still, it was nice.

It was dark outside and the temperature had dropped enough for her to slip on a light coat. There was no sign of Wallace's EV, but the hum of the television told her that someone was home. A couple of times she'd seen his father driving out in Wallace's car so there was a chance Wallace might be at home, and it was his anti-social father who was out.

Her nerves prickled but she tried to embrace Edgar's energy of not caring what anyone thought. She walked down the path and rang the bell, once, twice, three times.

There was a shuffling noise, and footsteps, but it sounded like they were heading deeper into the house. Ginny's shoulders sagged. No doubt it was his father, escaping to the safety of the garden. She checked her phone. No messages, and it was eleven minutes past seven.

She brought Wallace's number up and pressed.

'This is Wallace. Leave a message.'

Ginny opened her mouth and shut it again.

Why *was* she calling? To report her friends were late? To

get an update on the investigation? To tell him that his father should answer the front door when someone knocked? Or none of those things?

She ended the call without leaving a message, just as headlights cut through the night and a sensible silver car slid to a halt outside her house. It was closely followed by two more small cars. Her heart slammed into her chest as the engines were silenced and the three driver's doors opened in sync.

Hen, Tuppence and JM all stepped out, and relief flooded through her. Whatever had happened to them, they were safe and unharmed. Questions danced on the tip of her tongue, but she swallowed them down as the passenger door of Hen's car opened and Connor emerged, untangling his long legs from the confines of the small seat.

'Quick, we can't talk out here on the street,' JM said in a low voice as her gaze darted in the direction of Wallace's house. 'I take it he isn't home?'

Ginny shook her head, not trusting herself to speak as she ushered them into the front room. None of them took their coats off or sat down.

'We found him. His name is Ben King, but he isn't Harlow's business partner. He's an estate agent of sorts. Though it sounds like he specialises in doing things under the table. Harlow hired him to find a building.'

'Under the table?' Ginny's throat tightened. 'Is he dangerous? I've been so worried about you all. Which is why I was looking for Wallace.'

'We should have sent you a text message.' Hen's face flushed. 'We didn't mean to worry you.'

'I'm okay. But tell me what you found out,' Ginny said, still not sure what Connor was doing with them. She'd always prided herself on being able to piece things together quickly, but her mind was finding it hard to think.

'It's a long story,' Tuppence said.

'Nonsense. It's quite simple,' JM corrected. 'The man you saw is Ben King. We paid him a visit and he admitted helping Harlow find an industrial property for a separate business that he had. Said that Harlow was getting kicked out of his current place and that he needed somewhere else in a hurry. But that he wasn't keen for people to know about it.'

'Was this before or after Harlow approached Ants Mancini?' Ginny asked.

'After. King said that Harlow only went to see Mancini because one of his barns was only accessible by a dirt track,' Hen explained. 'But King refused to tell us what the business actually was.'

'I reckon the business is illegal,' Tuppence added. 'He said that Harlow promised him some money up front for the work he was doing, and that's why he turned up at the shop last Saturday. But when King saw the police, he freaked out and left.'

'That's why he was at the press conference,' Hen added. 'He wanted to speak with Megan about the money Harlow owed him.'

'But she wasn't there. And maybe he was worried I recognised him from the day of the murder, which is why he ran away from me?' Ginny mused. The idea of an illegal business explained the bag of cash Harlow had shown to Ants, and why Ben King hadn't wanted to speak to the police, but it still didn't give them a lot to go on. 'Did he say anything at all about Harlow's business?'

'In a manner of speaking. King secretly followed Harlow once to a place outside Rochdale. Tucket Farm. But after visiting it to get his money... he thought better of it.'

'What do you mean, he thought better of it?' Ginny asked.

'Silly man was scared by a bit of tough-talking. Ben King doesn't have much backbone.' JM waved off the concern. 'The important thing is that we know where Harlow's business partner lives.'

The one that Harlow had feared.

And quite possibly, the one who killed him.

The words were left unspoken as Ginny swallowed and gave Connor a questioning glance. 'How did you end up in this?'

'I was waiting for my brother at the gym when they came in. There was an argument.'

'Misunderstanding,' Tuppence and JM corrected at the same time.

Connor's lip twitched. 'Right... a misunderstanding. Anyway, my brother was there, so I asked him who the guy was. He also gave me Ben King's address, and said I should visit him if I had a death wish. Which, for the record, I think your friends *do* have.'

'Nonsense. We needed to speak to him. Connor insisted on coming with us, which was quite lovely of him,' Hen added, and a sheepish smile pulled at Connor's mouth.

'I didn't think they should go there alone. Ben King lives in a place that makes Halton Park look like a gated community. As for the farm where Harlow's business partner lives, that doesn't look much better.' He held up his phone to show an aerial photograph. The property was covered in towering pine trees, their branches interlocking like fingers, to hide whatever was below.

JM harrumphed. 'Now he wants to come along to the farm. I think he's enjoying himself.'

'He is *not*,' Connor corrected, before turning back to Ginny. 'I told them to go home and stop looking for trouble. My brother reckons Ben King isn't easily scared off. Whoever the business partner is must be bad news.'

Oh dear. Ginny knew Connor's family had a deep distrust of the police and that he was trying to walk a different path.

The last thing she wanted to do was drag him into anything. Plus, Connor's account of Ben King's character was at odds with JM's, and while Ginny didn't doubt how formidable her friend was, it didn't make him any less dangerous.

'What if we go on our own?' she suggested.

He shook his head. 'Bad idea.'

'But we have no choice. Megan could be trapped there.' Hen clutched her fingers in lieu of her knitting needles.

'Or she might be a killer, waiting to murder you all?' Connor deadpanned, before reluctantly turning to Ginny. 'Seems risky. And they told me about your brakes being cut.'

Oh. It suddenly felt like a long time ago.

'Don't worry, we've thought of that. It's why we've all brought our cars. Safety in numbers,' Tuppence explained, glancing at the clock on the wall. 'We need to get moving.'

Indecision flickered through Ginny's mind. Did the police know about the farm? Should they be handing that information over? But what if Wallace was tied up with his other case? It would explain why he hadn't picked up her call.

And Hen was right. Megan might need their help. Now.

'I think we should go,' Ginny said, and followed them back out the front door to where the three cars awaited. She just hoped they were doing the right thing.

The moon was hidden behind a bank of clouds as the fields flashed past them on the narrow A-road. It was more isolated than Ginny had expected and made her think that whoever Harlow was working with, had picked the location on purpose. She shivered as long shadows danced against the dull grey night.

Tuppence leaned forward in the driver's seat, focusing on the road, while Ginny sat next to her, clutching her phone. Hen was ahead of them, along with Connor, and JM was the rearguard of the convoy. While it made sense to Ginny to take three cars in case something happened, she wasn't sure it was the best way to approach a potentially dangerous situation.

Hen indicated left and turned down a dark driveway, hardly visible under looming pine trees. They parked the cars and climbed out, but without any lights now, the darkness pressed in as if a blanket had been thrown over the moon.

Ginny shivered, wishing she'd brought an extra jacket.

'It's very dark,' Tuppence whispered, gripping the torch she'd retrieved from the boot of the car.

'It is. I can't even see the house,' Ginny said, as the pine needles rustled in the wind. She turned on her own torch, but all it did was create a narrow column of light that seemed to make everything else darker. They headed towards three other beams of light.

'According to the map, this is an old service road and Tucket Farm is on the other side, there.' Connor pointed towards the wall of pine trees. 'We should walk the rest of the way. But—' He gave them all a doubtful look. 'I'm not sure how far it will be.'

'Far?' JM swung her torch light down to her feet to illuminate her stout leather walking boots. Hen and Tuppence did the same, while Ginny peered at her thick gardening shoes. Then they all focused their torches on Connor's black sneakers that had gone tattered with age. 'We're the ones with the sensible footwear.'

Connor opened his mouth to retort, before seeming to think better of it.

Hen's voice came through the dark. 'It's okay, from now on we can keep a spare pair in my car for next time.'

'Next time?' He coughed before JM zipped up her jacket with a decisive *ziiiip* and marched into the looming darkness. It put an end to the debate.

Connor muttered something under his breath and moved to catch up with JM, but Hen put a hand on his arm.

'Best to let her lead. She knows what she's doing.'

'She knows about sneaking through woods in the middle of the night?' he checked, and then let out a sigh. 'Never mind.'

'Shhhh,' JM hissed and silence fell as they carefully picked their way through the dense pines. Years of fallen needles crunched under their boots, creating soft thudding sounds. It seemed to last for ages and without being able to see anything but the torch light in front of her, Ginny felt disorientated. She would have kept walking if JM hadn't put out her arm to halt her progress.

The others had turned off their torches and Ginny did the same, before looking around. Ahead was a large outbuilding and a rundown farmhouse. Her stomach dropped. Was this where the killer was? Where Megan might be?

Was she even alive?

Tuppence nodded towards the outbuilding. Soft light leaked out from under the door, accompanied by a faint hum of machinery, and off to one side was the red glow of a cigarette. Someone was there. Ginny's panic ramped up as she scanned the area. To the right was at least six cars, all neatly parked on the field. *Does that mean there are more people?*

JM nodded towards the outbuilding and touched Ginny's arm to follow. 'We need to see what's in there. But we won't all go. Just in case things take a bad turn. We will leave on the count of three and if I tap my nose we need to abort the mission.' She held up three fingers, lowering them one by one, before stepping out of the protective embrace of the pines.

Ginny took a steadying breath and followed.

The ground was uneven as they hugged the faint shadows provided by the tree line and made their way across the clearing, skirting clear of the unknown smoker on the other side. The humming noise increased, and JM pointed towards a small window. The glass was coated with years of dust, but it couldn't stop light from pouring out.

Ginny stepped to one side of it and JM ducked low to reach the other side. Then they both peered in.

One half of the space was crammed with high shelves, rolls of fabric and stacked boxes, while the remaining floor area was taken up by rows of industrial sewing machines. Each one had a bright light shining down on the material that was being worked on, as tired-looking women moved like automatons.

A cutting table was also squeezed in, littered with several pairs of sewing scissors. Behind it were rolls of lace and sheer fabrics and a shelf full of jars of buttons. Ginny's breath caught as her gaze settled on one jar in particular. Silver. They were too far away to tell if they were Roman coin replicas, but the idea wouldn't shift from her mind.

JM nudged her in the direction of another long table that had piles of brightly coloured lingerie on it. A woman was mechanically checking them over, her face drawn and pale, and finally Ginny understood what they were looking at.

A sweatshop.

She met JM's eyes and without speaking they both silently slipped back to their friends.

'What did you find out?' Hen whispered, as JM pulled them all into a huddle.

'Nothing good. It looks like a sewing factory. But I'm not sure anyone wants to be there.'

'I saw a jar of silver buttons on the shelf,' Ginny added, her heartbeat erratic. 'This must be Harlow's new business, though it seems very crammed. It would explain why he wanted to lease a building. Maybe this one wasn't big enough.'

'If it's an illegal operation, it also explains the cash,' Tuppence said in a low voice. 'So, what happened? Do you think the partner turned on Harlow?'

'It's possible. Maybe they wanted the profits for themselves?' Ginny said as a figure stepped out of the outbuilding and walked towards the glowing cigarette.

They fell silent as a floodlight switched on, revealing a heavy-set woman. She was tall with broad shoulders and dark springing curls that bounced with each footstep. Her hands were clenched into two fists and tattoos graced each knuckle. She looked terrifying.

The smoker, who they could now see was a slim woman in jeans and a T-shirt, obviously thought so as well and she cowered as the woman got closer.

'Lolly? Is everything okay?'

'Don't you Lolly me,' the woman growled. 'You think this is a Butlin's retreat? That you can come out for a quick ciggy break whenever you want? You've got one job to do. And let me tell you, miss, that things are messed up enough without you getting cold feet. Now get back in there, and I don't care if you take all the skin off your fingers, I want that blood gone. All of it. You hear me?'

Blood?

Whose blood?

Oh, please. Not Megan's.

Ginny clutched at her handbag as she pieced it together. Lolly was the mystery business partner that Harlow had feared. Ants Mancini had said the person in the car with Harlow had been well-built. This woman certainly fitted the description.

Had Lolly killed him, and then gone after his daughter?

Did that mean they were too late? Horror climbed up her throat as she turned to her friends, who seemed equally transfixed by the looming presence of the woman.

'We need to call Wallace,' she whispered.

'I just checked, there's no reception here,' Hen replied, her voice quivering. 'W-what if Megan's still alive? Should we go inside?'

'No,' Connor said in a firm voice, but before anyone could

protest, the door to the farmhouse opened and another woman stepped out. Her dark hair was pulled back, but there was no mistaking her jawline and dark eyes.

Megan.

Hen let out a little gasp and stepped forward, but JM hauled her back with a sharp shake of her head.

'What's all the racket?' Megan asked. 'And are you coming in for a cup of tea soon?'

'Wouldn't that be nice?' Lolly retorted, her words heavy with sarcasm. 'Unfortunately, some of us have to keep this business on track.'

'Don't have a go at me. I played my part, now it's your turn.' Megan folded her arms and glared at Lolly, clearly not afraid of her.

And very much alive.

Ginny's stomach plummeted as the sickening realisation hit her.

The police had been right. Megan wasn't a victim at all.

'We need to go,' she whispered to her friends – before a strong hand pressed down on her shoulder.

'Not so fast. You lot are going to need to come with me. The boss won't be happy about this. Now... move.'

TWENTY-FOUR

Saturday, 22nd March

'You're making a terrible mistake,' JM warned as they were herded to the outbuilding and into the floodlights.

When she saw them, Megan's brown eyes widened, and she sucked in her breath. 'W-what are you doing here?' she asked, though there was no menace to it, just confusion. Some of Ginny's panic subsided.

'We could ask you the same question,' Tuppence retorted, before waving her hand at Lolly and then at the outbuilding. 'Running a sweatshop and killing your father... and for what? Money?'

'Killing my father?' Megan's body jerked in surprise.

'Running a sweatshop?' Lolly sounded just as shocked. 'I'll have you know that I pay well above minimum wage to all my girls. As for accusing Meg of killing her father, as irritating as the man could be, it ain't true.'

'It's okay, Auntie Lo.' Megan patted the angry woman on the arm and for the first time Ginny could see the resemblance between the pair. While Megan had her father's jawline and eyes, her complexion and mouth were almost identical to her aunt.

Ginny recalled the single photograph that hung on the wall of Harlow's cottage. It was of him; his wife – Megan's mother – Jessica; and the aunt who had wanted to take Megan in after Jessica's death.

'You're Megan's maternal aunt,' Ginny said, not sure whether to laugh or cry at what appeared to be a huge misunderstanding.

'She is,' Megan admitted, before giving them all an apologetic grimace. 'I'm sorry I didn't tell you the truth about the business my father and aunt had set up.'

'But *why* didn't you?' Hen blinked as if she'd just walked out of a storm and was trying to get her bearings. 'I don't understand why you kept it all hidden.'

'That's because you don't know what happens when police discover that a murder victim's sister-in-law has an extensive criminal record,' Lolly said in a blunt voice.

'And what about the blood you mentioned?' JM folded her arms together.

'She cut her finger and didn't stop to treat it. Ruined three bodystockings because of it,' Lolly said, before gesturing towards the rundown farmhouse. 'I think we're all overdue a cup of tea. Jamelia made coconut cookies this afternoon. Girl can't sew to save herself, but she's a treasure in the kitchen. If we're in luck, there might be some left.'

JM scratched the side of her face, which either meant they should abort the mission or that she was as confused as the rest of them.

They exchanged glances then followed Lolly and Megan into the house.

.   .   .

In a surprisingly short amount of time, they were settled on a collection of old sofas with cups of tea and a large plate of cookies on the battered coffee table. A young girl with a cheerful Jamaican accent, who wasn't much older than Connor, hovered in the doorframe, before slipping out of the room.

After a long silence Megan put down her teacup, the porcelain rattling against the saucer. 'I suppose we'd better start at the beginning. Two years ago, Auntie Lo called, asking for us to visit her. We hadn't seen her in a long time, so we said yes.'

'That's because I'd been locked up for fraud,' Lolly added, her chin high, as if waiting for someone to challenge her. But it didn't come, and her shoulders softened. 'It's hard to get a job with a criminal record. And without a job it's hard to eat. So, I called Harlow to see if he'd help me set up a sewing business. I've always been good on a machine.'

'Not good... brilliant,' Megan interjected. 'My parents met at fashion school in London, but Lo was better than either of them. She and my mother were the ones who sewed my father's first collection.'

Lolly's mouth twitched. 'Not sure I'd go that far. And I certainly wasn't better at making good life choices. Mainly with men, which led me from one idiot to the next. But we're not here for that. Harlow and Megan came to visit me at my mother's house in Preston. I refused to come to them – didn't want to tarnish their reputation by having a criminal in the family.'

'My father tarnished our reputation all on his own. I don't care what people think of you.' Megan's eyes flashed with more spirit than Ginny had ever seen before. And why did Preston sound familiar?

Her eyes widened. It was where Juliana had gone to get her quilt finished that first year of the spring fete. The woman's name had been Charlotte.

She turned to Lolly. 'You're the one Juliana Melville paid.

And that's how Harlow knew she'd cheated and why he disqualified her?'

Lolly lifted a thickly drawn eyebrow. 'Impressive. Of course he didn't want to tell anyone how he knew me. Even then he was a snob. But, lucky for me, by the time I got in touch two years ago he was a broke snob. Terrible gambler. So, after I showed him my business plan, he agreed to help me set it all up as long as I had the capital to pay for the machines and rent a space. I did, and things took off quickly.'

'Because it's brilliant,' Megan added. 'It's called Break Free Lingerie, and we make it for all sizes and body types.'

'And ages.' Tuppence jumped to her feet and darted over to a pile of catalogues that were stacked on a sideboard. 'I've seen them on YouTube. Loads of people record themselves opening their parcels. You can see how excited they are to get something pretty that will fit them.'

'That's the whole idea.' Megan smiled round at the friends. 'So many companies only provide for a small section of the population. And Auntie Lo only hires women who need a fresh start. But we've been growing so quickly, and the lease runs out on this place next month, which is why my father was trying to find a new premises. These jobs are changing lives.'

'But why at night-time?' Hen asked. 'Wouldn't it be better to sew during the day, with the natural light?'

'Of course,' Lolly agreed. 'It would also be better if my girls could afford childcare, back massages and trips to the dentist. In the meantime, we make do with what we can. Some work days, some nights. That way no one is penalised for having a life and other responsibilities.'

'That's the most inspiring thing I've ever heard. What a wonderful woman you are.' Hen dabbed her eyes, and the formidable Lolly suddenly seemed lost for words.

'Yes, she is,' Megan agreed proudly, wrapping her arms around Lolly's strong shoulders.

'Does that mean Timothy Harlow had turned over a new leaf?' Tuppence sat down.

Lolly pressed her lips together. 'I wouldn't go that far, but we had a mutually beneficial partnership and we were going to start the paperwork, until he was murdered.'

'You really didn't have anything to do with it, then.' JM folded her arms and stared directly at Lolly.

'Nope.' Lolly mirrored JM's body language. 'Nor did my Meg.'

Which still leaves us with the question of who did kill him.

Ginny pressed her lips together, almost wishing Hen's little felt murder board was in front of them so they could rearrange the pieces and see what they had left. Then she realised she didn't need it. Nothing had changed. It was still just two things.

A button and the ides of March.

'Where does Milos fit in?' Hen asked, before reaching out and touching Megan's hand. 'And why did you disappear after he was released?'

'It's okay, love. I can answer that for you.' Lolly took Megan's other hand. 'I'll tell you where that two-timing no-good cheat fits in. He broke my girl's heart. Seems she inherited our family habit of picking bad men.'

'I feel so stupid.' Megan sobbed, pain fogging her eyes. 'I had no idea about the affair until Juliana came forward to the police. It was humiliating, and I couldn't bear to face anyone. But I'm sorry, I shouldn't have disappeared like that.'

'You're not the one who should be apologising,' Tuppence growled.

'That was badly done of him,' Hen added.

'What a player.' JM let out a disgusted snort and Lolly nodded in agreement.

'No arguments from me.'

'So, if neither of you killed Harlow, why not tell the police

where the cash came from and his involvement in the business?'
Hen's brows were drawn together.

Connor, who had been sitting on a corner of the sofa, spoke
for the first time. 'Because police only see the record, not the
person.' His voice was low, and Ginny knew he was speaking
from experience. He'd grown up on a rough estate and while his
uncle had gone down a wrong path and was on the run from the
law, Connor had worked hard to stay out of trouble.

'The boy's right.' Lolly nodded. 'And I ain't in no hurry to
look for trouble.'

As much as Ginny wanted to assure Connor, Lolly, and all
the women she'd seen in the outbuilding that it wasn't the case,
she really had no idea. Despite her fear of being arrested, until
recently she'd never been on the wrong side of the law.

Yet, they couldn't hide forever and still run a business.

'What are you going to do?' Ginny finally asked.

Lolly's eyes filled with worry as she turned to her niece.
'There's another reason she's been laying low. Show them the
note.'

Megan finally looked up, her face pale as she fumbled in her
pocket for a piece of paper. She smoothed it out and handed it
to Hen.

Hen scanned it and passed it on to JM and then Tuppence,
before it finally reached Ginny. She read it and too late thought
of all the fingerprints that now covered the only evidence that
might be able to lead them to the real killer.

Leave town, if you don't want to be next.

For a long time, they were silent. In the end it was Connor
who spoke the words they'd all been thinking.

'You need to call Wallace, and hope like hell that he's in a
good mood.'

TWENTY-FIVE

Sunday, 23rd March

Wallace was, in fact, *not* in a good mood, as Ginny discovered the following morning when she and her friends stepped into the small office at the back of the police station.

His text message had arrived an hour before, and while it had been shrouded as a request to come in and see him, Ginny had fully recognised it for what it was: a summons.

'Thank you, PC Bent. That will be all.'

'Yes, sir.' The young constable who had brought them through from the reception nodded and retreated from sight, leaving them to face Wallace's wrath on their own.

Ginny couldn't blame Wallace, and was just relieved that Connor hadn't been included. She would have hated to have landed the teenager in any trouble. Especially when she wasn't sure just how much trouble they were in. All she knew was that the police hadn't found anything when they'd searched the farmhouse and workroom, and Megan and Lo had given their statements before being sent home.

But as to who the killer might be, or where the police were

in the investigation, Ginny didn't have a clue, and there was nothing in Wallace's expression to suggest he would be giving them an update.

Once again, she wished Eric was still alive.

Surely if he'd been with her every evening, she never would have been drawn into a world that was so different from the one she'd always known. She interlaced her fingers together, trying to imagine his hand in hers.

'You wanted to see us?' JM ventured. But Wallace just pointed at the four plastic chairs that had been placed in front of his desk. It had the ability to silence even JM, which was unnerving in itself. Why did Ginny feel she was back in school?

They all took a seat, carefully walking around the tall stacks of paperwork and folders that covered half of the floor. There were more stacks on his desk and a large mobile whiteboard was pressed against the wall. Nothing was written on it and Ginny had the feeling he'd either flipped it over, or rubbed it clean for their benefit.

'Up until this point, I feel I have been *very* lenient,' he said, without preamble. 'But that ends now. Are we clear?'

JM opened her mouth and then closed it again. Ginny swallowed and clasped her fingers even more tightly together as silence filled the office.

It seemed to be the response Wallace had wanted and he leaned back in his chair. 'Good. Because if I catch any of you near a piece of evidence again, I will do my best to throw you all into jail. I don't care who you are trying to help... or what you think the police are doing. All I care about is not having my investigations compromised, and that no one else is hurt on my watch.'

This time Tuppence started to speak, before Wallace glared at her. Then he held up a clear folder that was filled with bank statements.

'It is not my habit to explain what we do, but so that there is *no* misunderstanding in the future, let me show you what a day in my life looks like. These are Timothy Harlow's financial records, which a forensic accountant has gone through. They are what led us to his involvement with Break Free Lingerie. However, to build a case, we need to do things like get search warrants and follow correct procedure.'

Hen leaned forward, her lips parted, but then thought better of it as Wallace dropped the folder onto the desk and selected another one.

'This is PC Singh's report on the CCTV footage that she went through at Mancini's farm to see who Harlow's companion was the day he visited.' He tossed it onto the pile and selected yet another. 'Here are the social media accounts for Harlow, Megan, Milos and several other suspects. And here we have the door-to-door *interviews* my team conducted on the day of the *murder*. My *very* small team who worked overtime *despite* my lack of budget. Would you like me to continue?'

Ginny quickly shook her head and was soon followed by her three friends. The information he'd told them was nothing they didn't know, which confirmed he'd only done it to prove his point. It also highlighted just how different the police's process was, compared to their own haphazard approach.

The room sank back into silence as Wallace continued to shift his gaze between them. A dull throb started in Ginny's temples. It was the shame of having assumed he wasn't doing his job. She peered around at the sea of files. How many cases were there? How many was he actively trying to juggle?

Staring back at his grey complexion and tight jaw, she realised that under his layer of anger, he really didn't want anyone else getting hurt. Or murdered.

She shuddered as she thought of her own cut brakes and the threatening note that Megan had received. She owed him an apology. They all did.

'I'm sorry.' Ginny swallowed and forced herself to look up

at him. Her shame increased as she met his dark eyes. She'd been right. Despite the façade, Wallace was more concerned than angry. The throb in her brows increased.

'I told you before, don't be sorry, be safe. And there is *nothing* safe about being involved in a murder investigation. Now, if you will excuse me, I need to get back to work.'

'O-of course.' Hen got to her feet, face flushed. 'And like Ginny said, we're ever so sorry.'

'It won't happen again,' Tuppence promised, while JM fumbled around her large tote bag and passed over the felt murder board that they'd spent so much time using.

'We'd better give you this.'

Wallace lifted an eyebrow at what – Ginny could now appreciate – probably looked like a craft project rather than a murder investigation. Then he gave them one final levelling stare before returning to his computer screen.

They trailed out of the office in silence and back through to the front of the station, where Megan and Lolly were waiting for them.

'How did it go?' Megan asked as they trooped out the doors before Wallace could change his mind. 'Was he angry?'

'Like a volcano about to erupt.' Hen shuddered as she turned away from the group of tourists who were looking at them with interest, phones held high. 'But what about you? Is everything okay? Are you or Lolly in any trouble? Or your girls?'

'Don't you worry about us. The police have been' – Lolly's face wrinkled into a grimace, as if it pained her to admit it – 'excellent. It made me realise we should have gone to them sooner.'

'And the note? Do they have any leads about who sent it?' Ginny asked, not because she wanted to ignore Wallace's warning, but because she was worried that the killer was still out there, and that Megan might not be safe.

'No. But they've tested it for fingerprints. In the meantime, they've suggested we close the workroom and stay in the cottage. They're going to have patrol cars going past at regular intervals until they find out who's behind it.' Megan leaned further into the protection of Lolly's broad shoulder. 'Aunty Lo is right, though. We should have gone to them sooner. They've been nothing but supportive. I-I'm sorry I dragged you all into this. It's like my mind went into panic mode.'

'And no wonder. Your amygdala takes over when it thinks you're in danger. That's what makes you go into fight, flight or freeze mode,' JM explained, and they all turned to her. She gave them a sheepish smile. 'The reason I only did half a law degree was because I became interested in psychology. I still am.'

'Well, I'm pleased someone understands it,' Megan said. 'It's still a lot to process, and we haven't had the funeral yet. I'm not sure how I'm going to feel then.'

'One step at a time.' Lolly squeezed her niece's hand. 'It's hard to plan anything until the police catch whoever is behind this.'

Ginny swallowed and they all went silent. It was clear they were all thinking the same thing. That the killer was still out there... and that they might have inadvertently made it harder for the police to catch them. And there was nothing that they could do but stand on the sidelines and hope that no one else died.

TWENTY-SIX

Wednesday, 26th March

Ginny took her cup of tea out to the conservatory and settled down in her favourite chair. Edgar was curled up on the footstool, his black fur gleaming in the late afternoon light. The library had been busy, and yet the day had passed with unbearable slowness, leaving Ginny heavy-limbed, as if she'd been walking through mud. The lack of sleep probably didn't help.

She took a sip of tea and sighed. In the three days since Wallace had read them the riot act, Ginny had been forced to watch his car come and go, helpless to do anything but jump at shadows and hope that Megan and Lolly were safe.

Not to mention herself.

She put down the teacup, trying not to think of her car brakes that had been cut.

'That's what comes from sticking my nose in where it doesn't belong,' she told the sleeping Edgar. Her voice was light, but she was finding it harder to stop her mind from spiralling into worry every time she thought about it.

A buzzing noise came from next door's back garden, as Wallace's father continued to work through a never-ending list of DIY projects that usually involved power tools. Clearly, he wasn't tempted to help his son pursue a killer. *Maybe I should have taken a leaf out of his book.* In the meantime, all she could do was try to distract herself.

From the kitchen came the rich scent of pears and cinnamon as her next batch of jam simmered away. Soon it would join the dozens of jars still waiting to be delivered for the upcoming fete. There hadn't been any announcements about the new celebrity judge, but Peter Skye had confirmed that nothing would stop the thirtieth Little Shaw spring fete and gala from going ahead. Which was good, because otherwise Ginny would be stuck with a *lot* of jam.

Sighing, she headed back into the kitchen, inhaling the rich, earthy sweetness. The tension in her chest eased, and she spent the next hour putting it in jars, writing labels and washing up. Her face was warm by the time she finished, and she was contemplating some dinner when the doorbell rang.

She walked down the hallway and opened it. A man with salt and pepper hair and a well-groomed beard and moustache was standing there. He had on old jeans rolled at the ankles, brown steel-capped boots, and a checked shirt with a faint smattering of wood shavings clinging to it.

Wallace's father.

Ginny blinked and turned towards the back of the house. Hadn't he just been in the garden? However, the familiar hum of power tools and the radio was no longer there. And, of course, the most obvious clue was his presence on her doorstep. But why was he here? He'd been next door for almost two weeks, yet she'd only seen him once at the pub, where they'd been distracted by Connor's ex-flatmates and their very loud music.

Her confusion must have shown on her face.

'I'm Ted. From next door.'

'Yes, so I gather.' Ginny nodded before remembering Harlow's suggestion that she get a car alarm installed. Was that what it was about? She had only received her car back on Monday and hadn't given it much thought. 'I take it Wallace... I mean James, told you about my car. But I'm not sure I need an alarm.'

'You do,' he countered bluntly but, unlike his son, it wasn't accompanied by a frown. 'That's not why I'm here though. It's your cat.'

Ginny groaned, feeling foolish.

He wasn't there to offer his help at all. Just to hammer the nail into what had been a long and trying few days.

'What's he stolen now?' she asked as Edgar, with impeccable timing, padded down the hallway and settled at her feet. He looked up, amber eyes unrepentant.

Ted scrubbed the back of his head with his hand, as if it would help him explain something more easily. Then he seemed to give up. 'I'd better show you. There's a gate at the bottom of your garden fence. I'll meet you there.'

'Why?' she asked cautiously, trying to imagine what Edgar could have stolen that required a field trip. But Ted was already disappearing back into the house next door.

Unsure what else to do, Ginny shut the front door and retrieved the set of keys for the garden gates before venturing outside.

Between the back fence and the fields was an overgrown hedgerow of honeysuckles, hawthorns and brambles, but she'd never attempted to open the gate, happy to merely view the wild strip from her bedroom window.

A squeak of hinges she heard told her that Ted had already gone through from his side and was waiting for her. Edgar, not sure what the holdup was, gracefully jumped to the top of the fence and disappeared. If it was meant to be a character endorsement, she wasn't convinced. After all, Edgar didn't seem to like anyone. Ted Wallace could be dangerous. Out of control. Or even a killer. Of course, he'd have to be a very average killer if he tried to commit a crime behind his son's own back garden.

The padlock was stiff with age but eventually gave way and the gate swung open. The brambles were wild, and she made a note to come back later in the season to forage the fruit.

Ted was a bit further along, studying the ivy that had laid claim to a half-dead tree below.

'What's this about?' she said, feeling irritated. Ted Wallace was just as rude as his son, yet now expected her to be interested in whatever he wanted to show her. 'I don't understand why I'm here.'

He pointed to below the tangled canopy. Crisp packets, beer bottles and old cans, all weathered with age, were caught in the undergrowth. To one side was a circle of charcoal and scorched earth. Edgar was padding around it, almost concealed as his black fur blended into the ash, before nudging his nose at a half-burnt sports bag.

Her annoyance was immediately forgotten, and she leaned forward. She'd studied archaeology at university and had always been fascinated by digs. A faint breeze rushed through the undergrowth, lifting layers of ash and sending parchments of paper floating up. Through the remains Ginny could pick out the cover of a book. *Oh.* Her hand flew to her mouth. Someone had burned books.

Any kind of book burning was distressing: to destroy knowledge and prevent others from accessing it went against everything she believed in – whether it was a political treatise or a picture book about teddy bears. It was a cruel and violent act.

'When did this happen?' she whispered.

'Couldn't say. I've seen your cat out here a few times. But

half an hour ago, while I was stripping back the patio furniture, he brought me this.'

From his pocket Ted produced a small Ziplock bag full of handwritten recipe cards and passed them over. The first one was for a date and carrot triple layer cake, with a cream cheese icing. While it sounded like something either Lily or Brenda would make, Lily's recipes had been typed and Brenda's were printed, unlike the scrawling cursive on this card.

At least it explained how Edgar had found the recipe cards in the first place, though not how they'd ended up half burned under the hedgerow. Her gaze danced between the charcoaled remains, then back to the cards in her hand. Clearly Lily and Brenda hadn't been the only ones who had been victims of a theft.

Her brows furrowed.

'Why aren't you showing these to the police?' she asked. Ted had been at The Lost Goat the night Brenda had demanded Wallace do something about the thefts. And while his hearing aids might've been turned off, she didn't doubt he knew at least some of what had happened.

'Not sure they've got much free time. Figured you might know what to do with them.'

Ginny winced. She could only imagine what Wallace had told his father about her. *That silly woman who thinks she can solve crimes.* But he was right. Wallace and the entire force were still in the middle of a murder investigation. They had better things to do than sort out a baking war.

Glancing around, she caught sight of a broken branch and used it to hook through the handle of the sports bag. Edgar immediately batted the stick away.

'I know it's your toy, but I need to see what else is in there. And stop rolling in that or I'll have to give you a bath.'

The word 'bath' stopped him in his tracks and he backed

off. Ginny gave the stick another tug and dragged the bag out from the undergrowth.

'Let me do that. I'm already in my work gear and you're still dressed in your nice library clothes.' Ted crouched down and picked up the sports bag. Ginny was so shocked at having her wide-legged brown linen trousers and plain white T-shirt called 'nice' that before she could protest, he'd already upended it and was using the stick to sift through the contents.

Several old ring binders tumbled out, along with years of carefully collected recipes, burnt and blistered from the fire. Ted used the stick to flip one of them open, but the pages crumbled with the contact from the air.

She closed her eyes to think it all through. Whoever had stolen the recipes hadn't just been targeting Brenda and Lily. Opening the Ziplock bag, she looked at the next recipe, hoping to find who the owner might be. Pistachio layer cake with salted persipan.

'My guess would be these belong to whoever got third prize in the fete,' Ted suddenly said, as if Ginny had spoken her questions out loud. She hadn't, had she?

'Why do you say that?'

'Persipan isn't something all bakers would attempt,' he explained. *It wasn't?* She stared at him, which he answered with an apologetic shrug. 'After James's mother and I broke up, I moved to New Zealand and ran restaurants and bars for many years. I met my fair share of pastry chefs.'

'I see.' Ginny nodded, not sure what to make of being privy to his personal history. *Probably best to ignore it and focus on the problem.* He'd made a fair point. Whoever had stolen the recipes was clearly targeting the winners, and so it would make sense they'd included the person placed third.

She retrieved her phone from the pocket of her linen trousers and did an internet search, but like so many other things she'd been researching lately, nothing came up. Either the local papers only reported first and second place, or she still needed to improve her online skills. Ginny made a mental note to enrol in an evening class... and filed it alongside the mental note to start exercising more. *Though not at the same time.* Then, realising that Ted was watching her, she wrinkled her nose.

'Sorry, I was trying to find out who usually won third place. There's nothing online, though I'm sure one of my friends will know. Or someone at the library.'

At that moment Edgar reappeared, carrying with him the remains of a driver's licence. He ignored Ginny and dropped it at Ted's feet, clearly still annoyed at the threat of a bath. Slighted by her own cat. It really was summing up her day.

Ted wiped it against his work jeans and then used the palm of his hands to clear the last of the ash and dirt. The plastic had bubbled up so that the photo was destroyed, apart from a glimpse of long hair. A woman?

The name was also unreadable, but there was an address. He held it out for her to see.

Number 8, Timberly Place.

'That's on the other side of the village. Eric and I looked at a cottage there—' Ginny broke off, not sure why she'd mentioned Eric's name. Apart from with her friends or Nancy, it was still something she preferred to keep to herself. As if saying it too many times might untether him from her side. She swallowed. 'I know where it is. I suppose I'd better return them.'

'I can do it.' Ted held out a hand, but Ginny didn't release the recipes. She had the feeling this was the most he'd spoken to anyone since he had arrived in Little Shaw. How would he handle an agitated amateur baker?

'It makes sense that I follow it up. Then I'll visit Lily and Brenda and let them know what you found. It might finally put this business to rest and stop them from bothering your son.'

Ted rubbed his chin then shrugged. 'Fair enough.' And

without another word he disappeared back through the fence and into Wallace's garden. *Oh yes, the apple most definitely didn't fall far from that tree.* And with that she walked back into her own house.

Ginny still didn't have a name, and she toyed with the idea of calling Hen, but thought better of it. It was quicker to drive straight there and give the recipes back. After all, the sooner she went, the sooner it was done.

TWENTY-SEVEN

Number 8 Timberly Place was a sandstone detached house with an arched entry over the front door, and a nameplate introducing it as Myrtle Cottage. A charming name for a charming place.

The garden at the front had made way for a black Audi, which seemed a shame, but there were several large tubs of tulips and early irises dotted about.

Ginny parked on the street and made her way to the front door. She just hoped whoever owned the recipes wouldn't be quite as obsessive as Lily and Brenda.

The brass door knocker made a thudding sound, and from somewhere in the bowels of the house came the soft pad of footsteps, before the door opened and Peter Skye appeared on the threshold.

Still looking like a gentleman farmer, he was wearing a neat blue button-up shirt, moleskin trousers and heavy brown brogues. His pupils, however, were dilated and fogged, as if he hadn't slept in a long time. Ginny, who had been in the process of retrieving the recipe cards from her handbag, stared at him. He seemed equally surprised as he rubbed his sleep-deprived eyes.

Poor man. This was probably the last thing he needed, and suddenly Ginny wished she'd left the task to Ted Wallace.

Still, she was there now. The recipes must belong to his wife Sandra. What had Cleo said? *She's a jolly good baker in her own right.*

'Peter, I'm so sorry to turn up on your doorstep. I found these, along with a partially destroyed driver's licence. The only thing I could see on it was the address.' She held out the recipes and what was left of the licence.

It seemed to shake him out of his confusion and he let out a rueful groan. 'You must think I've lost my wits. We just never thought to get them back again. Sandra will be so relieved. But how on earth did you find them? This is, what...? The third lot you've returned? One would almost think you were playing detective.' There was a note of gentle censor in his voice and Ginny could feel the heat travelling up her neck.

'I'm afraid it does seem a bit like that. My cat's the real detective though, not me. Someone dumped them in the hedgerow behind my house and set them on fire. But not everything burnt, and he kept bringing bits and pieces inside.'

'How extraordinary.' He blinked, then peered out of the door past her shoulder, much like Brenda and Lily had both done. 'Where are my manners? You must come inside. Sandra will want to thank you.'

'Of course,' she reluctantly agreed. All Ginny really wanted to do was give Lily and Brenda an update and go home. But since most of the village knew she'd spent time with both other bakers, it would be rude to refuse. At least she'd be able to confirm the best time to deliver the marmalades and jams for the upcoming fete.

The cottage was just as lovely on the inside. A small mudroom filled with gumboots, Barbour jackets and a collection of straw market bags led through to a light and airy hallway. The sitting room was at the back of the house and was tastefully decorated with a large velvet sofa and a wingback in one corner, covered in a delicate blue and white toile that Ginny was now very familiar with.

She raised an eyebrow. 'I take it Harlow also convinced you that "Deer in a Woodland Delight" was the only textile worthy of someone with exceptional taste.'

'Not exactly.' A flicker of something crossed Peter's face and he sighed. 'Sandra spent months going over fabric swabs before deciding on it. We asked Harlow to order it in specially for us, but instead of ordering one roll, he got thirty. And when he couldn't return them, he set about convincing everyone to buy it. Poor Sandra was devastated.'

Ginny raised an eyebrow. Megan hadn't mentioned that it wasn't her father who had chosen the fabric. Nor had Peter or Sandra's name appeared on the list of disgruntled customers she'd called.

'I can imagine. Did she ever say anything to him?'

He closed his eyes, as if pained. 'No. But I wonder now if I should have let her complain. It might have helped her get over the upset. As it was, I encouraged her to think of it as a compliment. After all, the great Timothy Harlow – arbiter of style – was being swayed by our humble choice.'

'You both have lovely taste,' she said truthfully, since while Harlow might have traded on his reputation, the house he shared with Megan was virtually devoid of character, unlike Myrtle Cottage.

'Thank you. We muddle along quite well as far as these things go. Anyway, please sit down. I'll put the kettle on and find Sandra. Last time I saw her she was sorting out the judging cards.'

With that he disappeared back down the hallway, leaving Ginny on her own.

There were several prints on display, and a golden oak writing desk. A turned-leg chair was tucked under it, with a navy corduroy jacket thrown over the back. But her attention was quickly caught by the twelve yellow rosettes that hung from a pinning board above the desk.

Third place. So, Ted's guess had been correct. Judging by the number, Sandra Skye either hadn't entered each year, or she didn't always place. But she'd obviously received enough rosettes to have drawn the attention of whoever had been behind the thefts.

Over on a side table was a collection of silver-framed photographs. One was from outside the Little Shaw church. Peter Skye looked much the same, just younger, while his bride, Sandra, had large doe eyes and glossy brown hair as she clutched a bouquet of wildflowers. The rest of the photographs were of the couple over the years, each time standing in front of the 'Spring Fete and Gala' sign.

At that moment, Peter reappeared holding a tray with a stunning set of Royal Albert teacups and matching pot, as well as a plate of delicately coloured macaroons. Catching Ginny looking at the photographs, he put down the tray and wrinkled his nose.

'You must think Sandra and I are terribly boring. Most people have photographs of their travel adventures and grand-children. But for us, our life seems to revolve around only one thing.'

'I think it's lovely,' she assured him as he poured out the tea and held up the milk jug with a questioning glance. She nodded and he splashed some in before handing it over to her. There was still no sign of his wife, but Ginny assumed she must be coming to join them soon. 'Thirty years is an amazing legacy.'

'I admit we're proud of ourselves.' He offered her the plate of macaroons, but she shook her head and stirred the tea. The spoon clinked against the delicate porcelain. The tea smelt faintly of pepper, and she wondered if it was a special blend. Considering the lovely tea set, it was easy to imagine. She took a sip and warmth flooded her limbs.

Peter smiled at her. 'But I mustn't rattle on. Tell me again how you found the recipes?'

She opened her mouth to explain but her jaw had suddenly turned to cotton wool and the room began to spin. Peter's face blurred as he stood and shrugged on the navy jacket hanging over the chair. Silver buttons gleamed at her, catching the late afternoon light as a wave of nausea rose in her throat.

Why were they familiar? Wait... she knew the answer. But as soon as she tried to reach for it, it disappeared.

The room began to swim as Peter Skye loomed over her. She lurched to one side. Something was wrong.

He snatched the cup from her hand and snarled. *Oh dear, he's angry now.* But the thought came from far away as she was dragged to her feet. Her shoulder made a popping noise and she cried out, before slipping gratefully into the cold, numb darkness that was beckoning.

Everything hurt. Ginny's first thoughts were that she must be in hospital. It would explain the terrible aftertaste of medicine in her mouth, the sharp throb running along her right arm, and why she was lying down. Her eyes fluttered open but she quickly shut them again as a wave of dizziness washed over her. It took several more goes before she could finally keep her eyes open.

She was lying along the backseat of a car, though her legs were pushed to one side, as if someone was worried about getting shoe marks on the upholstery. There was no movement or sound of an engine, which meant it was parked. Groaning, she tried to shift into an upright position. Pain ricocheted through her, but she bit back a yelp as she fumbled with the seat belt that had been strapped across her torso.

Her eyes adjusted to the darkness and she peered towards the front seats but no one was there. Who had driven her here? Peter? Sandra? Or both of them?

It was dark outside, and shadows swept across the car windows. Ginny's throat tightened as she grasped the door handle. It was locked. She had no idea where she was but knew that she had to get away. Where was her handbag? Her phone? She groped around with her left hand, not daring to try moving her right. But they weren't there. Panic rose in her chest, but she pushed it down.

There would be time for panicking later.

First, she needed to think. Why had Peter drugged her? Not because of the recipes, surely? But what else was there? Had he been offended that she'd commented on the deer fabric? She tried to remember. No. He'd said Sandra was the one who'd been upset, but he'd taken it as a compliment.

The great Timothy Harlow – arbiter of good taste – was being swayed by our humble choice.

Was Sandra the one who'd drugged her? Had she stayed out of sight on purpose? Or were they both responsible? Had they resented Harlow for overshadowing the hard work they'd done year after year? It was certainly what had happened to Megan.

Was it enough to kill him, though? But why now? And why the ides of March? The only connection she'd been able to find between Harlow and the fifteenth of March was the newspaper article with him on the cover. The only other thing on the entire front page had been the list of other headlines. One of them had been for a marriage.

She thought of the photo of Peter and Sandra Skye standing outside the church.

Blind Date Leads to Wedding Bells... more on page nine.

Had Peter and Sandra's wedding been pushed off the front page because of Harlow's need for attention? Yet, it still seemed so petty. Ginny tried again to open the car door. Even if she was right about the wedding, she'd only reached that conclusion because they'd drugged her. If they'd let her leave the house, she might not have thought anything of it. So why take the risk?

Orange torchlight cut through her thoughts as a key fob chimed and the car door was yanked open. Peter Skye's face loomed over her. There were streaks of dirt on his hands.

'It's time for a walk.' He gripped her arm. Pain flooded her damaged shoulder as Ginny stumbled out and stared at her own car. Her stomach tightened. Had he used it to pretend she'd left his house of her own volition? But his face was a hard mask and she swallowed back the question. And where was his wife?

If Sandra was involved, why hadn't she shown herself?

They were near some kind of woods. To the left were the remains of a building, almost buried beneath a wall of gorse. Ginny's throat tightened as she recalled the dilapidated factory the estate agent had shown her and Hen. It hadn't been far from Timberly Place, but she doubted anyone would think to look for her there.

The air was damp, and the ground was soft beneath their feet. Peter pushed her forward to a small clearing in the trees where a large hole was looming.

A mound of soil was piled at one side. Ginny began to sway. She'd seen enough graves since arriving in Little Shaw; once when she and her friends had tried to dig one up, but also in their work at the cemetery.

But this was in the middle of the woods. At night.

If she ran, how far would she get? Not very, if her attempt to follow Ben King was anything to go by, and her shoulder still throbbed with pain. Wallace's numerous warnings rang in her ears. How many times had he told her about the dangers of getting involved in a murder investigation?

And how many times did I ignore him?

Too late she realised that she'd brought it all on herself. Fear buzzed in her ears and the blackness tried to sweep her away again. No. She dug her nails into the flesh of her arm. Had she spoken to Eric today? She couldn't remember. What if she had? Did that mean she had to wait until tomorrow to say something else to him? Except she had a terrible feeling there might not be a tomorrow.

Sorry, love. I seem to have got myself in a muddle, and I'm not sure what to do.

He didn't answer but a flicker of warmth swept along her arm, reminding her of their many evenings together. Side by side, reading their books. Sometimes he'd look at her and smile.

You never get sick of reading those stories, even though you know what will happen. And she would return his smile and tell him that it wasn't the ending that mattered, it was how the characters got there.

Oh. Ginny's spine straightened.

Many of those books had been mysteries, and at the end the villains always liked to boast about what they'd done. Was that what the memory was trying to tell her? To make Skye talk?

At the very least it might delay him.

'Please, you don't want to do this,' she gasped, the words burning in her throat.

'You're right. I would have preferred you crashed your car the other night, and died from a tragic accident,' he agreed, coolly. 'But life always has its challenges.'

'That was *you*? But why?' Ginny froze. She assumed he'd drugged her because he'd panicked. But her brakes had been planned.

'Why? Because you ruined everything. Milos was in jail. Arrested. Case closed. It was so simple. So easy. Until you came along. And then... *then*... not only did Milos get an alibi, but it was because he'd been having an affair with Juliana Melville. Who was meant to be *my* new celebrity judge. Do you have any idea how humiliating that was? How many plans you ruined?' Now there was an unhinged edge to his voice and a glitter to his eyes, made worse by the flashlight that he kept sweeping across his face.

Ginny was going to be sick. So, he had killed Harlow and framed Milos for the murder. And tried to kill Ginny because she'd helped prove the young upholsterer was innocent. *Stop it*, she mentally chided herself. *Just keep him talking.*

'How did you frame him? Did you pay someone in the bedsit to plant the evidence or did you do it yourself?'

He raised an eyebrow at the question but then shrugged. 'Why get my hands dirty when I don't have to? The secret to my success has always been that I'm a good delegator. And negotiator. It only cost me thirty quid.'

Ginny swallowed down her disgust. How could he be so casual? 'You won't get away with this.'

'Now you really are sounding like a librarian who has read too many stupid stories. Of course I'll get away with it. Though I must admit I didn't think it would be so nicely done. I should thank you for delivering yourself to my door. Can you believe I wasted an entire evening trying to work out how to arrange this?'

'Arrange *what*? How to kidnap and kill me?' Ginny asked, trying to keep the rising panic at bay.

'Yes, exactly that,' he agreed. Ginny sucked in a breath. She had to keep him talking. Stop him from doing anything worse. But her head was swimming, and it was hard to focus.

'Is that why you dumped the recipes behind my house?'

'The recipes?' he spluttered. 'You women are all the same.

Sandra was obsessed with them, stupid cow that she was. Can you believe I found them hidden at the bottom of her handbag? As for dumping them behind your house, that was just dumb luck. Not that I intended anyone to find them. But I suppose it's turned out for the best.'

The cool of the evening was starting to seep into Ginny's bones and the darkness pressed in. She had to keep him talking. Buy herself time. Not that anyone was coming. No one knew she was there except Ted Wallace, who only had Skye's address.

And her car was no longer there.

'Why did Sandra steal Lily and Brenda's recipes?' she persisted.

Peter glared at her as if she was stupid. 'She stole them thinking it would finally be her chance to win first place. Delusional. As if I'd suddenly respect her, after she's been a failure for so long,' he snapped, and the chill spread through Ginny's bones.

It was such a cruel way to speak about his wife. But he was looking past her shoulder, his regular features twisted into an angry mask.

'You think Sandra's a failure because she doesn't have any red rosettes? That's hardly a good way to judge character.'

'Says someone who's never won any. Still, that's no longer a problem.'

Ginny clamped her lips together. Over the years she had won several ribbons and certificates at local fetes, but had no idea where they were, nor did she care.

His gaze was still fixed somewhere in the distance and Ginny's skin prickled.

'You killed her? You killed your wife?' She took a step away from him, for the first time fully appreciating how unhinged he was.

'Sandra has never been anything more than a chain around my neck. Dragging me down to her own mediocrity.'

'Why did you marry her, then?'

'Because I could,' he snapped. 'Harlow wanted her, you know. I suppose she was pretty enough back then, enough to hide her stupidity. And he pulled out all the stops to get her – smug git that he was. But she couldn't stand him. Told me that he made her skin crawl. So, I took her out from under him. Just to show him that I was better than him.'

'Someone said he didn't like playing second fiddle,' Ginny said, and Peter's face contorted with the truth of it. She took another step back, her heart going out to Sandra, who'd married a monster. Had she always known what her husband was like? Had she spent her whole marriage unloved?

'Instead of being jealous, though, he simply moved on to Juliana Melville. A woman so far above his reach. She was a genius, until he corrupted her.'

'Harlow must have been a little jealous, though. Because he was on the front page of the newspaper the day after your wedding. That *was* yours, I presume. *Blind date leads to wedding bells.*'

His eyes suddenly narrowed. 'Well, well, haven't you been busy? The stupid pig probably didn't even realise he'd backstabbed me on the ides of March. But then again, with my intellect I was always his cultural superior. From then, I knew that when he did die, that would be the day.'

'So why wait thirty years?'

'Indeed. It's a question I've asked myself every year come the fifteenth of March. But I would always think to myself, "No, Peter. Just one more year. One more year to put up with his insolence and then it can be over." But he forced my hand with that bloody fabric. To know that every sitting room in this wretched village now has *my* "Deer in a Woodland Delight". And all thinking it was Harlow who had chosen it? No. Unacceptable.'

'You killed him over some upholstery fabric?' She couldn't hide her horror.

'It wasn't just *some* upholstery fabric. It represented me and my style. It was personal,' he said, before suddenly noticing how far she'd moved away from him. He strode over and dragged her back to the lip of the hole, his smile malicious. 'Besides, Juliana Melville's return had been quite the triumph, and we had several frank conversations, which made me realise just how suitable she'd be to take Harlow's place. *And* Sandra's.'

'So you planned both murders,' Ginny whispered, fear taking her voice.

'Of course I planned them. How do you think I've managed to run the most successful village fete in the county? Because I'm exceptional at what I do. I made sure Sandra was seen at the public meeting and then brought her here the night before I killed Harlow. Stupid cow was almost excited – as if we were going on a date. After that I burned her passport and wallet as well as the recipe cards.'

'Except they didn't burn properly,' Ginny pointed out, and a flicker of irritation flashed across his face.

'Damn spring weather. It must have rained,' he muttered, before collecting himself. 'Still, that won't be an issue for much longer.'

Ice crept through Ginny's veins, leaving her numb. *Just keep him talking. And think of an escape.* 'But what about Harlow? Surely that wasn't as easy. How did you get in and out of the haberdashery without being seen? And manage to plant the evidence in Milos's bedsit? Not to mention the scissors.'

'It wasn't difficult. I went to visit Vanja on the pretence of getting our wingback reupholstered after I discovered how many people had used the same fabric. While I was there, I took the scissors. As for killing Harlow, the weather was on my side. There was hardly anyone around, and I wore one of Sandra's coats and a sunhat. Even if anyone saw me, they wouldn't have known who I was. Not that Harlow noticed. Arrogant prick that he is. Still, I suppose I should be thankful he was so self-absorbed. He was so busy boasting about some business venture that he didn't even see me lock the front door before following him into the back room.'

Bile rose up through Ginny's cold stomach at his calm, casual account of two murders. The last thing she wanted to do was continue the conversation, but she dared not let it go silent.

'Why do you hate him so much?'

'Why do I hate him?' Skye snapped, his calmness deserting him. Ginny shivered, hoping she hadn't made things worse. 'Because he was an arrogant know-it-all who was devoid of talent yet tried to convince the world he was a genius. I almost think he believed it himself. Clearly, he forgot that it was *my* designs that he stole. My designs that got him into the fashion school in London. And then, when he came back to Little Shaw, he had the gall to act as if I was beneath him.'

Finally, it all came together.

The brilliant designs that had gained him entry to the prestigious fashion school. Meeting Jessica and Charlotte, the two sisters with exceptional sewing skills, who had helped him craft that first collection. The success that led to a job on a television show. Everything Timothy Harlow had achieved had been at someone else's expense.

Yet it didn't mean he deserved to die.

'You made him a judge. Why do that if you couldn't stand him?'

'Because we couldn't get funding without a celebrity attached to the fete. Then he attracted so much attention it was impossible to get rid of him.' His fingers dug deep into her injured shoulder. 'But as you're about to discover, I always get my way in the end.'

'Not this time.' A woman's voice sounded out from the darkness and PC Anita Singh stepped forward. She was holding a warrant card in her hand, and next to her was the young PC Bent. 'Let her go.'

Never had she been so relieved, and Ginny's body almost crumpled as the two PCs raced towards her. Help was there. But her hope was short lived as Skye snarled and pushed her closer to the looming hole. *No.* She tried to wrench his hand away, but his grip was like iron on her useless arm.

'I don't think so,' he hissed as he suddenly let go of his hold and Ginny lurched forward.

She braced herself to fall, but instead found herself being gently yet firmly pulled sideways, and out from Peter Skye's reach.

'It's okay. Don't try and move. You're probably in shock,' Wallace said from next to her, and moments later the clearing was flooded with light.

Ginny squinted at the brightness until her eyes adjusted. She was just in time to see Skye being tackled to the ground by Singh and Bent, who cuffed him, all while his face was pressed into the soft soil.

Once it was done, she turned back to Wallace, who looked angry, irritated and more than a little worried.

'Thank you,' she managed to say as two paramedics burst through the trees, closely followed by Hen, Tuppence and JM. 'A-and I'm sorry. I really didn't mean to get involved this time. I thought I was just returning a recipe.'

'Yes, so my father has been telling me. Though how you managed to drag the most antisocial man in England into your adventures, I've got no idea.'

'Did he call you?'

He nodded. 'When you didn't return in your car, the old man went back out to the hedgerow and found Sandra Skye's passport and wedding ring. He called me straightaway and we went to Skye's house. A neighbour had seen him drive off in your car but had no idea where you'd gone.'

'But I still don't understand how you found me. I don't have any fancy gadgets in my car, or on my phone, and I was unconscious the entire drive, so even I didn't know where I was until I woke up.' Her brows pressed together as she studied his face.

She'd expected him to grimace or dismiss it as unimportant, but instead colour ran up his neck.

'Actually, I have your murder board to thank for that.'

'Our murder board?' Ginny parroted, trying and failing to picture Wallace carefully studying the felt board with tiny Velcro figures and small scraps of paper pinned onto it. Then her eyes widened as she remembered they'd written down the names of the estate agents they'd visited, and the address of the factory, thinking it was a lead. 'You read our notes?'

'Call it an occupational hazard,' he ruefully admitted. 'Not that I thought much of it at the time. People have been trying to sell this place for the last twenty years, so I figured the agent had just brought you here on the off chance.'

'She did,' Ginny admitted. 'But I still don't understand how you made the connection.'

He ran a hand through his dark hair. 'It's only four miles from Peter Skye's house on Timberly Place, and there's a back road that cuts through to it. It made sense to try it first, and I guess I just had a gut feeling about it.'

'Oh, I-I see,' Ginny stammered, not sure whether to be relieved or terrified that DI James Wallace, who did everything by the book, had only found her because of a gut feeling. Or that, unlike the stacks of meticulous research piled up in his office, it was all down to the little felt mat that she was still alive.

Her thoughts must have shown on her face and his expression softened. 'And thank *you*. While I would still much prefer to solve a murder without civilian interference, I'm pleased you're okay. Now, I'm going to hold off your friends while the paramedics check you out.'

He marched towards the three women who had become so

much part of her life, his arms stretched out wide like a barricade. But instead of stopping them from getting through, they seemed to think he wanted a hug, and before he could protest, Hen, Tuppence and JM had thrown their arms around him, burying him from sight.

For the first time in ages Ginny burst out laughing.

TWENTY-EIGHT

Saturday, 5th April

'Can you believe there hasn't been a drop of rain all day? Turns out that Harlow wasn't the weather guru after all,' Cleo marvelled, as Ginny tidied up a pile of handmade bookmarks that Esme and William had made for the Friends of the Village stall.

It was true. Despite a week of gossip and worry about April showers, hailstorms, and, according to one obscure almanac, a snowstorm straight from the Arctic Circle, the sky was a pale blue with a few smudges of marshmallow clouds.

'I told you there'd be a blood sacrifice,' Connor retorted from the other end of the stall, where he'd just finished selling three pairs of hand-knitted bed socks. Unlike the stunning Nordic patterns Hen used for her knitted socks, these ones had been made from a lurid green acrylic wool, with black trim and several pompoms around the top. Somehow Ginny doubted that any of the supplies had been bought at Harlow's Haberdashery, where Timothy would have probably chased the person out for even considering the combination.

'Blood sacrifice?' scoffed the man who had just paid twenty pounds for the three pairs of socks. 'Nonsense, it's that new head judge, Juliana Melville. She's a right weather guru, she is.'

'Let him believe it if he wants to. You know what folks around here are like.' Slim joined Connor at the table and began to unpack another box of Ginny's jams and marmalades. The likeable rogue hadn't quite got around to borrowing any books yet, but had volunteered to help around the library, and seemed to be enjoying himself. He'd even washed his hair, though she suspected that was in case his Russian honey cake won a prize.

Ginny smiled as he finished setting out the jams, which had been selling out as quickly as they could put them on the table. And so had all the wooden salad bowls, the hand-painted rocks and the lovely collection of organic soaps and face creams. Though nothing had done as well as the thirty-one mouth-watering cakes that graced the cut-glass stands in the middle of the stall. They'd been made by Lily Rogers and Brenda Larson, who had spent five days together, baking up every award-winning entry for the last twenty-nine years.

The extra two were the ones they had each planned to enter in this year's competition, before deciding to step down from competitive baking to take over the running of the entire fete.

Though they managed to keep a tally of whose cakes sold out first.

Ginny adjusted her sling as Andrea and two other library volunteers appeared from the crowd, ready to take over at the stall. After pointing out a few items that were waiting to be collected, she managed to slip out of her apron, using only her good hand, before stepping around to the other side of the stall.

It had turned out that her shoulder had been dislocated and while the pain had subsided once it had been reset, she would have to wear the sling for several more weeks. But she'd been determined not to miss her first Little Shaw spring fete and gala and was so far enjoying herself immensely.

'What are you going to do now?' she asked Connor as he joined her. 'Will you stay and look around?'

'Yeah, but not for long. My nan is here somewhere, and I promised to show her my new place—' He broke off and frowned. 'Unless you don't think I should. I don't want to get off to a bad start.'

'If you're really worried about it, you could always just ask your new landlord. There she is.' Ginny nodded towards the rotunda where Hen was happily sitting in what looked like William's fishing chair, teaching a group of young children how to cast on. She'd tentatively agreed to teach some classes at Greenhill Barn, but wanted to practise first. 'But I'm certain that she'd want you to feel at home and invite your friends around. Though... maybe not Spider and the rest of the band.'

'No fear of that.' Connor rolled his eyes. 'Last I heard they'd broken up due to creative differences. Anyway, I'd better go and find Nan before she gets into too much trouble at the coconut shy. She really hates losing. But thanks again for convincing Hen to let me move in.'

'I hardly convinced her,' Ginny protested. 'Ever since Alyson went travelling overseas, I think she's been wanting someone else in the house. And you get on famously with her dog, so it couldn't have worked out better.'

He gave a half-smile and then loped off, not even bothering to pull his hoodie over his head as he went. Ginny looked around. Across the grass was Megan and Lolly's tent, with racks of colourful lingerie to fit all sizes. A dressing room had been set up behind the tent and to one side was Ants Mancini, who was deep in conversation with Lolly about something. According to Megan, he'd not only promised to act as a mentor to Lolly's growing business, but had offered to rent out his barn so the workroom could be moved to a more secure, comfortable location.

Megan still looked pale as she spoke to a customer, but had

said that with the funeral behind her, she was starting to come to terms with her father's death.

In the distance she could see Tuppence wearing a pair of linen overalls and a pink wig as she helped paint faces, and JM was over by the art tent, entertaining a group of out-of-towners who had mistakenly thought she was a tour guide.

Next to her was Juliana Melville, who had been spending time with JM, talking about art and design when not busy overseeing her panel of judges.

Ginny thought about going to say hello, but they were due to meet at The Lost Goat in an hour to try the lunch special that the new (new) manager had instigated. Which meant she had just enough time to slip into the main tent and look at the sixty-five categories of arts, craft, produce and baking. It still seemed a staggering amount for such a small village, but, as she was quickly learning, Little Shaw didn't seem to do anything by halves. And with a smile, she went on her way.

A LETTER FROM THE AUTHOR

Huge thanks for reading *A Widows' Guide to Backstabbing* – I hope you were hooked on Ginny's journey as she and her friends solve another murder. If you want to join other readers in hearing all about my new releases and bonus content, you can sign up for my newsletter.

www.stormpublishing.co/amanda-ashby

If you enjoyed this book and could spare a few moments to leave a review that would be hugely appreciated. Even a short review can make all the difference in encouraging a reader to discover my books for the first time. Thank you so much

When I wrote the first book in this series, I mentioned that the village of Little Shaw had a haberdashery shop that looked like the Bennet sisters might step out of. And while I wasn't sure what would happen in this charming shop, I knew I wanted to open the door and let Ginny step inside. So, this story was really inspired by my love of beautiful fabrics, and my desire to throw Ginny and her friends yet again into some mystery and mayhem. And of course, knowing how particular sewers are when it comes to their scissors, I never had a doubt of just how the villain would commit the murder.

Thanks again for being part of this amazing journey with me and I hope you'll stay in touch – I have so many more stories and ideas to entertain you with!

KEEP IN TOUCH WITH THE AUTHOR

www.amandaashby.com

 instagram.com/authoramandaashby

ACKNOWLEDGEMENTS

As always, a big thank you to Sally Rigby, Christina Phillips and Rachel Bailey for your continued support through the ups, downs and the occasional hysterics. You had no idea what you were signing up for, but you still all stuck around.

Thank you to Oliver Rhodes and the entire team at Storm for helping bring this story to life. I'm so grateful to be working with Emily Gowers and her brilliant understanding of story-telling, puns and murderous intentions. To Alexandra Begley for her love of grammar and all-around fabulousness. To Belinda Jones for once again diving into the world of Little Shaw and making sure it all holds together. To Amanda Rutter for helping catch all the last-minute surprises I left in! And to Emily Courdelle for another wonderful cover.

Finally, to my father, Gerald Ashby, who never got to see any of my books in print, but who helped fuel my love of stories every Saturday morning at our local bookstore.